THE CHRISTMAS HOUSE

THE CHRISTMAS HOUSE

A Novel

VICTORIA JAMES

alcove
press

Published in the United States by Alcove Press, an imprint of The Quick Brown Fox & Company LLC.

Alcove Press and its logo are trademarks of The Quick Brown Fox & Company LLC.

Library of Congress Catalog-in-Publication data available upon request.

ISBN (hardcover): 978-1-64385-772-5
ISBN (ebook): 978-1-64385-773-2

Cover design by Lynn Andreozzi

Printed in the United States.

www.alcovepress.com

Alcove Press
34 West 27th St., 10th Floor
New York, NY 10001

First Edition: September 2021

10 9 8 7 6 5 4 3 2 1

To James and Victoria,

May you always hold dear the bond that you share. One of life's most precious gifts is having a sibling who is also a trusted and loyal friend-never take each other for granted. You are both my most treasured blessings. I love you forever. xo

PROLOGUE

"Ken and Barbie are going to have five kids and live happily ever after."

Charlotte Harris Palmer bit her tongue in an effort not to ruin her younger sister Olivia's idealistic view of the world. At the advanced age of twelve, Charlotte had already figured out the way the world worked; five kids would be a nightmare, five kids would *not* lead any adult to happily-ever-after. It wasn't Olivia's fault for being so naïve—she was only nine. In a way, it was Charlotte's fault that Olivia didn't get how the real world worked, because she was always trying to protect her younger sister from the reality of their home life.

Frowning as she surveyed the worn hardwood floor filled with Barbie clothing and random pieces of pink plastic furniture, she added this to her list of things to clean up after school. Maybe she'd sort the clothing into piles and then into shoeboxes, complete with labels. "Liv, we don't have time for this now. We're going to be late for school," she said, crossing the small room and picking up her hairbrush.

Charlotte had bigger problems today than the usual ones. She envied Olivia's little-kid problems. Seventh grade had made everything different. Seventh grade meant everyone changed. It was like all of a sudden none of her old friends wanted to hang around her anymore.

She frowned at her reflection in the mirror, taking in the frizzy hair that she'd hoped she'd be able to blow-dry away, the pimples that seemed to dominate her once perfect skin, and the chubby cheeks that never seemed to get smaller as she aged. No wonder no one thought she was cool. She tugged at her shirt that had fit just a month ago. Everything about her body felt weird now.

"Meet me at the door when you're done, Liv," she said, grabbing her backpack. She had to hurry up; their father had just come home.

"Damn it, Wendy, would it kill you to clean this place up?"

Charlotte winced at the irritation in her father's voice. She closed the bedroom door, not wanting Olivia to hear their argument, and ran down the narrow hallway of their apartment and into the kitchen, hoping to intervene before it got bad.

"I'm not your slave, Mac. Why are you always working nights anyway? It's almost Christmas," her mother said, her voice low and slurred.

"You know I have no choice. We're behind on rent, and if I want to get a few days off so we can go to your mother's for Christmas, then I have to work more now."

"Hi, Dad!" Charlotte yelled, bursting into the room. She ran by her mother who was drinking coffee with a bottle of some kind of alcohol beside it.

Her dad opened his arms and gave her a hug. He was wearing his police officer's uniform, which she loved because it always reminded her that her dad was a super important person who took care of people. He was everyone's hero, but especially hers. He never let her down. "I'm sorry I didn't have time to clean up in here this morning, but I will after school for sure."

Her dad pulled back and smoothed the hair off her face. His dark brown eyes stared into hers and she held onto the gaze and all the promises she read there. For a second it almost looked like he was going to cry. She knew that was impossible, of course. Her dad didn't cry. No police officers cried. "You don't have to say sorry. It's not your job to do all that," he said in that voice that always made her feel safe, his large hands on either side of her cheeks.

"It's no one's job," her mother said in that awful voice again.

Charlotte turned around to look at her mom and her stomach churned. Why couldn't she just smile and be happy, or pretend to be happy? Just for a day.

"Whoever is home and doesn't have a job outside the house should be in charge of the home and chores," her dad said, gathering dishes from the counter and placing them in the sink.

He always made sense. It sounded fair to her. "I can do it, Dad. Liv is almost ready to go. How about I make you breakfast? I can clean up the kitchen real fast too," she said, hurrying to open the fridge.

"Charlotte, honey, you are so thoughtful. Don't worry about me, I already ate. Do you need help packing lunches?"

She shook her head. Her heart felt like it was going to burst. He saved people and he saved her, every day when she thought she couldn't handle her mom's sadness. Charlotte stuffed the lunches she'd made for herself and Olivia in their bags and looked up at her dad. "Already done," she said, holding up the paper bags. "I told everyone at school that you're coming to career day today."

He flashed her a smile. "You bet."

She couldn't wait. All those mean kids would finally meet him and no one would ever make fun of her again. Anyone who had a cop for a dad had to be cool. "I told them about those kids you rescued last week. I told them you're a hero."

He frowned for a second. "You give me too much credit, Charlotte . . . but I'm happy to be coming to speak to your school today."

Charlotte beamed up at him before continuing to clean the kitchen, trying to brush off the sadness she felt as her mom left the room without saying goodbye. "Liv, hurry up!" she yelled, grabbing her jacket and setting out Olivia's. She was in a hurry for another reason—or a person, really.

She was hoping that they'd be able to walk with Wyatt. Last year he and his family had moved into the apartment down the hall, and from day one she'd fallen for him. He was two years older than she was and had become the most popular guy in school without even trying. But he always treated her like she was cool. Most days they walked to and from school together. Olivia tagged along behind them. Sometimes they'd even talk about their messed-up families. Maybe she talked more than he did, but he did tell her that his dad was messed up.

A few minutes later, with Olivia in tow, Charlotte spotted Wyatt in the hallway and her heart did a few summersaults. He was closing the door on the sound of yelling and something being smashed. Olivia gasped out loud and Charlotte tugged on her hand and gave her a frown, a silent command to keep quiet. She understood the arguing and the yelling. She had never really had to deal with things being smashed, though. Wyatt turned around and walked toward them. His face went from sad to a smile when he saw them.

"Hey," he said as they met at the stairwell.

He held the door open for them, and Charlotte loved that even though he seemed tough, he was always nice to them. Even to Olivia, who always had her head in the clouds. He was tall and so gorgeous, not an ounce of awkward in him. "Our dad is coming to school today," Olivia blurted out when they reached the bottom of the stairs.

"Oh yeah? What for?" he said as they walked outside.

Freezing cold wind and icy snow attacked them as made their way to school, but it was a short distance so it wouldn't be too bad, Charlotte thought. The sidewalks had been plowed, and rush hour traffic buzzed around them. "Career day," Charlotte said, taking over the conversation before Olivia said something embarrassing.

"He's a cop, right?" Wyatt asked.

Charlotte nodded and smiled proudly. "Yup."

"I'm going to be a cop when I grow up," he said.

"Charlotte, you forgot your gloves!" Olivia burst out, completely interrupting their conversation.

"Oh, you want mine?" Wyatt said, frowning as he looked at her bare hands. She was pretty sure she might be in love.

Yes. Yes, she wanted his gloves. But she would never take them. She shook her head and smiled. "Thanks, but I have an extra pair in my bag. I'll grab them later," she said.

"Wyatt!" Wyatt turned from her to the direction of the school ahead and the group of kids waiting for him. All the cool kids.

"I'll see you later," he said, with a flick of his chin before he jogged off to meet his friends.

"Are you going to marry him?" Olivia whispered loudly.

Charlotte frowned at her. "Quiet, Liv. Of course not," she said. She would never get married. Not in a million years. But if she were to get married, it would be to someone like Wyatt.

Hours later, Charlotte stood in front of the entire school on the stage. A bead of sweat trickled between her shoulder blades as she introduced her dad, even though he wasn't actually there yet. Everyone else had already had their turn. She pulled on the hem of her shirt, very aware of how snug it felt, how it didn't quite reach the top of her jeans. Her stomach brushed uncomfortably against the harsh denim, and her gaze scanned the crowd for Wyatt. He would smile at her. Except he wasn't even looking at her. His brown eyes were staring in the opposite direction.

"Charlotte, why don't you sit down? Your father might be running late," the principal said, approaching her.

Charlotte shook her head. "Can we just wait another minute?" she asked, confident that her dad was about to burst through the gymnasium doors, apologize for being late, and tell everyone about all the heroic things he'd done last night while he was working. Her principal frowned slightly and spoke into the microphone. "Students, we will wait quietly for Officer Palmer to get here."

"Thank you. Just five more minutes. He's really important," she choked out. He was her hero. He would never leave her in front of the entire school to be embarrassed like this.

She shifted from one foot to the other, ignoring the snickers and smirks. She blinked rapidly, fighting tears as Wyatt stood up, not sparing her a glance, and left the gym. Why would he leave?

The principal approached a few minutes later, shaking her head. An emergency. She should tell her he was probably rescuing someone. She opened her mouth to do that, but no words came out and she hiccupped into the microphone by mistake. Laughter from the crowd made the tightness in her throat worse as she backed away. She wouldn't let them see her cry.

If she had known that the boy she had a crush on was going to just disappear that day, she would have had the courage to tell him how she really felt about him.

If she had known that this would be the last morning she'd ever see her father, she wouldn't have let him leave.

She would have begged him to stay. She would have asked for one more hug, one more kiss, one more chance to be a better kid.

She would have asked what she could have done better, how she could have been better, how she could have made him love them enough to stay.

CHAPTER ONE

Charlotte Harris had three things to accomplish during the holidays in Silver Springs:

1. Take an *actual* break from her business—not the fake kind that she usually preferred.
2. Repair her relationship with her sister, Olivia.
3. Survive the holidays with her entire family.

Grabbing her suitcase from the trunk of her white Volkswagen SUV, she took a deep breath of the cold, clean, country air. She set her gaze on the beloved Christmas House and, instead of breaking out into her customary march, she actually stopped. Stood still.

Something washed over her, prompting her to just pause. *Grace will lead you home, Charlotte.* That memory, the one that dripped with Grandma Ruby's confident, self-assured voice, bubbled to the surface. She didn't know how that happened. There were parts of her childhood she successfully blocked out daily, but that day, after their father had taken off, when they were standing on Grandma Ruby's doorstep, always rushed to her mind when she came here. She'd been so lost. Grandma Ruby had taken one look at her, at Olivia, and wrapped them up in her arms like they were the most precious things in the world, and had whispered that in her ears. And she'd held those fiercely whispered words close to her heart. Grandma Ruby had been security in an insecure world.

The Christmas House was a place where you could stop running. The Christmas House was a place where you belonged, no matter who you were.

She rolled her shoulders, refusing to dwell on that memory from a time in her life when she was so sure she was broken, when she had given the outside world the power to break her. But Grandma Ruby had shown her that she could be courageous.

She walked from the circular driveway where she'd parked her car to the shoveled and salted flagstone path that led up to Grandma Ruby's front porch. The usual cedar roping was hung meticulously, spanning the tops of each of the twelve pillars on the Victorian porch. The white lights twinkled cheerfully and blanketed the area with just enough light that she didn't have to worry about where she was going. The glossy black shutters were spotless, as were the oversized parlor windows, each one boasting a fresh green boxwood wreath and bright red bow.

The Christmas House B&B looked exactly as it always did. Time stood still here, the season never changed; Christmas clung to everything, bringing hope to everyone who visited. This was the house that welcomed everyone and anyone, and her grandmother's heart touched all the guests. Legend had it that the house brought people together—even made them fall in love.

Ringing the doorbell, Charlotte's heartbeat quickened at the thought of seeing her grandmother again. She stared at the bright red door adorned with another deep-green boxwood wreath as she waited, thinking she should have made a point of coming here more often. But the last two years, she'd let her new business as a professional organizer take priority over visiting the only person who'd always been there for her. Or maybe she'd just been avoiding what this place did to her—The Christmas House was all about feeling. And somewhere along the way to adulthood, she'd stopped trying to feel.

Maybe she'd stopped believing in the magic here. Maybe she didn't need magic anymore. Nothing was the same or could ever be the same. Even she and Olivia had drifted apart. She didn't know how the two of them could ever restore their closeness. Olivia's rejection had cut deep, had triggered long-buried feelings of abandonment which Charlotte thought she had dealt with through years of therapy.

Now she pulled the edges of her wool coat together and swung her red and green plaid scarf over her shoulder as a gust of wind kicked up the icing-sugar thin snow, swirling around her body and making her shiver.

The door swung open and her stomach dropped at the sight of the man standing there. It couldn't be *him*.

He was tall and his dark hair was short and slightly mussed at the front. Dark brown eyes that were achingly familiar stared into hers, and his face was so different, so much more handsome than she could ever have imagined. Five o'clock shadow darkened the hard lines of his firm jaw. She snapped her gaze up to his when she realized he hadn't said a word.

They stood there, memories and time past hanging palpably between them, and she wondered if he remembered her, if he remembered their talks, their walks. She wanted to jump into his arms, to grasp onto that person who had meant so much to her once. She wanted to ask him where he had gone, what had happened. All of a sudden, she was twelve again, staring at the boy she had connected with, the one who'd disappeared from her life on the same day as her father. "*Wyatt?*"

"Charlotte," he said, his deep voice thick with the warmth she still remembered. He stepped aside and held the door open for her, and the gesture triggered memories from when they were young.

"What are you doing here?" she asked, belatedly realizing he didn't look surprised to see her.

He shoved his hands in his front pockets, his brown eyes studying her. "I, uh, I'm a friend of your grandmother's, actually," he said, as though that could somehow explain how of all the houses in all the towns, he had found this one.

"Wyatt, dear, I'm all out of your favorite scones, I'm afraid. But I do have some freshly baked cranberry muffins with a tangy orange glaze!"

Charlotte tore her gaze from Wyatt's to see her grandmother and a woman she didn't recognize walking down the long corridor together. The woman was holding her grandmother's favorite antique silver tray laden with muffins and china cups. Grandma Ruby looked as robust and happy as Charlotte remembered. Her gray curls were perfectly coiffed, her red and green holly-printed dress hung perfectly over her full figure, and her cheeks were rosy with good health. She didn't look a day over sixty. "Oh, my dear Charlotte! I didn't even hear you come in! You're early!"

Charlotte ran forward and threw her arms around her grandmother, momentarily dismissing Wyatt and all the emotions and questions he brought with him. Her grandmother hugged her back with the ferocity of a much younger woman, and relief gushed through Charlotte that all was well, that she was as tough as ever. She squeezed her eyes shut, welcoming the nostalgia and memories that came with the hug. She and Olivia had loved spending their summers here with Grandma Ruby. Their days had been filled with swimming at the lake, fishing in the river, and evenings sipping homemade lemonade on the porch and catching fireflies. Those were days of hope and daydreams, of whispered promises and absolutes, when all the problems of their everyday home life seemed to skulk away into the shadows until it was time to go home again.

Pulling back, she smiled into her grandmother's blue eyes. "I thought I'd surprise you."

Her grandmother grasped her hand. "I'm glad. Wyatt. This is my granddaughter, Charlotte. Charlotte, this is our brave deputy sheriff, Wyatt Holt. He also happens to be a good friend and neighbor."

Deputy. Law enforcement. *I'm going to be a cop when I grow up.* Charlotte tried to push the memory aside. How did she remember so much about him? She was happy for him, that he'd achieved his goal, despite the immediate wariness that profession brought out in her. It was a juvenile reaction. His job, his career, should mean nothing to her. After all, they'd known each other for barely a year before he and his family had moved away. Her infatuation had been just that and nothing more. She forced a smile and turned to her grandmother. "Yes, we know each other . . . knew each other. It was a long time ago."

"Well, isn't that just providential," Grandma Ruby said, a little too enthusiastically, as Wyatt coughed and looked away. "Oh, and how rude of me, this is his dear Aunt Mary, and my good friend as well."

Mary's brown eyes shone with warmth, and she smiled. "It's so nice to finally meet you, Charlotte. I had no idea my nephew was so secretive about who his friends are."

Wyatt took the tray from her as Charlotte extended her hand, but the older woman swept her up in a hug. "I wasn't being secretive, Aunt Mary. It really has been a lifetime since we've seen each other," he said. A lifetime indeed. She wondered what had happened to him in all those years.

Charlotte smiled at his aunt and played along, not wanting to look like the only one shaken up by this random coincidence. "Wyatt's right. This was very unexpected. But I'm so glad Grandma Ruby has such caring friends looking out for her. I've heard so many wonderful things about you."

"We just adore Ruby. Now, come and take your things off and get settled in. You're just in time for coffee, so come and join all of us. Wyatt, set the tray down on the coffee table," Mary said, wagging her finger in the direction of the parlor room, while Charlotte pulled off her boots and hung her coat and scarf on the coat rack beside the front door.

A few minutes later, they were settled in the large sitting room and Charlotte was seated on one of the dark-green, velvet couches, while her grandmother filled the holly-patterned china cups with coffee. She already knew tea wouldn't be coming out of the teapot because her grandmother was an infamous coffee lover. Adding a splash of cream to her coffee once her grandmother handed her the cup, she settled into the deep, overstuffed cushions. The two parlor rooms off the front entrance had always been her favorite rooms. When the house was built, one of the rooms had been for ladies, while the other had been for men. Now one room was used as the main sitting room while the other was a library. The high ceilings and ornate tin molding never ceased to inspire awe. The ten-foot Christmas tree sat in the large bay window, just as it always did. Vintage ornaments twinkled under the multicolored lights. When they were children, Charlotte and Olivia would spend so much time in front of that tree, looking at the various ornaments, some of them given to their grandmother by guests of The Christmas House.

"Thank you, Ruby," Wyatt said, smiling at her grandmother as she handed him a cup of coffee. He sat across from them in one of the matching armchairs, looking perfectly at home here. She didn't know if it was his looks or his size, but he seemed to dominate the room. His face was hard, lean, and every inch the capable law enforcement officer.

For years after her father left, whenever she saw a man in uniform she would break out in a sweat and her heart would race at the possibility that it might be her dad. She'd scour the sidewalks, the malls, wherever they happened to be, in case he was there. Somewhere in her early teens she stopped, with the gutting realization that, even if she could find him, she didn't want to anymore. Nothing he could say would ever justify his leaving.

"Your grandmother talks about you and Olivia all the time. It's so wonderful to finally get to meet you. I hear you've started a successful business too," Mary said with a wide smile.

Charlotte already liked Mary—she seemed just as outgoing as her grandmother. She rested her coffee cup on her lap and nodded, trying to appear relaxed even though she felt almost jittery, and it had nothing to do with the dark roast coffee she was sipping. "I have. Business is going very well so far. There's a growing need for professional organizers as people are getting busier and busier and just don't have someone at home with time to devote to that."

"Yes, it's so true. What an invaluable service. There are so many people who are overworked and deserve to come home to a nicely organized space. Don't you agree, Wyatt?" she asked, with a pointed glance at her nephew.

He shifted in his chair. "Sure, Aunt Mary."

Mary gave him a satisfied smile before turning back to Charlotte. "Do you have gift certificates available? I have a person very near and dear to me who could really use some help. I'm thinking it would make a wonderful Christmas gift," Mary said, her smile growing even wider, her eyes sparkling.

Charlotte cleared her throat, stealing a glance at Wyatt. He was staring dispassionately at his aunt, not looking at all surprised. The last thing she wanted to do was go over to Wyatt's house and clean out his pantry at his aunt's insistence. This whole situation wasn't something she was even remotely prepared for. He looked at her as though he barely knew her. The warmth he'd showed her when she first walked in had disappeared and she felt silly for being so impacted by him. She wasn't about to make a fool of herself around him. Wyatt was the last person she needed to be spending time with. "I do have gift certificates, but I usually suggest that the person doing the gifting confirm that the receiver is open to having their space organized first."

Wyatt opened his mouth, but his aunt beat him to it. "Oh, but some people don't know what they need until it hits them over the head like a cast iron frying pan."

"Yes, that's true, Mary. Sometimes you have to insist," Charlotte's grandmother said, nodding.

"I'm sure Charlotte is here to relax and spend time with Ruby for a few weeks and doesn't need to be organizing pantries," Wyatt said, his gaze fixed on his aunt.

"Well, why don't we let Charlotte decide?" his aunt said, and everyone turned their heads to stare at her.

Charlotte clutched the cup of coffee and forced a smile. How was she going to get out of this one? "Maybe I'll take a day or two to think about it? How are you doing, Grandma? Anything new at The Christmas House?" She held her breath, hoping that her dodge would be accepted and the topic of conversation would shift.

A few odd looks were exchanged. "Well, I suppose. But not in a good way," her grandmother said.

Wyatt leaned forward, bracing his forearms on his thighs and holding his coffee cup in both hands. "There's been a rash of break-ins in the neighborhood. Nothing too serious. Mostly looking for cash, purses, or anything valuable at the front door. I just wanted to let Ruby know and remind her to keep things locked, even during the day."

Charlotte's stomach dropped. She tore her eyes away from Wyatt's intense gaze to gauge her grandmother's reaction.

Grandma Ruby stirred her coffee and gave them all a forced smile, her gaze darting between Charlotte and Wyatt. "Oh, now, don't give me that look, Charlotte. It's nothing to worry about."

Charlotte's muscles tightened at the obvious downplaying. "If there wasn't anything to worry about then Wyatt wouldn't have stopped by."

Her grandmother's sweet, weathered face was suddenly showing its years, and Charlotte leaned across the couch to clasp her grandmother's hand. She shouldn't be in this big old house by herself any longer. Just the idea that someone could burst in here was horrible.

Her grandmother put down her cup and saucer, the cup precariously tipping to the side before settling. "Please don't make this a big deal, dear. I just want to enjoy our time together."

Charlotte's heart squeezed. "You're right. Let's drop it. I'm here now, so you're not by yourself," she said softly.

"And I'm right next door, so if you see anything suspicious, just reach out. There's only one Ruby Harris, and I'll never let anything happen to her," Wyatt said, the affection in his voice mingling with a clear protectiveness that Charlotte found endearing.

"I will second that!" Mary said.

Her grandmother's face actually turned pink. It seemed Wyatt's charisma was not lost on her. "Oh, Wyatt, you are a charmer."

Wyatt gave a low chuckle as he unfolded his large frame and stood, placing his empty cup back on the tray. "It's the only way I can get you to agree with me. All right then, Ruby, we'll just stay alert."

Charlotte stood as well, not completely satisfied with the resolution but not wanting to upset her grandma any further. "I'll walk you out," she said.

"That's okay, I can see myself out," he said, looking even more at home there than she did. She tried to brush off the hurt of his dismissal. Maybe she was the only one who'd thought they'd had some kind of bond as kids.

"It's no bother," Charlotte said, glancing at her grandmother. She wanted to know more about how serious the burglaries were.

Ruby nodded. "Yes, yes, see him out, dear."

"All right, well, I know there's no arguing with Ruby. Thanks for the coffee and the muffin," he said, shooting her grandma a smile. "Aunt Mary, I'll see you later."

It was one of those casual, warm smiles that shouldn't have been anything special . . . but on Wyatt Holt it was pretty spectacular. It took an otherwise hard, purely masculine face and made him seem almost boyish for a second. It made her forget to breathe, it made her forget she wasn't twelve anymore. He gestured for Charlotte to pass, and as she walked to the front door, she mentally rehearsed what she was going to tell him.

She stepped out onto the porch, Wyatt following behind. It was cold and dark, and snow fell in swirling patterns, aglow against the twinkling Christmas lights.

"I know you must be concerned about your grandmother— trust me, I am too. She's very dear to me. I'll always look out for her."

Charlotte shivered against the cold wind, feeling exhaustion and worry start to set in. Of course, she was worried about her grandmother, but she also couldn't help feeling slightly hurt by his seeming indifference toward her. She wanted to jump into a conversation of a thousand questions and catch up like old friends would. She shrugged off her irrational disappointment and followed his lead of impersonal conversation. "Are these break-ins really as innocuous as you said in front of my grandma?"

He glanced away for a moment, and she couldn't tell if he was irritated by her questions. "Not really. But I also don't think Ruby is in any danger. This place is lit up like Vegas, and she has deadbolts on all her doors, and her main floor windows are all secure."

Charlotte shivered and rubbed her hands together, feeling slightly appeased by his statement. His gaze followed her motion and she remembered that last morning, when he'd offered her his gloves. His jaw clenched and she wondered if he was remembering it too. She needed to break the silence before nostalgia took hold. "Lately I've been worried about my grandmother running this place by herself."

He gave her a nod. "I can understand that. Silver Springs is a safe community, but you never know. I'm glad you're here spending the holidays with her," he said, taking a step toward the stairs, away from the past they'd shared.

She forced a smile and glanced away from his handsome face. Her heart raced and her hands turned clammy, knowing she couldn't just let him walk away without more. "Thank you. I'm happy to have this time with her."

He gave her a nod. "It was good seeing you. I need to run. I've got to get my daughter to ballet."

Her heart squeezed. He had a daughter.

Apparently she was the only one who'd been hiding from life. She barely knew him now. After all these years, she didn't even know if she liked him, but here she was, disappointed that the man might be attached. "Nice to see you too."

He smiled back at her, a half-smile that caused her breath to lodge somewhere in her chest. For a second something flickered across his eyes, but it was gone before she could tell if she'd imagined it. "Have a good night, Charlotte."

He turned and walked down the long porch, his boots leaving large prints in the snow.

"Wait! Wyatt?" she called out, approaching him as he paused on the last porch step. She couldn't let him leave again. Not just yet.

"Yeah?"

"Just, um, thanks for looking out for my grandmother," she said, feeling silly to have called out only to tell him that. But it was true, despite her own feelings being hurt, he was looking out for her grandmother.

"I owe her," he said before giving a slight nod and walking away.

He owed her? What did that mean? She stared at his retreating figure longer than necessary, not quite ready to let go of him again. She wanted to run after him and ask him what had happened, why he'd left without saying goodbye. But that would be silly. They were adults now. With lives. People loved and people left. People didn't come back to Charlotte, and she was foolish for thinking Wyatt was any different.

CHAPTER TWO

DECEMBER 24, 1968
TORONTO

Ruby Harris clutched the doorframe of her bedroom and craned her neck carefully to hear but not be heard. Her hands were so clammy that she worried she might slip and fall into the hallway. So far, this wasn't the way tonight was supposed to go. Richard and his parents were supposed to be at the door, not on the telephone. She tiptoed into the hallway because her parents' voices were so hushed it was impossible to understand what they were saying.

Dread knotted her stomach as she caught the words "tragic" and "devastating" and "prayer."

"Ruby, come downstairs please," her father called out. His voice sounded heavy, worried. Alarm coursed through her body at the thought that he could somehow know. That would be impossible. She and Richard were going to tell both of their families together. Well,

Richard had promised that he would do the talking, which was fine by her because she didn't have the courage. Richard did. She could put her faith in him. He was the brave one.

She straightened her red sweater and then clutched her hands, composing herself as best she could. "Yes, Father," she said, already walking down the stairs.

Her parents met her at the bottom of the stairs, both their faces white and drawn. "What's wrong?" she whispered, saying a quick prayer that they didn't know the truth already, hoping that someone up there actually still listened to prayers from her, despite what she'd done.

"Dear, we've received some horrible news about Richard," her mother said.

Panic flooded Ruby's body and she stood stock still.

Her father walked forward, placing his hand on her arm. "His parents found him this morning, in his room. It appears . . . he took his own life."

Ruby floated to the ground, or that's what it felt like, when her legs stopped working, when her skirt billowed out around her like a parachute. She stared up at her parents' faces, and it felt as though she was looking at them behind a window, where their words came out muffled and they remained out of reach. Her mother's gold cross dangled in front of her, and Ruby tried to focus on it, to focus on the promise of what it symbolized. As she tried to stay alert, the realization that the man who'd promised to marry her, to explain to their parents that she was pregnant, but that he would do the right thing, slowly strangled her, making it impossible to breathe. If she had known . . . if she had known Richard was going to do this she would have begged him not to.

She would have begged him to stay. She would have tried harder to be the woman he needed.

* * *

"Why don't you go on over and give that gift certificate to Wyatt while I put the finishing touches on dinner?"

Charlotte tried not to let her discomfort show at the mention of Wyatt or that gift certificate she'd gotten roped into. After Wyatt had left yesterday, Mary had insisted on buying him one. Charlotte had gone out to the car to bring in her work bag, where she always kept a supply of her most important items.

Grandma Ruby glanced over at her from where was standing in front of the stove, stirring a large pot of her famous Italian minestrone soup, which she adamantly refused to ever hand out the secret recipe for. Her grandmother had made so many friends over the years, gathering their recipes and life stories along the way.

Charlotte forced herself to continue setting the table and pretend she wasn't bothered that her grandmother and her grandmother's friend were trying to set her up with Wyatt. She had barely slept last night. She had tossed and turned, finally falling into sleep only to find herself dreaming about her childhood, her father, Wyatt, Olivia, her mother. All these people who were so important to her had, at one time or another, all left her. As much as it hurt to think about it, somewhere along the way she'd come to the conclusion it was her. There was something in her, something that wasn't good enough. *She* wasn't enough.

Seeing Wyatt had sent the avalanche of insecurities tumbling through her dreams. But they weren't kids anymore, and he had probably never even thought of her until yesterday. He had been desperate to leave the porch, and she would never beg to be close to someone again.

"Judging by the look of horror on Wyatt's face when Mary suggested I organize his house, I don't think it would be a good idea."

"Wyatt *does* have a wonderful face, and he is a wonderful man. What a surprise it must have been to see him. Tell me again how you know each other?"

The entire thing was ridiculous, as was the obvious reference to Wyatt's looks, even if her grandmother was right about his face. Charlotte fiddled with the edge of her napkin. "He lived in our building for a year, and he also went to our school. One day his family just took off," she said, not mentioning it was the same day her dad had left too. She didn't want to get into all that.

Her grandmother turned to her, her eyes pensive. "It can't be a coincidence after all these years that he just happens to be the man who bought the house next to mine."

Charlotte crossed her arms, refusing to agree. "Grandma, that's exactly what it is."

"Of all the small towns and properties . . ."

Charlotte rolled her eyes but softened her rebuff with a smile. "Coincidence."

"Providence."

Oh, *no*. "Grandma, please. He was born in Silver Springs before he moved to Toronto. His aunt lives here. That's why he's here."

"Still. You have to deliver that gift certificate. It would be fraud if you didn't. You accepted money from Mary."

Charlotte let out a choked laugh. "I wasn't planning on pocketing the money. I was just going to . . . mail it."

"Charlotte, you will do no such thing. Deliver it. He would never be upset by you bringing over a gift from his aunt."

"Well, why didn't Mary just give it to him?"

"She wants *you* to give it to him," her grandmother said, lifting the wooden spoon to her lips and taking a taste.

"Why do I get the feeling that I'm being set up?"

Her grandmother smiled. "Because you are! Mary is just trying to look out for Wyatt, and she wants to see him happy again. I've talked a lot about you and how proud I am of everything you've accomplished with your business. It's harmless. You should be flattered. Wyatt is a man many women have pursued, but with no luck."

There was no way she'd ever pursue a man, let alone a cop. Charlotte took down two white china bowls with holly rims and placed them on the counter beside the stove. She had no idea how she was going to reply to this one without hurting her grandmother's feelings. "I'm flattered Mary likes me and thinks that I'd be a match for her nephew, but you can't just throw two random people together and think magic will happen. I've told you before, I have no interest in a relationship. I like my life the way it is."

Grandma Ruby pursed her lips and silently filled each bowl with the hearty soup. "First of all, you are not *random people*. And you know I'm all for pursuing your dreams and having ambition. I wouldn't be here if I didn't. But when you're not admitting things to yourself and hiding from the truth, you need to examine why."

"Hiding from the truth?" Charlotte said as she picked up the soup-filled bowls and brought them to the table.

Grandma Ruby nodded, her hair bopping with the motion as she sat down across from her at the large farmhouse table. "Yes. The truth is that you hide from people and meaningful relationships.

And I'm not one to judge . . . I've pushed important people away too and I'm not sure that was right, in fact I'm certain it wasn't right. Don't be like me and figure it out too late. We were not made to be alone, Charlotte."

"I don't need a man to make me happy, Grandma," she said, trying not to sound defensive.

"Lord knows we don't need men. I'm talking about people in general. You have no one. Next thing you know, you'll be coming here on your visits carting five cats with you."

Great. Her grandmother thought she was going to become a lonely cat woman. "I'm allergic."

"You know what I mean. I never hear about you going out with friends or going on vacation with people or any kind of meaningful relationships. Your sister, on the other hand, dives headfirst into relationships and makes bad choices."

Charlotte ignored the bit about her, because she was still reeling from the cat-lady assumptions and leaned forward. "You think Will was a bad choice too?"

Grandma Ruby lifted a filled spoon to her mouth and raised her eyebrows. "I think we both know the answer to that."

"Have you heard anything from Olivia?" Charlotte asked, relieved that she hadn't been wrong about Will. Not that she wanted her sister to be married to a jerk, but she didn't want to be the only one who thought so. She hadn't heard from her sister in weeks. Up until Will, they had been in contact daily. Phone, text, they always knew what was going on in each other's lives. But Olivia had slipped away from Charlotte so gradually that she hadn't even noticed at first. A day became a week, then a month. She understood that being a new mother was difficult, but the distancing had started even before baby Dawn was born. Charlotte had been pushed out. She didn't really feel welcome in their home, and Olivia's husband, Will, hadn't ever been conversational or warm with her. Olivia would rattle off excuses about Will being an introvert or stressed out from work. Charlotte had wanted to throw Olivia a baby shower but had been emphatically turned down.

"No, I didn't manage to talk to her but I did leave a message. Hopefully she and that adorable little baby will still be able to come for Christmas. It would be wonderful to have you all home," Grandma said, stirring freshly grated Pecorino Romano cheese into her soup. The comforting aroma of the soup and freshly baked bread in the old kitchen filled Charlotte with an unexpected longing for her childhood. There had been a simplicity to it—even though it had been far from perfect, it had been simple in comparison to now. There had been absolutes—she had a sister who was also her best friend, she had a mother, a grandmother . . . and no father. But they'd been happy when they visited The Christmas House. She blinked back tears and tried to focus on the warmth and sounds from the fire crackling in the room, the view of the snow-covered hills that ran into the frozen-over river out the window. That feeling, the one that had gripped her as Wyatt had walked away last night, snuck up on her again. She didn't like it. It was this house, her grandmother. Too much . . . feeling.

"I guess she's just busy with Dawn," Charlotte said, forcing a smile. She didn't want to expand on any of it because it would hurt to talk about how rejected she felt.

"Well, new babies are a lot of work, and the transition to motherhood isn't a piece of cake for most," her grandmother said, tasting a spoonful of the soup.

"I'm sure. Maybe I'll text her tonight and see if we can get an answer," she said.

Her grandmother put her spoon down and frowned at her. "Pick up a telephone, child, and hold it to your ear. You should let her hear the softness and concern in your voice. A text is void of emotion and feeling."

Charlotte brushed off her embarrassment. "That's what emojis are for, Grandma."

Her grandmother's eyes narrowed. "Stop ignoring your problems, Charlotte. Face them."

Charlotte's mouth dropped open. "What? I thought we already established that Will was the problem."

Her grandmother let out a muffled laugh. "Will may have his issues, but *you* are the one I'm concerned about."

Charlotte leaned back with a huff. "What? I'm the one who has my life together, Grandma."

"Yes, sweetheart. All you young people have your lives together. Wyatt too."

She knew better than to argue. She toyed with her spoon. "Wyatt said something about owing you one. What did he mean by that?"

Her grandmother raised an eyebrow, a small smirk appearing on her mouth. "Maybe you'll find out if you deliver that gift certificate."

"I don't need to know that badly," she said with a laugh.

Her grandmother raised her eyebrows. "We'll see. Oh, also, your mother called this afternoon. She'll be arriving any day now."

Oh no. She had counted on having the entire week leading up to Christmas Eve with just Grandma Ruby. "Mom's coming before Christmas?"

"Yes. She promised she would be here the day before Christmas Eve at the latest. Apparently she's very busy at work."

Charlotte tried to swallow the soup that had tasted amazing just a minute ago, but which she now had trouble getting down. Her mom would bring holiday drama, hidden resentment, and anger. Of course Charlotte wanted to see her . . . kind of . . . but the thought of a low-key Christmas was also appealing. She wasn't going to tell her grandma that her mother was most definitely not working herself to the bone—last she heard she was off "finding herself" for the tenth time in her adult life. Charlotte wanted to change the subject. "Right . . . This is all delicious, Grandma."

"Good. I'm glad you enjoy it. It's always nice to cook for a loved one."

Charlotte fiddled with her spoon for a moment and then took a deep breath.

"How did you become such good friends with Wyatt?"

Her grandmother broke off another piece of bread and chewed slowly before answering. "Not how you would imagine, probably. But when I met Wyatt, he was a very different man. He came back here to start over with his daughter about two years ago. His wife just plain walked out on them one day. His Aunt Mary helps out as much as she can. He had a lot on his plate, getting over the end of a marriage and moving forward with a very grueling career."

Charlotte swallowed the flavorful soup too, with difficulty. That wasn't what she'd expected. A pang of sadness hit her. He deserved more than that. But what did she know? Maybe he had turned out to be someone very different from the man of her twelve-year-old dreams. "That's a lot to handle," she said, finally.

Her grandmother nodded. "It is, but he did it. Wyatt is one of those people that I consider family. As I always say, blood is a cheap substitute for true love."

Charlotte's heart squeezed at the old saying. She knew enough about her grandmother's past to know why she could say that. They didn't know all the details, but whenever her mother or Grandma Ruby would talk about the past, she and Olivia would cling to the tidbits and try to piece together the real story. Whenever they'd asked for the details, they were told it was in the past and no one wanted to discuss it.

"So, Grandma, how are you feeling? I didn't want to get into things with Wyatt here earlier, but are you okay?"

Her grandmother reached for the bottle of Perrier, but Charlotte grabbed it first and poured her grandmother a glass. "Thank you, dear. Yes, I'm fine. Still fine enough to run a big old place like this if that's what you're getting at."

Charlotte took a drink of water and stared at her grandmother from across the rim of the glass. "Of course. I'm just looking out for you. I was thinking that while I'm visiting I can help you get ready for the season at Christmas House."

Her grandmother's eyes widened, her sky-blue eyes sparkling. "I was hoping you'd say that. I would love the time with you. But I also know you have a career and a business to run, so I don't want you to put yourself out."

Charlotte shook her head. "Not at all. This is long overdue. Starting my organizing business was crazy, but honestly, the month of December is dead. No one has time to organize their life in December."

Her grandmother's lips twitched. "Except Wyatt."

Charlotte took a long sip of water, wishing it was wine. "Well, we'll see. Now, January, *that* will be chaos, but I already have all my ads set up. So I am all yours for the whole month!"

Her grandmother beamed. "Excellent! We will catch up. I want to hear all the details about your company and life in the city."

She loved that her grandmother had always supported entrepreneurship and having big dreams. When she'd started her company three years ago, her grandmother had been the one to give her that final push and confidence boost. While it hadn't exactly been easy, she was able to support herself, and her business was growing. She had every reason to expect that she'd be able to pull this thing off. "Well, I'm happy to give you all the details. Should I get us a bottle of wine?"

Her grandmother's eyes lit up. "Yes! Find something that you like in the cold cellar. Good idea. A little wine is exactly what we need."

Charlotte stood, ready for a glass of wine. "I'll be right back." A minute later, Charlotte placed her foot gingerly on the old wooden steps leading to the basement and flicked on the light switch. Unfortunately, the light only emphasized the dust and cobwebs along the stairwell. She hated this basement—she and Olivia had spent many summer nights under makeshift tents telling ghosts stories with their grandmother's basement as the setting. It was decent—as decent as a basement predating the 1850s could be—but it was unfinished and rough by today's standards.

She gripped the wobbly handrail, as the stairs were uneven, and took a sharp turn at the end. Stopping once she reached the bottom, she surveyed the area, her gaze taking in the groupings of cardboard boxes and random pieces of old furniture. More importantly, she scanned for any sign of mice, bats, or spiders larger than a quarter; the ghost stories had also starred life-sized rodents that attacked. She hadn't been able to rid herself of that particular childhood memory.

Walking to the cold cellar as efficiently as possible, Charlotte entered the small room, leaving the door open for light. She scanned the full rack for the right wine and quickly grabbed a bottle, relieved she didn't have to spend longer than necessary down there. Making her way across the dusty cement floor, she paused as her gaze caught something in the usually empty space. Frowning, she approached the opening in the wall—which she'd always assumed would be the perfect place for an ax murderer to hide.

She held her breath, her eyes on a box with her mother's name written on it, sitting on the ledge. Chewing her lower lip, she wrestled with her conscience. She should just walk away. It wasn't hers. It was probably an empty box anyway. Or maybe just filled with loose change and hair clips or something insignificant like that. Then again, if it was so insignificant, it probably wasn't that big a deal if she opened it. And it was odd that it was down here. Maybe her grandma had misplaced it and was looking for it. Then Charlotte could give it to her.

There, she was going with that. She touched the smooth surface of the wooden box and opened the lid.

Her breath caught at the sight of a pink, knit baby's dress and hat; her mother's, no doubt. An envelope with her mother's name in her grandmother's cursive writing sat on top. She tugged on her lower lip and gingerly opened it. A copy of her mother's birth certificate, with her mother's birthdate along with her grandmother's name stared at her. It took her a moment to pick up on what seemed odd about the name staring at her . . . *Miss* Ruby Harris. She had thought that "Harris" was her grandmother's married name. And she'd thought her grandmother had been married when her mother was born. The space beside the father's name was blank. Charlotte's heart rattled around furiously as she held the paper in her hand.

"Charlotte, are you all right?"

Charlotte gasped and hastily shoved everything back in its place, her cheeks burning as though she'd just committed a crime. As she walked back upstairs, her hands were still shaking at what she'd uncovered. The box of mementos from her mother's birth . . . the missing information on the birth certificate, all secrets from a past that was obviously supposed to remain hidden.

CHAPTER THREE

DECEMBER 24, 1968
TORONTO

Ruby opened her eyes, the sensation of the cool washcloth against her forehead calming and reassuring.

"Dear, please say something. Are you all right?"

Ruby nodded slowly as her parents grasped her arms, helping her sit.

Her father leaned forward and brushed her hair from her face. "I know this is a shock, sweetheart. We know how much Richard meant to you. We were all expecting the two of you to announce your engagement."

She shut her eyes again as a wave of nausea hit her. Richard. Why hadn't she been enough? A part of her wanted to just go back up to bed and cry herself to sleep, but she knew that wouldn't be possible. He had left her here to face the shame alone.

She needed to tell them the truth. Before she could grieve Richard, she needed to tell them the truth. "He was going to tell you," she began but paused as she stared into her parents' concerned eyes.

Her mother placed her arm around her shoulders and Ruby wanted to turn into her and clutch her like a child. She wanted to believe that her mother would hold her closer when she found out the truth, that she would whisper that it would all be okay. "We know. He was a fine young man, darling."

They helped her stand, and she reached for the staircase railing as she wobbled slightly. She wasn't sure if it was the same faintness that had been following her for the last two weeks or whether it was knowing that the man who was supposed to be her fiancé had left her alone.

"Let's get you off to bed, Ruby. We can talk about this in the morning. You need your rest," her father said, his typically stern face filled with sympathy.

Ruby wanted to take that offer to just put everything on hold until the morning, but she knew it wouldn't get better in the morning. The truth would loom in the darkness tonight, turning itself into an ugly, grotesque monster. She would survive. Her parents would help her. "I . . . I don't know how to tell you this. Richard . . . he was supposed to come here tonight to ask for your permission to marry me . . . but also, to tell you that I'm pregnant."

She watched, with growing horror, as her parents did not move toward her with sympathy, with unconditional love, but instead recoiled as though she were some kind of monster instead of their own flesh and blood. She waited, maybe with the last bit of naïveté left in her body; she waited for the love and grace she had been led to believe would always be there for her. In those few moments she learned what it was like to not be good enough, good enough for anyone to fight for.

*   *   *

"You don't have to sit and watch me, you know," Samantha said.

Wyatt ignored the jab straight through his heart, delivered by his preteen daughter in one short sentence, practically dripping with irritation. But it was a welcome distraction, because he'd been living in the past since the moment he'd opened Ruby Harris's front door to find Charlotte standing there last night. Charlotte was the past he'd been trying to forget his entire adult life.

"Dad, hurry," Samantha said as they walked through the dark parking lot of the bustling ballet studio, forcing him to concentrate on the present. He'd been a cop for over a decade and had seen a helluva lot of nasty stuff, but nothing had prepared him for having a twelve-year-old daughter. There were some days he didn't know if he was cut out for this—like his daughter going through puberty and all the sass that came with it might actually kill him. He glanced down at the top of her dark hair, pulled back into a perfect bun, as he held open the door to the dance studio and tried to play it cool. "Okay, thanks. I'll just pay for your class and hobble back under the rock I came from."

He was rewarded with an eye roll before she ran off and caught up with her friends. The studio was swarming with dancers ending and starting their classes. Making his way through the sea of parents and kids, Wyatt tried not to remember the day Sam had started ballet after begging him for a solid month. The receptionist at the front desk had quickly hopped out of her chair and rushed over to them, horrified by his sorry-ass attempt at a real ballet bun. Penny had taken the time to show Wyatt how to do a proper ballet bun and, after only half a dozen more sessions with her, he'd mastered it. He could now proudly do a bun in his sleep, except Sam did her own buns now.

He wasn't so sure when it had happened, but somewhere between eleven and twelve he'd become . . . embarrassing to her. Of course, he knew preteens were self-conscious and all the memes about them were basically on point, but somehow he'd thought maybe he'd be exempt from that. He had naïvely—which was ironic because he wasn't naïve about anything—thought that because they were so close she would never be embarrassed by him. What was even more surprising was that his feelings were actually hurt. Not so hurt that he made an issue of it, but it made him nostalgic for simpler days. Like the days when he would instinctively place his hand out and know that within seconds her smaller one would clasp onto his like a magnet. Now, he knew if he held that same hand out, he'd just feel air on his skin. No one had prepared him for that. No one had prepared him for guiding a daughter through adolescence.

He sought out the empty bench in front of the viewing window of the ballet studio, ignoring Sam's statement that he didn't need to watch.

"You look like you could use something a hell of a lot stronger than coffee."

Wyatt turned in the direction of the voice and smiled up at his oldest and best friend, Scott Martin. Scott joined him on the bench and handed him a coffee and placed a giant basket wrapped in cellophane and a red ribbon between them. "Yeah, probably until Sam's in her twenties. What's with the basket?"

"Oh, yeah. Here, you can have it," he said, shoving it closer to Wyatt.

Wyatt glanced inside. It looked like . . . cheese and crackers and a bunch of other random things he had no use for. "What is this?"

Scott stared straight ahead and took a sip of coffee. "An early Christmas present or something. Aunt Mary made me buy it."

Wyatt pondered where to start with that one. His Aunt Mary was also "Aunt Mary" to Scott and his daughter. "She's forcing you to buy cheese baskets?"

Scott turned to him and pointed to things in the basket. "Uh, yeah, with ulterior motives I guess. I had just picked up a coffee at the Main Bean next door and ran into your aunt outside. She basically shoved me into the cheese shop and made a beeline to the back in order to introduce me to the new owner, Meghan, I think. I felt bad so I had to buy something."

His aunt needed to be stopped. Clearly she thought he and Scott were in need of her help. "Wow, sorry, man. I'll see if I can tell her that we're perfectly happy alone."

Scott snorted. "Yeah. So happy. Who would have thought the two of us would be sitting here one day, two girls the same age and single?"

"With a random basket of cheese between us," Wyatt said before taking a drink of the coffee. He and Scott had become friends in the first grade when Scott had shared his sandwich with him when he noticed Wyatt didn't have a lunch. Wyatt repaid the favor later that day when he spotted a third-grader bullying Scott at recess and decked the kid. From that point on they had been inseparable, even when Wyatt's family had moved from Silver Springs to the city.

And when Scott's wife died, Wyatt had dropped everything to be there for him. When a job opening was available, he'd jumped on it. His aunt was happy to have him back in Silver Springs, and his best friend was grateful. Sam had been the only holdout.

Now, their daughters were best friends and instead of having a beer by himself on Saturday nights, or pretending he didn't need a beer when Aunt Mary was around, he had a beer with Scott while their daughters hung out in any room of the house that the dads weren't in. He'd thought their days of feeling like idiots in high school were over, but their preteen daughters had managed to rekindle that particular emotion.

He'd almost go so far as saying they were thriving, but he knew that would be a stretch. He didn't know if Scott would ever get over the loss of his wife. They'd been the real deal, and many times Wyatt had found himself envying the kind of relationship they'd had. Scott's wife's death had shaken all of them.

"Saturday morning coffee is on me," he said, taking a sip of piping hot coffee.

"Damn right. This is my second time in a row picking up coffee," his friend said, sitting beside him on the bench. "Also, you should know that Aunt Mary is trying to set you up with Ruby's granddaughter."

Wyatt shut his eyes briefly, only to find the image of Charlotte Harris in his mind, where she'd remained since he saw her yesterday. Her dark, glossy hair had tumbled around her shoulders and her blue eyes—that he was pretty certain were the same as Ruby's—had been inquisitive and sharp. Her seriousness had seemed almost severe on an otherwise beautiful face, so much so that it had almost taken him aback. He could still picture her back in Toronto. Charlotte had been a ray of sunshine in his otherwise shitty life. There were things he had never talked about with anyone except Scott, but on his walks to and from school with Charlotte, he'd found himself opening up to her without intending to. She had always seemed to understand. He knew her home life had been shitty too, and maybe that's why he'd opened up to her . . . but there was more to it than that.

He hadn't been prepared for the emotional hit when he saw her standing there last night. But he'd been kind of an ass. He hadn't given her a proper reaction, he hadn't been warm, and then he'd brushed her off. She deserved more than that. She had been important to him and he had disappeared and never saw anyone from that school or building again. He owed her an explanation. But he didn't want to get into it, he didn't want to dredge up the past. He'd spent years outrunning it.

Charlotte had been as sweet as he remembered—her affection for her grandmother had been obvious, as had her disappointment in him. But she'd been very gracious to his persistent aunt. At least she hadn't fallen for the gift certificate scheme hatched by Aunt Mary.

"Apparently, Ruby's granddaughter is a gorgeous and talented entrepreneur," Scott said.

"Yeah . . . She's actually someone I knew in Toronto when I was a kid," he said, bracing himself for the reaction he knew this statement would illicit. He wanted off this topic.

"Seriously? What are the odds of that? I'm sure Aunt Mary is going to put some kind of destiny spin on that one."

Wyatt shrugged, already knowing what was in his future. The coincidence hadn't been lost on him either. When he'd first spotted

Charlotte's picture in Ruby's house last year, he'd dismissed it, thinking it must just be a faint resemblance to the girl he used to know. But then Ruby had talked about her granddaughters. And he'd seen the picture of Charlotte's little sister, and he'd known. Hell of a curve ball life threw sometimes.

"She can try. I'm not interested though, and I'm pretty sure Charlotte isn't either. We were kids. We're basically strangers. I'm not looking to complicate my life right now with someone from my past . . . or any woman at all. You get it. There's just too much going on. I made a mistake once, and I'm not going to do it again. I can't do that to Sam."

Wyatt turned back to watching the class and the students jumping around the room. He didn't want to introduce a woman to Sam, to have her go through the insecurity of allowing a woman into their lives that would be some kind of mother figure. He had seen shows where divorced parents started over again, and it looked like hell. He'd been to hell, and he was thankful he was back. He had no intention of revisiting it and dragging his daughter with him. As long as he could make Sam happy, then why the hell would he go searching for something that could ruin everything for them?

Scott let out a rough sigh. "I know. It kind of sucks."

"It does."

"When did we get this old and pathetic, Wy?"

Wyatt sat upright and glared at his friend. "Speak for yourself. We're not old, and I'm definitely not pathetic. We're just being good dads and we're busy with work. I'm barely hanging on, man. It's work or the dance studio. I can't even cook a meal or keep up with laundry. There's no time for anything else."

Scott nodded. "Okay. You're right, let's go with that; we're too busy. You update Aunt Mary on our position."

Wyatt nodded. "Done. I'll tell her. We have no interest in relationships."

"That's a great plan. She won't buy it. But good luck."

Wyatt shot him a look and turned his attention back to the window. He was right.

An hour later, Wyatt was arguing with Sam as they walked up the front steps of their house.

"I don't get why I can't wear makeup," she said as he held the door open for her and balanced their takeout pizza and stupid cheese basket in the other.

He hung up his coat and tried not to lose his temper when she threw hers on the hallway chair and it flopped to the floor. They had been circling this same argument for the entire car ride home. Or maybe the entire year. Seventh grade was a crash course for both of them. It was so bad that he'd kept scanning the sides of the roads in the hopes there might be some kind of non–life threatening accident, a car in a ditch, or anything that would get him out of finishing this conversation he wasn't qualified for. He just wanted to say, "because I said so" and open a bottle of beer. "Because you're twelve. You don't need makeup."

She rolled her eyes and stomped into the kitchen. "You don't even know what it's like to be a kid these days. I'm not even allowed to have any social media accounts, which has basically solidified my social status as loser. You don't get it because when you were a kid people used flip phones."

He nodded, placing the takeout pizza on the table and cramming the large cheese basket into the already messy fridge. He handed Sam a plate when he turned around and found her already eating. "Yes, it's your generation that has it all together. Clearly. Judging by the teenagers coming into the station, you guys have all the answers."

"I don't even want this pizza!" she said after eating a slice and then throwing her crust down on the table.

He spoke through clenched teeth. "You know it's only kids who don't eat crust. So as much as you think you're all grown up, you're still a kid, Sam. *My* kid. And it's my job to make sure you're safe and happy."

"Well, you failed at the happy part!"

* * *

Charlotte had no idea how she'd agreed to deliver a gift certificate to Wyatt next door. Oh, she did know—his aunt and her grandmother had bulldozed her into doing it. That was fine.

Charlotte buttoned up her navy wool coat in front of the front hall mirror as she bundled up to walk over to Wyatt's house and deliver the gift certificate. She needed the fresh air, and a nice little walk was perfect. It's not like she had to talk to Wyatt or anything. She'd just slip the envelope with enclosed gift certificate under the front rug and run away like a child. Except as a child she never would have run away from him.

She picked up her hat and then placed it back on the coat rack. It would be a shame to ruin the hair she'd actually taken the time to curl into soft waves. Not that she'd styled it on the off chance that she *would* run into Wyatt, because she didn't know what that said about her.

A few minutes later she was breathing in the sharp smell of pine and winter as she walked along the road that led to Wyatt's house. Now this was a street of dreams; century-old homes were scattered along the winding roads like stately symbols of a bygone era that was filled with propriety and prestige. Enormous oak trees, with leaves long lost to the fall wind, bordered the properties, and towering pines majestically lined the streets, their branches bowing under the weight of the freshly fallen snow. Some houses had professionally strung lights, reaching all the way up to the towering evergreens, creating a sparkling landscape.

She knew so many people complained about the winter weather, but she loved it. She loved how crisp the air was, how it was almost startling when you first breathed it in after coming from the warmth inside. She loved the feel of snow under her boots as she walked, the way it coated and topped the grass. She could watch the snow fall for hours, and it always brought a smile to her face, even when things were at their worst. Even after her father left.

There was a point in her life when she had fixated on the day her father would come home. Lying in bed at night after Olivia had fallen asleep, she'd imagine hearing the reassuring sound of his footsteps approaching their room, and she could practically feel his lips pressed on her forehead whispering goodnight. Other nights she'd dream about opening the front door after hearing a pounding and have her father tumble in, blood soaking the front of his police uniform and him mumbling about how he'd gone undercover to save a family and that was why he'd stayed away. She'd run and call 911 and would save his life and they'd all be reunited.

But her favorite fantasy was the Christmas Day one—the one where she and Olivia would run into the family room, and sitting beside the tree would be their father, drinking coffee with their mother and smiling. That fantasy didn't even have an explanation about where he'd gone. In that one, her hurt, her pride, her anger didn't matter because he'd come home to them. After a year, she'd stopped going to sleep dreaming of him, angry with herself when she'd have a bad day that she'd want to revert to those old comforting thoughts.

The world could be so cruel, and her father, her hero, had been a part of the cruelty. Maybe that was the worst of all of it, because he'd instilled this deep sense of mistrust in her, this belief that people were inherently selfish beings, that when the going got tough, love, blood, honor meant nothing compared to one's own needs. She had blamed herself for so long—that she hadn't been good enough for him to stay.

Which was why she never made relationships a priority. She didn't need men . . . just like her grandmother. She needed to find out about the box of memories. The women in their family were basically cursed. Grandma Ruby had been on her own forever, and now with what Charlotte had found in the basement, she knew there was something even bigger in her grandmother's past, which she was planning on discussing with Liv. Their mother had been a single mom for a long time. Olivia was the only one who seemed to be managing as a married Harris woman. But then again, it's not like Olivia's husband, Will, was a gem or anything. Not that Charlotte would ever express that to her sister—the time to voice any thoughts about Olivia's love life was long gone.

Pausing at the end of the driveway that led up to Wyatt's house, Charlotte quickly surveyed the house and grounds. The misty blue siding stood out boldly against the white snow and white trim of the front porch. White lights were strung along the roofline and on the front bushes that lined the walkway. A Christmas tree was visible in the front window, with twinkling lights. The Cape Cod–style home seemed cheerful and casual and very much the idyllic family home. The house was nestled and protected from the road by the rows of massive pines and was pretty enough to be on the front of a postcard. It was a far cry from where they'd grown up, and Charlotte was happy for him.

She made her way up the walkway. What was she going to say if Wyatt saw her? It would be awkward. She hated awkward conversations.

She paused on the bottom step of the porch when she heard a young woman's voice yell from inside: "*Well, you failed at the happy part!*"

Charlotte cringed and decided to hurry. This clearly wasn't a good time. Wyatt's deep voice boomed: "*Well, at least I'm trying, and I don't roll my eyes so much that they're in danger of disappearing into the back of my head forever.*"

Charlotte looked around frantically for a place to just leave the envelope and run. The rug had snow on it, and the gift certificate would be soaked and ruined. Maybe she could slip it in between the screen door and the frame. Carefully opening the screen door, she winced at the loud creak it made as she tried to get the envelope to stay.

The door swung open, and she looked up to see Wyatt standing there. "You just saved my life."

Maybe it was that display of vulnerability, or that half second before they both burst out laughing, or the way he'd run his fingers through his already mussed-up hair, or the way his five o'clock shadow seemed to accentuate the strong lines of his handsome face, or that genuine sparkle in his eyes, the one that hadn't changed after all these years, that made Charlotte very happy that Aunt Mary had roped her into delivering this gift certificate.

CHAPTER FOUR

DECEMBER 24, 1968
TORONTO

Ruby leaned her head against the cold front door of her home and cried like a child. She pounded her fist on the door again and again, begging for them to let her back in, letting any pride in her body seep out of her until she was a pathetic shell of the woman she had thought she was. She wept for Richard, for her childhood that was gone, for the rejection that had ripped a hole inside her heart she knew would never heal.

After what must have been an hour, her knuckles red and throbbing from knocking, her throat parched and her body shaking with cold, she knew it was time to go. Pride broke through the sorrow, prodding her upright, and she stood on shaking limbs. Buttoning her wool coat, she stumbled down the front walk, her heels no match for the slippery layer of snow. She just needed to think of a plan, where she would go, who would take her in. Snow tumbled from the black sky and swirled around her, frenzied and hostile.

She stared down at her hands and saw her father's hand holding hers. How many times had she clung to his hand? How many times had he been a hero to her? And now? Now what? That hand wouldn't hold hers when she needed it most? That hand promised only conditional love.

She numbly felt for coins in her pocket as she walked down her street. Richard was dead. Her parents had disowned her, and in a few days it would be Christmas. In a few months she would be a mother. Without a husband, without family, without a job, and without a significant amount of money. She let out another sob, the dense, damp, winter air capturing her breath.

Walking without knowing where to go, wind whipped mercilessly around her and Ruby knew she would never let them win, she would never join Richard. She walked for what felt like hours, huddled inside her thin coat, her feet soaked, her face icy. She walked until one building beckoned, the lights inside glowing extra bright, almost pulling her forward even though she didn't think she could walk another step.

Through blurred eyes, Ruby read the words: The Sisters of St. Michael's. She knew of them. Their compassion and charitable work were legendary. But not for her. There wouldn't be grace for her.

The snow had turned to freezing pellets of rain, and her hair was heavy, matting to her head, filled with icicles as she slowly, painfully lifted her face to the sky and prayed to the same God her parents believed in. She closed her eyes and prayed for guidance, for grace, for salvation as ice battered her skin.

"Are you all right, dear?"

Ruby opened her eyes, alarmed to see a woman walking toward her.

"Do you need help? Do you have anywhere to go?"

Ruby's lip trembled, and she was mortified because the emotions she usually hid so well were bubbling to the surface. "I . . . I will find somewhere."

The woman tilted her head. "I'm Sister Juliette. Why don't you come inside and warm up? There's a hot dinner waiting inside by the fire, and if you need a warm bed tonight, we have those too."

Ruby held her gaze, reading the truth in her eyes. "Thank you, Sister, but I'm not . . . I don't belong inside. I've done something and . . ."

Sister Juliette reached out and placed her hand on Ruby's shoulder. "Come inside, my dear. No one will judge you here. You are safe. You are welcome."

Ruby clutched her hands together tightly, trying to find the strength to trust this woman, but refusing to lie about herself. "I'm pregnant. I don't have a husband. I'm alone."

Sister Juliette put her arm around Ruby's shoulders, pulling her in like a lost sheep. "You are never alone. Come inside, dear. Rest, eat, pray."

Tears ran down Ruby's cheeks as they walked up the steps, the kindness shown to her by this stranger, a warm blanket on her soul.

If she'd known then that Sister Juliette was going to save her life, to give her purpose and direction, she would have slept peacefully that night. Instead, she lay awake in the narrow but clean and warm bed, staring at the ceiling, hating herself, crying for her parents and Richard, afraid for her future.

After she finally whispered the prayers she'd whispered her entire life, she vowed that she would never again be weak, vulnerable, and would never again lose her soul for a man. And if she was given another chance, a new life, she knew that the way forward would be with the grace the sisters had shown her. She would never shut her door on a soul in need.

*   *   *

Wyatt held the door open a little wider. "Come on in," he said, a jolt of awareness rocking through him as Charlotte shot him a smile and entered the house. A memory hit him as he caught that smile; it was the one she used to give him when he'd hold the door open for her at their apartment building. She'd always made him feel like he was good enough. It had been a new feeling for him—in his home, he'd never been good enough. He had been shown with a hand or a belt or whatever object was lying around just how little he meant. He *had* learned how to be a man, though, by being the exact opposite of his father.

"This is weird, isn't it?" Charlotte said softly, looking up at him with those blue eyes that seemed to take him right back to Toronto and the eighth grade.

He shoved his hands in his pockets, knowing he owed her more than he had given her last night, even if it made him uncomfortable. He didn't want her to ask why he'd disappeared. He wouldn't lie, but he hated looking back to those days and how powerless he was. "It's one hell of a coincidence." Charlotte's dark hair fell in glossy waves around her shoulders and her neck, and the green scarf she was wearing deepened the color of her blue eyes to dark sapphire.

"I know . . . I'm sorry. I'll be quick. I didn't mean to just barge over here unannounced. I was just planning on slipping this under the rug and . . . It was just . . . your aunt was so persuasive . . ."

He wasn't being welcoming enough, and now she was doubting herself. He forced himself to relax and not act like an ass. The last thing he wanted was to make Charlotte uncomfortable. "Bossy. I think the word might be bossy."

She smiled up at him, a soft laugh escaping her mouth. "Maybe."

He smiled back. "Trust me. This was nice of you. Thank you."

She shrugged and took a step back toward the door. "You don't have to use it anytime soon. I know it's the holidays and totally not a time to be organizing your house."

"Dad, I can't find anything in this stupid pantry! Do you know where the peanut butter is?" Sam yelled before appearing in the doorway. Her eyes darted to Charlotte and her face turned red.

Wyatt stifled his grin of satisfaction at Sam's embarrassment. "Charlotte, this is Samantha, my daughter. Sam, this is Ruby's granddaughter . . . and an old friend."

Charlotte gave her a friendly wave. "Nice to meet you, Samantha."

Wyatt hoped like hell Sam wouldn't ask how they knew each other. He didn't want to get into that with Sam. The fewer questions about that time in his life, the better. He also didn't want to get into that day when he'd left school. There were things that were better off buried. "Nice to meet you too. Did you, um, say something about organizing? My dad really needs major help," she said, leaning against the doorjamb and crossing her arms like a seasoned sergeant.

Wyatt shook his head. For someone who was so concerned about being embarrassed all the time, his daughter clearly had no qualms about humiliating *him*.

Before he could defend himself and not appear like a giant slob, Charlotte spoke up.

"Well, it's hard to keep on top of everything. Your Aunt Mary was telling me how busy your dad is at work, and that was why she wanted him to get some extra help. I find a lot of times, people just need the right organizational tools and techniques and then it's smooth sailing. Anyway, I'll just leave that gift certificate with you. It was great meeting you, Samantha. I'll see you guys later," she said with a smile that made him want her to stay. That wasn't new. Charlotte had always had the sweetest smile, one that made him want to latch onto her light.

"Nice to meet you too," Sam said.

He cleared his throat and turned back to Charlotte. "Do you want to come in for a coffee?"

"Oh, no, thanks. I hate intruding and being that drop-in guest that everyone dreads. I really was planning on leaving it on the doorstep," she said with a small laugh and taking a step back, bumping into the door.

"That's okay. My dad has nothing to do tonight anyway."

Wyatt clenched his jaw but hoped that his smile did an adequate job of hiding it. Charlotte bit her lower lip and lifted sparkling eyes to him.

He shrugged. "It's true. I was just planning on arguing with a preteen about makeup and reminiscing about flip phones."

Her gaze darted to the door and then back to him, and he tensed, disappointment already filling him at the prospect of her leaving. "Okay, well then, I'd love to."

He shot her a smile, surprised by how happy he was. Maybe Scott was actually onto something about not wanting to be alone.

"Follow me, but no judgment," he said as they walked toward the kitchen, suddenly worried that he might actually be the slob his daughter made him out to be. It's not like he intended on being disorganized, it just happened somehow. He could never let things slide at work, but at home, there was just too much happening and he was usually too wiped by the end of the day to worry about the state of his kitchen cupboards. After Leanne had walked out on them, he'd been left struggling and had never really found a way to manage all of it. He assumed that when Sam got older, life would get easier. He hadn't counted on her love of dance and how much time all the extracurricular stuff would take up. There had never been enough money growing up for him to be able to pick up a sport, and he still remembered what it felt like to listen to all the other kids talk about their hockey or baseball games. He wanted more for Sam and wanted her to pursue whatever she wanted. But that left little time for all the other household tasks.

"Your home is lovely," Charlotte said, looking around.

There was a quiet confidence about her, and he liked the way she easily maneuvered her way around his daughter's comments. Sam was another surprise—if he didn't know better, he'd actually think that she'd wanted Charlotte to stay. "Thanks. It was sort of a move-in ready place. It was built in the fifties, but the previous own-ers did a lot of updating and renovations. Which is what I wanted because I had no time to tackle a reno," he said as they walked into the kitchen. "It's bigger than we need for just the two of us, but it's nice to have the space as well."

"Oh, this kitchen is gorgeous," Charlotte said. He had always liked the kitchen too, not that he was much of a cook. Even if he was, there just wasn't time. The kitchen had been updated with painted, white, Shaker-style cabinets and white quartz counters. Unfortunately, the counters were currently covered in schoolwork, books, dishes, and half the groceries he'd brought home last night that hadn't needed to be refrigerated. But Charlotte didn't seem to notice or mind.

"A heck of a departure from our building back in Toronto," he said with a rueful laugh.

Charlotte placed her hands in the front pockets of her jeans and nodded. "Definitely. I'd say you've done well for yourself."

He held her gaze for a moment, very aware that Sam was watching their exchange and knowing he couldn't get more personal with Charlotte about their shared past without having to answer a million questions.

"Dad, you should use the Christmas cups for the coffee," Sam said, grabbing the mugs Aunt Mary had bought for him last Christmas from the back of the cupboard. He had no idea they were even in there. Who was this girl? He was surprised by his daughter's sudden shift in mood and her interest in what mugs he used.

"Those are so cute," Charlotte said, smiling at Sam.

Sam was holding up the mugs that had a little Christmas Village design on them and beaming. He had no idea what was happening, but it was great to see Sam smiling. And it felt nice to have Charlotte there, despite his initial reservations.

"What a gorgeous view," Charlotte said, walking to the window over the kitchen sink.

"We see deer here all the time in the morning," Sam said, joining her.

"I love deer! I see them at my grandmother's house too," Charlotte said.

Wyatt listened to them as he set the coffee to brew and smiled. It had been a long time since they'd had an adult woman in the house besides his aunt. But the biggest shocker was that Sam was hanging on Charlotte's every word. She'd had such attitude lately that it was strange to see her like her old self. "What do you take in your coffee, Charlotte?"

"Cream or milk would be great," she said.

He opened the fridge and peered inside, hoping like hell he'd remembered to buy milk. He couldn't see anything past that stupid basket of useless cheeses.

"See, that's what I'm talking about, Charlotte. Look at the fridge! There's so many expired things in there, I can never find anything. And now this random cheese basket has taken over."

Wyatt grabbed the carton of milk and shut the door quickly, cringing as the cellophane from the cheese basket crinkled against the door. He needed new friends. "Thanks, Sam."

Charlotte was smiling, and he could tell she was trying to hold back her laugh. "That's an easy fix. Seriously."

Wyatt poured Charlotte her coffee in the preselected mug and handed it to her. He couldn't actually take her up on the offer to organize his house. Sure, a part of him was intrigued by the idea of making life run smoother at home, but the other part was weird . . . because he was drawn to Charlotte, just as he had been when they were kids. Except back then she'd just been the sweet girl down the hall. Now she was this incredibly gorgeous woman who still made him want to be around her, even though he had too much baggage.

"Thank you," Charlotte said, adding a splash of milk.

Much to his humiliation, he noticed she quickly glanced at the expiration date. *Thanks, Sam.* What had happened to him? He used to be cool. Suave. Now he was just this single dad with a fridge full of expired food, cheese baskets, and a sassy tweenager.

"Do you want to sit in here?" Wyatt asked, pointing to the kitchen table.

"Sure, this is great," Charlotte said.

He watched in wonder as his daughter quickly removed the pizza box and her homework in record time. He made a mental note that she actually *did* have the energy to clear the table, unlike the story she kept trying to feed him every other night.

Sam sat beside Charlotte and stared at her with the same amount of interest she gave her phone. "So when are you going to come over and work on our house?"

Charlotte glanced over at him. "My schedule is pretty flexible because I'm here for three weeks. So it's really up to your dad."

Wyatt sat back in his chair, crossing one leg over the other. He didn't know how he was going to handle this. Thanks, Aunt Mary. It would feel awkward to have Charlotte over here cleaning up his kitchen cupboards. And the reality was that the longer Charlotte was around, the greater the odds that they would have some kind of a personal conversation.

He cleared his throat, both women waiting for his answer. "Well, my work schedule is pretty hectic for the next few weeks until I take my week off for Christmas, so if you don't mind coming over here while I'm at work, then you can come whenever is convenient for you."

"I get home from school at three thirty. You can come over then if you want. I have ballet every night, but that's not until seven," Samantha said, leaning toward Charlotte with an expression he hadn't seen from her in a long time—vulnerability.

Well, hell. He hadn't expected that.

Charlotte smiled before taking a sip of coffee. "That's perfect, I'd love the company."

Sam's phone rang with her latest favorite ringtone—glass smashing—and Charlotte jumped in her chair. Wyatt smiled at her and rolled his eyes. She lifted her mug, but not before he saw that gorgeous smile again.

Sam had already made a beeline to the island to check her phone. "I've got to go and answer this," she said, taking her phone and walking to the door. She stopped abruptly and turned around. "Oh, um, it was nice to meet you, Charlotte. I'll see you tomorrow?"

He didn't even know who this girl was standing in the door-way. *It was so nice to meet you.* He was thrilled by the manners he rarely saw, but it was that vulnerability again, when she confirmed that Charlotte would be coming over tomorrow, that gutted him.

"Sounds great!" Charlotte said.

Sam left the room, and Wyatt knew he had to keep the conversation going before things felt awkward. "Thanks for agreeing to this and for not minding having Sam around while you work."

Charlotte waved a hand. "Are you kidding? She's great. And I'd much rather work with Sam here than all by myself. She might actually really like it. There's a sense of satisfaction that comes with getting organized."

He grinned. "I haven't exactly experienced that yet, but I'll take your word for it."

She laughed, and he found himself smiling at the sound. She was incredibly attractive, but it was more than that. There was a warmth she exuded that made him want to be around her. Maybe that's what Sam had picked up on. Her lips were still curled in a smile and he noticed again how full they were and how perfectly shaped. He quickly averted his gaze. They couldn't go there.

"So, is your whole family coming for Christmas?"

Charlotte glanced down at her cup and stood, that warmth gone. "Uh, yeah, at some point. I should get back though. I hate leaving Grandma Ruby for too long. I especially want to have some time with just her before family descends," she said, placing her mug in the sink.

He knew avoidance when he saw it. He prided himself on being a keen observer of human behavior. He'd learned that at a very young age, instinctually, because of the environment he'd grown up in, and then he'd mastered the skill in his professional life. Charlotte had suddenly closed herself off, and he didn't know if it was because there were issues in her family or if she just didn't like personal conversations with him. "I'm sure Ruby is thrilled."

She nodded, walking toward the door, clearly dying to get out of there. "It's been a while since we've all been together for Christmas. My sister and my mom. So, full house," she said, shrugging into her jacket.

He didn't know what it meant that the place suddenly felt emptier as she prepared to leave it. "Olivia. How is she?" He had a distinct memory of Olivia trotting along behind them on their way to school, sort of lost in her own world. It was hard to imagine they had all lived this other life, this messed-up childhood, and now they were all adults.

She zipped up her coat, still not looking at him. "Good. She's good. Married. Has a baby."

"Wow, that's great."

She shot him a look similar to the one she had given him when he mentioned Ruby, one that clearly told him there was a hell of a lot going on in her life . . . and that she had no intention of sharing it—not with him anyway. "It is. Good night, Wyatt."

He held the door open. "I should walk you home," he said, noticing dusk was descending.

She stepped outside, her face lit by the glow of the porch lights. They stared at each other a moment and he remembered all those walks together when they were younger. She avoided his gaze. "That's nice of you, but I'll be fine."

"Charlotte," he said, wanting to be the guy she remembered.

She stopped. "Really, it's barely even dark out and it's not far. But thanks."

He gave her a nod and watched her walk away, a sense of loss washing over him again. The day he'd walked out of that gym had been the beginning of the worst year of his life. He had never been the same, and the memory of Charlotte had been a source of comfort for him on many shitty nights.

He took a deep breath as she rounded the corner toward Ruby's house, inhaling the fresh, cedar-tinged air. Maybe he was the one out in left field with all these feelings. Maybe it was the nostalgia of the season. Maybe he just needed to concentrate on Sam and getting through the holidays unscathed.

Maybe Charlotte coming back into his life was just a coincidence and nothing more, because he'd never believed in anything beyond what was right in front of him.

CHAPTER FIVE

DECEMBER 31, 1968

"Sister Juliette, with all due respect, I don't think this is a good idea. I just want to forget all these people and this part of my life," Ruby said. It was New Year's Eve, and Sister Juliette had urged Ruby to come forward and tell Richard's parents the news about the baby.

Sister Juliette turned to her, her dark eyes serious. "Why do you think we met on Christmas Eve?"

Ruby didn't know what she meant. "Because my parents threw me out."

She shook her head. "Of all the streets in the city, of all the corners, you were right where you needed to be for me to find you. That isn't a coincidence, Ruby. That's providence. Now let me take me the lead."

Ruby maintained her gaze for as long as she could before looking down at her shoes. She didn't want to offend Sister Juliette. She didn't want to tell her that maybe she didn't believe in any of that anymore.

Or worse, that she didn't deserve any of that anymore. But she owed this woman. "Okay."

"They have lost their son, they might be comforted by the thought that he will live on through his child, Ruby. I will be with you every step of the way."

A moment later, Richard's father opened the door. The tragedy had taken its toll on him; the usually polished man needed a shave, his slicked-back hair was messy, and his shirt was untucked. "Ruby. We didn't know what happened to you," he said, concern lining his deep voice as he opened the door wider. His gaze darted from her to Sister Juliette.

"I'm so sorry for your loss," she said, forcing herself to make eye contact with him.

"Thank you," Richard's mother said, appearing in the hallway. She looked pale and gaunt, but she reached forward to hug Ruby.

Sister Juliette introduced herself and Richard's parents led them into the dining room, where Ruby sat beside Sister Juliette and his parents sat opposite them. Ruby tried to concentrate on the chit-chat, but her mind wandered to all the times she had sat in this dining room when Richard had been alive. The house had been filled with conversation and laughter then. His older brother, Harry, was usually around. He'd always seemed more serious to Ruby, maybe even mysterious.

"I'm so very sorry for your loss," Sister Juliette began, glancing at Ruby from the corner of her eye before continuing. "But I'm hoping the news we have for you can bring you some light in the darkness."

"Thank you, Sister. We will gladly listen," Richard's mother said, with a slight shadow of a smile.

"Ruby and Richard were very much in love, and before . . . well, Richard had planned on proposing to Ruby."

His mother gasped and covered her mouth, her eyes clouding over with tears. His father put his arm around her. "He hadn't told us, but I'm not surprised. We were always very fond of Ruby. I'm so sorry it's ended this way. Ruby, you're a wonderful girl and we wish you the best," he said, his voice thick with emotion.

Ruby began trembling as she wrung her hands together in her lap.

"Ruby is a wonderful and brave woman. She is also carrying Richard's baby. Your grandchild," Sister Juliette said softly.

His parents didn't move, and Ruby was scared to breathe. They turned at the sound in the doorway. It was Harry. His handsome face was white, his strong jaw clenched, his hands in his pockets as he stared at Ruby. She didn't know if it was anger or revulsion in his eyes.

"Oh my . . . oh my . . . this all makes sense now. He was too afraid to tell us what you had done, Ruby. He was too ashamed. My baby," his mother moaned, placing her head on the table.

Shame and panic tore through Ruby and she moved to stand, she needed to leave, to run from the shame that followed her around like a shadow. Sister Juliette held her upper arms steady . . . "This was not Ruby's fault, and I urge you to think clearly. Maybe it will take time, but Ruby is carrying your grandchild. This can be a beautiful blessing," Sister Juliette said.

Richard's father stood, keeping one hand on his wife's shaking shoulders. "Get out of our house. Our son would have never acted that way. For all we know, this could be any man's child."

Ruby felt the room tip as what he was implying hit her with the impact of a train. Everything blurred and spun, and she was vaguely aware of someone's strong hands on her shoulders as she struggled to stay in the present. "Dad, that's a lie. Ruby wouldn't do that. She wouldn't lie and I know . . . I knew Richard. He never took anything seriously.

He partied. He drank too much. This is Richard's doing," Harry said harshly.

"How dare you speak of your brother that way?" his mother hissed, raising her head, her tear-streaked face pulled back into an angry grimace.

"It's the truth. He was an irresponsible, selfish drunk. Don't turn Ruby away," Harry said. His words, his presence, his belief in her managed to keep her sane and standing.

"We will give you some time to think about this. Ruby is staying with me at St. Michael's. Once you've processed all this, you may reach out to her through me," Sister Juliette said, her voice holding a note of something that Ruby had never heard in this woman in the last week. If she didn't know better, it sounded like a tinge of judgment, directed toward Richard's parents. And protectiveness, toward Ruby.

Harry's hand dropped from her shoulders and he followed them to the front door and stepped onto the porch with them. "Sister Juliette, if I can help in any way . . . Ruby . . . I believe you. I . . . I always thought you were the best thing to have happened to my brother," he said.

Ruby couldn't look him in the eye, shame making her want to never see anyone from this part of her life again. She glanced in his general direction and walked away from the porch. She heard Sister Juliette thank him and then quickly catch up to Ruby.

"I'm sorry, Ruby. But you will find your place in the world again," Sister Juliette whispered. Her arm around Ruby's shoulders, a shelter in the storm, a promise that Ruby would not be alone.

* * *

The following afternoon, Charlotte sat on the bed in her favorite room in The Christmas House, with her planner, pens, and notepads spread around her, but unable to focus. Three large windows over-looked the ravine and river, and with all the snow-covered trees, it looked a little like a magical forest. Now that all the leaves were gone, she could see straight to the frozen river. The window seat was filled with overstuffed pillows embroidered with snowmen and a coordinating red and green tartan blanket. It had always been her favorite spot to sit and read as a little girl—especially when it was raining outside. Snow was even better because she would sometimes imagine she was inside a snow globe and everything was picture perfect.

Her gaze wandered the room, nostalgia tumbling over her. The rattan chair was still in the corner of the room with a blanket draped over the back and a plaid pillow with a perfect V indent on the top. The white iron bed frame reminded her of Anne Shirley's bed in the original *Anne of Green Gables* movie. She had so many memories of Grandma Ruby tucking her in, praying over her. Charlotte would then inhale the crisp, clean scent of the sheets and fall into the best sleep. Sometimes Olivia would sneak into her room and they'd share the bed. She ran her hand over the patchwork quilt embroidered with little hollies, the texture warm against the palm of her hand, the memories comforting to her soul.

The Christmas House was home, and like every time she'd visited before, Charlotte reached for the magic it offered, even if it only lasted seconds instead of hours like when she was a child. She forced her gaze to her list of notes and ideas she had for Wyatt's house. But thinking about Wyatt's house meant thinking about Wyatt. And his daughter. It had been clear that he hadn't wanted to talk about their past, and she would never have brought it up in front of Samantha. But she wanted to know what had happened to him. Despite how many years had passed, he still had that special something. He still made her heart race, his smile made her palms sweaty, his voice made her toes curl. He was still *Wyatt*.

Wyatt had been so much more than she expected. So had Sam—she'd been so sweet and polite, but there was something about her that tugged at Charlotte's heartstrings. It wasn't some kind of maternal instinct, because she'd never had maternal leanings. She was fine with that. In fact, she preferred it that way because she didn't have to worry about letting anyone down, or dealing with the chaos that kids brought to one's life. She had grown up surrounded by chaos, and she wanted the opposite for herself.

Commotion and disorder caused stress and wreaked havoc on people and marriages. But as she spent time with Wyatt and Sam last night, their little family had seemed . . . enviable. She knew there must be heartache there, and she knew that life hadn't exactly been rainbows and ice cream for either of them, but Wyatt had created a home filled with love. His affection for his daughter was evident and endearing, and he hadn't lost his patience despite her comedic attempts at pushing all his buttons.

Charlotte was still aware of Wyatt in a way that she'd never experienced with anyone else, and that was crazy. He was undeniably masculine in a way that made her very aware of being a woman. But it was the other side of him, that easy laughter, the ready sarcasm, and the undeniable patience he showed when Sam was in the room. His asking about her family had been perfectly natural. She should have said something more. Instead, she'd clammed up.

But Wyatt . . . it was as though there was this unspoken mental photo album of that year they knew each other and he would do something or say something that could take her back to seventh grade; even her awkwardness rose to the surface, unfortunately.

She glanced down at her planner and the notebook with the color-coded headings she was making for the different areas to tackle in Wyatt's kitchen. The organizing would be the easy part; seeing Wyatt would be the hard part.

The doorbell pulled her from her thoughts and she scrambled off the bed, a few markers tumbling to the ground. There was always someone coming to visit her grandmother, but now that she was here, she was ready to help. She made it halfway down the stairs to see her grandmother opening the door and her sister and baby niece standing there.

Charlotte hid her panic and raced down the stairs, not caring that Liv had ignored her, not caring about all that might be between them, just needing to be there for her.

Olivia looked like hell.

"Come in, come in, my dear. Let me take this baby," Grandma Ruby said, pulling Olivia in.

Charlotte's gaze darted from her sister to the baby Grandma Ruby was holding. She was adorable. She was dressed in a red snowsuit-type thing and her cheeks were rosy. Her wide blue eyes searched the room quickly. Charlotte felt helpless and silly and like a stranger to her sister. But she couldn't just stand there when Olivia looked like she was going to fall apart. "Liv, I'm so glad you came," Charlotte said, swallowing her nerves and making the first move to hug Olivia.

The minute her sister's arms wrapped around her, Olivia burst into tears. "I'm so sorry, Char," she choked.

Charlotte pulled back, holding onto her sister's arms and really looking at her. Olivia's usually perfect, glossy hair was greasy looking and thin and pulled back in a messy bun—not the cute

Instagram kind. Her eyes were red, the bags beneath them deep and dark. But it was the sadness in her eyes that was the most gut-wrenching. Charlotte had seen that look a very long time ago, when it was just the two of them, when their dad had walked out and their mom had fallen apart and dropped them off here with Grandma Ruby. And just like then, they were standing here in the vestibule of Grandma Ruby's house, terrified and feeling like their world was falling apart.

"Oh, Liv, it's okay. We'll figure it out," Charlotte said, tears blurring her vision. She knew there had to be more.

"Now, come in, my dear, hang up your things. There is plenty of time to sort things out; right now you need rest," Grandma Ruby ordered.

"I'm so sorry, Grandma. I should have visited more. I've been a horrible granddaughter and sister—"

Grandma Ruby grasped one of her arms, staring into Olivia's eyes. "Enough. Stop. You have not been horrible. You've been surviving. You've been doing what you should be doing—taking care of this baby. You are always welcome here. This is always your home. As long as you are alive, you will always be welcome here. No strings. No conditions. My door is always open to you," she said, her voice raspy.

Charlotte's throat was tight with emotion as Olivia nodded and started crying again.

Olivia took the baby from Grandma Ruby's arms. "Thank you, Grandma. You always know just what to say, just what to do. I'm just so tired. Or hormonal. Or both," Olivia said, sniffling as she kissed the top of the baby's head.

Ruby glanced over at Charlotte, her lips in a thin line. Olivia was not well. It was so much more than exhaustion; they both knew it. "Why don't I get you a nice bowl of soup and freshly baked bread, and then you go and settle into your favorite room?" Grandma said.

Olivia gave her a wobbly smile. "I just . . . I should get Dawn's things set up and change her and then give her a bottle before her nap . . ."

Grandma Ruby took the baby like a pro. "Nonsense. We're here. We'll help. You need rest. You are good to no one if you can't even think or speak without crying, my dear."

Olivia nodded rapidly, looking like she was going to cry again. "I'll just unload the car," she said.

"I got it, Liv. You go into the kitchen with Grandma," Charlotte said, happy to have something to help with since she had no idea how to help with a baby.

Olivia nodded. "Thanks," she choked out, pulling her keys out of her coat pockets, Kleenexes and lip balm falling onto the floor.

"I've got it," Charlotte said, reaching down and picking everything up, wincing as the soggy Kleenex touched her skin.

Olivia choked out a sob and pressed her nose into a tissue. What the hell was happening? This was her sister's life now? "I'm so sorry, Char."

"It's nothing. Seriously. Go do whatever Grandma tells you to do before you get in trouble," she said, forcing humor into her voice.

A few minutes later, Charlotte was frowning at the contents of Olivia's car. First of all, there was crap everywhere. Coffee cups—empty and half-filled—napkins, Kleenex—tons and tons of Kleenex. Then there was the gear. How much did one baby need?

She pulled out what she assumed was the diaper bag and swung it over her shoulder, and then swung Olivia's bag over the other shoulder before making her way to the trunk. She was going to clean out her sister's car tomorrow morning. No one should be subjected to this kind of mess—no wonder she was a disaster. Charlotte would be in tears too if she had to drive around with stained seats and snotty Kleenexes everywhere. It was a horror show.

The trunk was no better. She managed to pull out a thing that resembled a folded-up crib and swung it over her shoulder, almost falling backward. This was insanity. She spotted the large pack of diapers and somehow maneuvered them under her arm and then managed to shut the trunk by swinging one of the bags on top.

A few minutes later, after having only dropped the pack of diapers three times on her way back up the walkway, she dumped everything in the vestibule and made her way to the kitchen. She was out of breath and very pleased with her own life choices.

Olivia had almost finished her bowl of minestrone, and Grandma Ruby was bouncing a very happy baby girl on her lap. Her snowsuit had been removed and she was wearing an adorable red and white striped velour pajama onesie with the picture of a reindeer on the front. Charlotte smiled at her and to her surprise, the baby gave her a wide, open-mouth, no-teeth smile that made her laugh and almost forget that she had been so hurt by Olivia. After seeing her sister she knew instinctively that the reason Liv had distanced herself had nothing to do with Charlotte. There was something going on. "She's so cute, Liv," Charlotte said, joining them at the table.

"Thanks," Olivia said, putting down her spoon.

"Come and hold her," Grandma Ruby said.

Panic hit Charlotte. "Oh, Grandma, I have no idea what I'm doing."

"Nonsense. Come here," she said, and shoved the baby at Charlotte. Charlotte instinctively wrapped her arms around the baby, and immediately a flood of warmth swam through her. Baby Dawn smelled as good as she looked, and her chubby little body felt squishy and huggable and oh-so-adorable. She positioned one hand on the baby's back and she leaned her head back slightly to look at Charlotte. She waved her hand wildly as drool pooled at the corner of her mouth and she smacked Charlotte in the face.

Charlotte laughed out loud and grabbed her little hand. "You are so cute," she whispered.

Dawn stared at her seriously, as though contemplating her sincerity, and then gave her that toothless grin again.

"See, you're a natural," Grandma Ruby said, standing and clearing Olivia's plate.

"Liv, seriously, go take a long nap. We've got everything under control," Charlotte said.

Her sister looked like she was going to argue but then nodded. "I'm so tired," she whispered, standing slowly.

"Is Will going to be coming soon?" Grandma Ruby asked while loading the dishwasher.

Olivia's face went red, and she walked to the door. "I'm not sure. I'm going upstairs. Thanks . . . thanks for being so welcoming," she said before leaving the room.

Charlotte waited until she heard Olivia walking upstairs before she turned to Grandma Ruby.

She was shaking her head. "Things aren't good. She's hiding," Grandma Ruby said, already moving on from the dishwasher to the coffee pot. "Now I'm going to make us some nice strong, afternoon coffee. That baby may look adorable, but she's going to put us through the ringer once she realizes her mom is taking a nice long break."

Charlotte pulled the baby closer and kissed the top of her head, just as Dawn started crying.

"That's what I'm talking about. Put that little pacifier that's clipped on her collar in her mouth," Grandma Ruby called out from the other side of the kitchen.

"I should cancel my plans to go over to Wyatt's. You have so much baking to do, and you can't do that and look after a baby," Charlotte said, awkwardly doing as she was told.

Dawn stared at her intently, and Charlotte wondered if the baby was judging whether or not her aunt was qualified for this. A second later, her niece made a sucking motion and looked content again. Charlotte let out a sigh of relief. She hated canceling, but her sister needed some rest, and it was too much to leave the baby with Grandma Ruby with all the Christmas prep.

Grandma Ruby spun around, her eyes sharp, making Charlotte doubt whether a baby was too much for her to handle on her own. "Don't cancel. Olivia will probably be awake by then if I know her. Besides, Mary is coming over any minute, and she loves babies. Oh! I have a batch of homemade shortbread cookies for Wyatt too," she said.

She had no idea where her grandmother got her energy from. The amount of sweets she produced during the Christmas season was legendary. No wonder guests were so happy here, they were in a perpetual sugar coma. Charlotte frowned and glanced at the time. "Well, I do have an hour before I have to go over there. If Mary says she'll stay and help you until Olivia wakes up, then fine."

Grandma Ruby chuckled as she turned the coffee maker on. "Oh, child, Mary would offer to spend a *week* here if it meant you going over to her nephew's house. And actually, you have forty-five minutes, because you should take fifteen of those minutes to get changed and freshen up. No offense."

Charlotte almost laughed, but her mind was on Olivia. "Okay. But, um, watch out for Liv while I'm gone."

Grandma Ruby crossed the kitchen and surprised her by pulling her into a hug, with Dawn sandwiched between them. Charlotte held onto her, welcoming the comfort.

"I remember that year after I became a mother, it was overwhelming. Nothing tried me more. But this house, the woman who took me in, she saved me. She showed me so much compassion, and that's what we will do for Olivia. Grace has led her home to us."

CHAPTER SIX

FEBRUARY 14, 1969
SILVER SPRINGS, ONTARIO

Ruby clutched the handle on the well-worn luggage that the sisters at St. Michael's had given her and stared up at the enormous house in front of her. The vicious February wind brought tears to her eyes and whipped around her, stirring up snow over her ankles and feet.

She tried to a draw a deep breath and walk toward the house, but it was as though her lungs couldn't expand to accommodate the size of her nerves. But this was her new life and she was grateful for it. Being a housekeeper to one rich, elderly woman in a small town where no one knew her was truly a blessing. Sister Juliette said she had been dear friends with this woman for years and had informed her of Ruby's . . . situation. The widow said she was happy to offer a room and salary to Ruby and to help a woman in need.

Ruby forced one foot in front of the other, slowly making her way up the stone path that led to the biggest verandah she had ever seen. Even though her family had been solid middle class in Toronto, it had been city living, and the houses weren't grand like this or surrounded by so much land. There must have been acres and acres of forest surrounding this . . . mansion. Right now, all the bare trees towered around the property, their branches thick and heavy with pristine white snow.

She ignored the fluttering in her abdomen, knowing it would only last a brief moment or two. She wasn't quite sure how she felt about that . . . or the baby. But she had time to worry about motherhood. First she needed to secure employment. Stepping onto the wooden front porch, Ruby prayed frantically for everything and anything she could think of before grasping the O-shaped iron knocker and giving it two quick raps.

She held her breath and a moment later the door opened. Shame snuck up on her as she remembered the other porches where she'd been tossed aside. She didn't think she would recover if it happened again.

A woman, maybe in her late sixties, answered the door. Her gray hair was in perfect curls and she wore a bright red dress and matching slippers, with a knit red shawl draped around her thin shoulders. But it was her eyes that gave Ruby the most hope. They were kind, green eyes, filled with such warmth and kindness that Ruby was able to finally release the breath she'd been holding.

"Come in, dear, you mustn't get a chill. Especially in your delicate condition," she said, moving to the side so Ruby could walk in.

The moment she stepped over that threshold from the harsh winter into the warm, richly furnished entryway, Ruby knew that this must be a magical home. But it was when the woman reached out to grasp

Ruby's cold hands in her frail warm ones and looked up at her with such compassion that Ruby knew she wasn't being judged. Her kind eyes confirmed what Ruby had come to realize during her months away from home, that family didn't always mean unconditional love, and that kindred spirits did exist. She also knew the kind of woman, the kind of mother she wanted to be: filled with compassion and empathy and unconditional love.

*   *   *

Charlotte stomped the snow off her feet as she stood on Wyatt's front porch, careful not to jostle the plate filled with shortbread cookies. She was stalling. It's not that she didn't want to go inside— she did. She really did. And she had followed her grandmother's advice and had gone to change and brush her hair. She was just going to attribute it to looking professional because this *was* technically a job. That's what she would normally do before going to a client's house anyway. The fact that she knew Wyatt was irrelevant. They barely knew each other now, and they had barely known each other back then. Obviously, she had been the only one who'd felt a connection with him when they were kids.

But there was no time for this kind of thinking anyway, because she had other things to worry about now, like her sister's problems and her grandmother's past. There was a part of her that almost felt like she couldn't really trust Olivia anymore. Their relationship had been great until Will had come along. They had been tossed aside by their parents in different ways, but being tossed aside by Olivia had gutted her. She had never expected that from her. Charlotte didn't want to be heartless, but she was a little hurt by the thought that Olivia might only be here because she was going through something and needed their help. But she'd follow her grandmother's example and help Liv. Of course she would.

She wanted nothing more than to just pick up where they left off, but she couldn't. It wasn't that easy. She knew nothing about Olivia's day to day life now. She had wanted to pick up the phone so many times in the last year, but she had stopped because she knew her calls would go unanswered.

A gust of icy wind gathered a puff of snow and sent it in her direction, reminding her of what she really needed to be focused on right now. She lifted the leather strap of her tote a little higher on her shoulder and rang the bell. Sam whipped the door open a minute later, giving her a giant smile.

"Hi! I just got home, perfect timing," Sam said, opening the door wider.

Charlotte held up the plate of homemade shortbread cookies and smiled. "Great, because I have the perfect after-school treat, courtesy of my Grandma Ruby," she said, walking into the house.

"That's awesome, she's so cool," Sam said, as Charlotte took off her coat and draped it on the hallway chair.

"She is," Charlotte agreed with a little laugh. She paused as she spotted what must have been Wyatt's uniform boots. The memory of her father's boots by the door brought a rush of feeling, and she shrugged it off. It was great Wyatt was a cop. It had been his dream.

She rolled her shoulders and joined Sam in the kitchen. Charlotte pulled out her notebook and the appropriate colored pens and placed them on the island. She had made her preliminary list based on memory and now checked it over to make sure she hadn't missed anything. She was happy to concentrate on organizing— it would force her to push aside all the unwanted memories and thoughts of Wyatt or her dad. "Feel free to do whatever you'd like, Sam. I don't want to intrude on your plans. I'm going to start by just poking around. Does that sound okay?" Charlotte asked.

Sam nodded and took a bite of one of the cookies, fixing her brown eyes on Charlotte. "Sure. Do you mind if I stay in the kitchen?"

"Of course not! I'd love the company."

Sam took another cookie and watched as Charlotte opened the pantry and made some notes in her book. She pulled out her measuring tape and almost knocked over three different cereal boxes in the process. "That pantry is a wreck," Sam said, coming to stand beside her.

Charlotte wrote in the dimensions before she forgot them and shook her head. "It's nothing that can't be organized and solved. Trust me, it's really not that bad."

She slowly made her way around the kitchen for the next fifteen minutes while Sam followed her around. She was surprised she had so much interest in all this. "I like all your colored pens, and that notebook is really cool too," she said.

"Thanks. I find it's really easy to break down the different areas that need help by color. I'm kind of a planner nerd," she said with a laugh as she crouched down and opened the cupboard under the sink.

"That makes sense. I kind of like my digital stuff, though."

Charlotte pushed aside some of the cleaning supplies to get a better look. "There's something very satisfying about making a color-coordinated checklist and then highlighting every task when it's done," she said, standing to finish off her notes.

"I can see that," Sam said, looking at her pens.

"You should try it. You can use it for anything. Studying for a test or just keeping track of things you need to do."

"Maybe I will. Oh, don't bother looking in the closet. It's supposed to be for like brooms and cleaning supplies but Dad ends up cramming in paper towels and stuff like that in there. Things might crash on you if you open the door," she said as Charlotte put her hand on the doorknob to the small closet in the kitchen.

Charlotte swallowed her laugh and hesitantly opened the door. She caught the mega pack of paper towels and then peered in the small space. It was a good little storage spot, it just needed organizing.

"So humiliating," she heard Sam whisper.

Charlotte joined her at the island again. "Seriously. It's not bad at all. I have seen so much worse, believe me. But your dad is a very busy man, and a lot of times organizing isn't a priority. When you have so much going on and you're the only adult in the house, it's really about just getting the immediate jobs done."

Sam leaned against the island. "We have a cleaning lady who comes over."

Charlotte shrugged and felt the need to defend Wyatt. "Sure, but she's doing the essentials. Getting to the other stuff isn't something she can do."

Sam crossed her arms. "So what are you going to start with?"

"What would you like?"

"The pantry! I can never find anything in there and it's even worse than the fridge," Sam said.

Charlotte made a note of that. "Okay, that's a good one. You'll be able to enjoy it right away too, instead of a boring pots and pans drawer. So why don't we clear off everything on the island and kitchen table? Then we're going to take everything out of the pantry and organize it by item. Does that sound good?"

Sam hopped off a bar stool and started clearing her school things off the table. "So, like, cereal in one group and, like, crackers in another?"

"Exactly," Charlotte said, starting to grab some boxes and place them on the table. They worked in silence for a few minutes and then Charlotte turned to Sam. "Hey, do you like Christmas music? Maybe we can put some on?"

"Sure," she said.

Charlotte continued with the pantry and a few seconds later the sound of Nat King Cole's smooth voice filled the kitchen.

Sam walked back to the pantry. "I put on the Christmas Spotify channel. Not sure what song this is, though."

"This is classic. Perfect choice."

They worked quickly and efficiently. Once they were done emptying the pantry, they surveyed their work. "Okay, now let's look at expiration dates. Anything old we toss in the garbage bag. While you do that, I can wipe down the shelves. Sound good?"

Sam nodded and got to work.

"So do you like your school?" Charlotte said, trying to make conversation.

"It's decent. Most of the kids are weird, though," Sam said as she tossed a crumpled, half-empty bag of Goldfish crackers in the garbage bag.

"Oh, yeah? How so?"

Sam shrugged. "I don't know. They're just different than the kids in the city. I have a best friend, though. She's actually dad's best friend's daughter."

"Really? That's amazing," Charlotte said, shooting the girl a smile while she wiped down the top shelf.

Sam nodded. "Yeah. We do ballet together too."

"That's great. How many years have you been dancing?"

"Since I was six."

"You must be really good now," Charlotte said, as she finished wiping down the last shelf.

Sam's face flushed slightly. "I'm okay, I guess. Our studio is doing their annual production of *The Nutcracker*—it's on the same night as Candlelight Christmas."

"I love *The Nutcracker*! I see it every year in Toronto. My sister took ballet through all the grades. Did you have to audition?"

Sam nodded. "Yes, but the older students get all the good parts. We weren't even allowed to try out for Clara."

Charlotte smiled. "A few more years and you'll be able to, I bet."

Sam nodded. "For sure."

Charlotte glanced at the time on the oven, surprised to see it was already six o'clock. "What time does your dad usually get home?"

"He said he'll be home around six today. This is his last week of work before the holidays, so he's kind of tired because he's going in early and stuff."

Charlotte chewed her lower lip for a minute. "Are you hungry? Should we get dinner going or something?"

Sam's eyes widened. "Do you know how to cook?"

Charlotte opened the fridge. She didn't tell Sam that she'd had to learn to cook because most of the time her mother wouldn't do it and, because Charlotte was the family peacemaker, she tried to not draw attention to that fact. Sometimes she'd even lie to her dad and say that her mom had made the food. She stared at the fridge, the image of Wyatt's boots at the door floating across her mind. Was she doing that now? Was she in a hurry to make dinner because Wyatt was coming home from a long day at work and she . . .

"I bet you can't find anything in there either," Sam said, clearly misinterpreting why Charlotte was just standing there blankly.

Get it together, Char. "No, no, this is fine. To answer your question, yes, I can cook—my grandmother made sure my sister and I could cook. She said it was an important life skill. Of course, it won't be anything fancy because we haven't really planned for it. Let's see what we can pull together," she said, opening the vegetable drawer. It was slim pickings, and she had no idea what either Wyatt or Sam liked to eat.

"Do you like brie?" she asked Sam. Charlotte was surprised to find a nice assortment of gourmet cheeses in the deli drawer of the fridge.

"Uh, I don't think so. But maybe I do. I never tried it," she said.

"Hmm, I actually think your dad might have the ingredients to one of my all-time favorite toasted sandwiches."

"Really?"

The shock in Sam's voice almost made her laugh out loud. She walked over to the table filled with the pantry items and started rifling through the jars, pretty sure she'd seen one of her grandmother's jars of red pepper jelly preserves. "Do you have apples and a loaf of bread?"

"Yup. Dad always keeps a loaf of sliced bread in the freezer and apples are on the counter," Sam said, opening the freezer.

"See, your dad is pretty organized," she said, giving Sam a little wink.

Sam brought the remaining ingredients to the island, where Charlotte was setting up a cutting board and lining up the ingredients. "Do you like cooking?" Sam asked, sitting on the other side of the island.

Charlotte paused for a second, brushing aside the memories. "Not really . . . but I kind of had to learn at an early age how to put things together. I was a sandwich master," she said with a short laugh as she began thinly slicing the apples.

"Really? How come?"

Charlotte paused, making sure to keep any bitterness out of her voice. She smiled as Sam leaned across the island and took a slice of apple. "My mom had a lot of . . . issues when I was growing up, and my dad had a demanding job. My sister was a few years younger than me so I used to make our school lunches and after-school snacks. I usually made some kind of simple dinner too."

"Wow, that's kind of rough. I'd be kind of pissed if I had to do all that," Sam said, staring at her with a strange expression.

Charlotte shrugged. "It wasn't so bad. It made me independent, that's for sure. I also didn't really have a choice. Your dad seems like he's amazing and has it all together, but that's actually really hard to do. He's got a tough job, and he's got a daughter he obviously loves more than anything. I didn't do any extracurricular stuff because there wasn't a willing parent and there wasn't extra money."

Sam's face fell and Charlotte hoped she hadn't pushed too far. "He's a good dad," she said softly.

Charlotte opened the sealed pack of ham. "Oh, I hope I didn't make you feel bad. I wasn't trying to. I just think it's so great you're involved in ballet and you have this dad who tries so hard for you."

"You didn't make me feel bad. Sometimes it's easy to forget all that," she said softly.

Charlotte held the girl's gaze and smiled. "I can understand that."

Sam nodded and fiddled with the apple slice she was holding. "Yeah. He is a really good dad."

"I also like to think that we learn from all our life experiences. If I hadn't had to be so independent from an early age, then maybe I wouldn't have started my own business."

"Good point. I'd like to be able to boss people around if I had my own business," Sam said.

Charlotte laughed. "Yeah, that always sounds better than it is."

"Can I help?" Sam asked.

"Sure. Why don't you spread the red pepper jelly on each slice of toast? Just a thin layer," Charlotte said, handing Sam a knife.

"Did you grow up in Silver Springs?" Sam asked while diligently spreading the jelly.

"No. In the city. But I came here a lot to visit my grandma. And my sister and I spent most summers here with her," she said, counting out the slices of ham.

"I miss Toronto," Sam said, with a slight frown on her face.

"I know it's hard to adjust to new places and people, but this a great little town. My grandma has said that she's met the kindest people here."

Sam shrugged and placed the knife down when she was finished. "They're okay."

"Except for the weird ones?" Charlotte teased, desperate to lighten the mood.

Sam let out a laugh. "Yeah, I guess. Things just keep changing."

Charlotte placed the ham over the jelly on half the pieces of bread. "I can't say I'm a fan of change either, Sam. I kind of like things to stay the same, but that's not realistic. Life is filled with change. We change. The better we are at accepting that, the easier it gets."

Sam nodded. "That makes sense."

It was strange, being in this kitchen and talking about life with a girl she'd only met the day before. But Charlotte felt like she understood Sam. She had pushed people away for so long, and suddenly she was back in Silver Springs surrounded by people who needed her on some level. Sam had a vulnerability she tried to keep hidden, but it came out in revealing sentences. Charlotte sensed that Wyatt was a great dad and was trying his best, but getting a teenage daughter through all these changes couldn't be easy. And for Sam, she was pretty sure that no matter how amazing her dad was, certain topics could be pretty awkward. She added the slices of cheese and pushed aside all these thoughts—these were thoughts of a person who was getting involved. These people were still strangers to her. Wyatt wasn't a fourteen-year-old boy anymore.

In a few weeks she'd be long gone. Back to living her perfect little life with color-coded weeks filled with nothing but work. The Christmas House had never really been home, only her little escape from reality. Just like Wyatt had never really been hers, just a schoolgirl's hero.

CHAPTER SEVEN

Ruby clutched the underside of her belly as a deep, gnawing pain coursed across it. She stood perfectly still and tried to breathe. After a few endless moments, the pain slowly eased so that she was able to continue pulling down the clean clothes from the clothesline. Her months at this home had been filled with growth and introspection. When she'd left home on Christmas Eve, she had been a naïve, sheltered girl. She'd had an idealistic view of the world. Now she knew what it meant to be an adult, to find her way in a world that could be cold and cruel. But she'd also learned that there were good people out there, people whose compassion was bigger than their judgment.

This house, this rambling, old, majestic home would be something at Christmas. It was truly a Christmas house and she felt very grateful to be a part of it. Her son or daughter would grow up here, and she would teach them every day to appreciate it. She would hold her head up high and she would never let them know the shame she kept buried deep down inside. She would never let them think that they were less than their peers with perfect families. She would tell her child their father had died of a heart attack. That he loved them and he was watching over them from above. If she had been a better person, she would have hoped that was true, but she wasn't and she hoped that he couldn't see them. She hoped that he was being punished for leaving her like this. Maybe one day she would be able to forgive Richard, but not now. The humiliation and hurt was still buried deep inside her.

"Ruby?"

Ruby stilled, her hand on a clothespin, ready to pull down a nightgown, when an unmistakable voice pierced through her thoughts. Harry. Richard's older brother. Her hands started shaking, and she couldn't bring herself to turn around. Why would he be here? How had he found her? His defense of her had been a soothing balm that night, but she was sure he would have changed his mind by now. She didn't want to see that in his eyes too. Not now, when she was healing.

"Ruby, it's me, Harry."

Ruby dropped her arms and turned slowly, squinting against the afternoon sun, and focused on the man standing there, hat in hand. Harry was as handsome as always, tall and fit. She finally forced herself to raise her eyes to his, her stomach churning, her muscles tightly wound, until she saw nothing but . . . surprise and then sympathy on his face.

"Hello, Harry," she forced herself to say, her voice sounding shaky to her own ears. She kept her chin tilted up, though, because she would never look down in disgrace again, no matter how hard it was.

"You're looking well," he said, holding his hat in her direction.

She put a hand on the small of her back, a new habit that had formed these last few weeks. "Thank you. I don't imagine you're here to see how I look."

His strong jaw clenched, and something flashed across his eyes. "Ruby, I'm sorry. For everything. For Richard, for my parents."

She swallowed past the lump in her throat and struggled to maintain her composure. She hadn't expected that. But Harry had always been different. He'd been more serious than Richard, who had thrived on being the life of the party and making people laugh. Harry had stood on the sidelines, serious, brooding maybe, but always a gentleman. "Thank you," she managed to say.

He winced. "It's not enough, I know. And if my brother were alive, I would have throttled him for what he put you through."

She almost smiled, but it was all so sad and . . . embarrassing. She didn't know what he must think of her. Certainly he thought she was someone with loose morals, even if he felt sorry for her. Really, she wanted him to leave so that she could go back to her new life. The one where she was a poor young widow with a baby on the way and no family to speak of. She didn't want to face the reality of who she really was unless she was alone in her room at night. "Thank you, but I'm doing just fine. It . . . is kind of you to say that, though."

He took a step closer to her and her pulse raced in a way that she hadn't expected. His green eyes were filled with something she hadn't seen before, and her mouth went dry as he reached out to grasp her hand. She pulled it back as though she'd been burned. A searing heat scorched her body at the feel of his large, warm hand on hers. It was something she'd never experienced before. She didn't know what it was. That had never happened with Richard.

"I'm sorry if that was too forward. Ruby, I came to ask for your hand. I will make this right, I will right Richard's wrong. I will give you a roof over your head and raise this baby like my own."

Her mouth dropped open, and the world tilted ever so slightly, but Harry was there, grasping her arms. "Are you all right?" he asked, his voice rough and filled with a worry that wrapped itself around her heart.

She shut her eyes for a moment and nodded. In that moment, she imagined what it would be like to be his wife, to play pretend family. It was enticing. Wonderfully so. But she'd learned her lesson. No man. She would rely on no man. Ever again. "I'm sorry, Harry. I . . . I can't accept your offer."

Surprise flickered across his eyes and maybe something else. But she couldn't wonder at it. She needed to stay focused and continue with the plan she'd laid out for herself. "I can offer you a good life, Ruby. I'm almost finished law school. We can be a good couple. I . . . wouldn't pressure you into anything if that's what you're worried about."

Goosebumps sprang up across her body at the realization that she had been a fool. This man was a real man. But she would never trust anyone again, and she wouldn't ruin his life. "Harry, you're a good man, but I can't expect you to raise your brother's child as your own. I can't ruin your life like that. You deserve to marry someone you love, to have your own family."

He looked down for a moment and then back up at her, the expression in his eyes making her forget to breathe. "Marrying you would not be ruining my life."

She fought against the heaviness in her chest, the fluttering in her heart. "I can't. Thank you, but I can't. I've become someone new in these last few months, and I'm determined to do this on my own. And

I will. Please just forget about me and live your life. I know you'll have a good one."

"Ruby," he said, his voice thick as he took a step closer to her.

She shook her head and took a step back, closer to the life she was going to live, farther from him and the life he was offering. "I can't. I'm sorry. I need to get back to work."

He pulled a thick envelope from his jacket pocket and handed it to her. She stared at it but didn't reach for it. "It's my savings from my job this last year. Please take it."

She drew a deep breath. "I . . . I . . . that is incredibly generous, but I can't take it."

"I won't leave unless you take it. I can't. I can't leave you like this, Ruby. Take it, even if you never use it. Have it for peace of mind. Or take it for my own peace of mind. Please."

She reached for the envelope, so very aware that her own parents hadn't done this for her. She was also aware that she would never use this money. She would save it for her child one day. "Thank you, Harry."

"Ruby . . . if you ever need me, you can contact me at P. Williamson Barrister and Solicitor in Toronto. I . . . anything you need, I'll be here for you."

Tears blurred her vision and she forced a smile. "I'll be fine. You go and have a good life, Harry."

He gave her a nod, his green eyes glistening, his jaw hard. "You too."

* * *

Wyatt walked through the front door after a day he'd rather forget and was dreaming of a cold beer and takeout pizza and maybe passing out on the sofa since it was the only night this week without ballet. But he was pretty sure he'd come into the wrong home. Christmas music was coming from the kitchen, his daughter was actually laughing at something that wasn't him, and he didn't trip over her usual heap of belongings.

But the biggest shock was overhearing the conversation happening in the kitchen. He'd assumed that Charlotte would be long gone by now, but her sweet voice was unmistakable, and he felt an odd ache in his chest when he heard her saying how hard he worked and what a good dad he must be. The emotional punch had then come from his daughter actually admitting that he was a good dad.

Just hearing that made the attitude he knew he'd face from Sam later on almost tolerable. He'd spent his entire adult life trying to give her the childhood he'd never had, even though it wasn't ideal. He and Leanne weren't supposed to be teenage parents. But he'd loved Sam more than anything in the world. Leanne walking out on them was something he blamed himself for daily. He'd thought that even though they were young, they had a chance. That wasn't the way Sam's life was supposed to go, and he didn't think he'd ever forgive himself for that. He had learned the hard way how to be a father—mostly following instincts and doing the opposite of what his father had done. It had worked up until Sam hit puberty. Now Wyatt was fumbling around in the dark.

He hung his coat in the hall closet, and for the first time in forever, hung it next to his daughter's already hanging one and then made his way into the kitchen.

He stopped short in the doorway, still unnoticed. A lump formed in his throat at the sight of Charlotte at the island with Sam, cooking together, as though this were perfectly natural for them.

His daughter's face was relaxed, and she was listening intently and following Charlotte's instructions on where to place the apples.

Charlotte glanced up, startled to see him there, and damn if eye contact with her didn't send a jolt of awareness through his body.

"Hi, sorry if I startled you," he said, remembering he wasn't a teenager anymore, and walked into his kitchen. "Hey, Sam," he said, leaning over to kiss the top of her head.

"Hey," she said, and lo and behold, she looked up and gave him a smile.

He had no idea what was happening, but if Charlotte was the reason his daughter was actually being warm and kind and like the kid he remembered before the hell of twelve, then he was indebted to her forever.

"Charlotte, you don't have to do all this. I think this goes beyond a gift certificate's worth of organizing."

Her cheeks turned slightly pink. "Well, not really. It's not a big deal because they're just sandwiches. I was emptying out the pantry and fridge and it was getting close to dinner, so . . ."

He shoved his hands into the front pocket of his jeans. "Really. This is very nice of you."

She waved a hand. "Seriously, it's not a big deal. I was just going to toss together a salad too. This tray can go in the oven for like five minutes," she said, walking to the fridge to get the package of pre-washed lettuce, which was, for him, basically even too much effort to open and put together some days.

"You're staying for dinner, right?" Sam asked, worry tinging her voice.

Charlotte glanced over at him then back at Sam. "Oh, I wasn't planning on it. It'll be really easy for you and your dad to put this together."

Sam made a face. "He burns everything."

Wyatt choked out a laugh. He wasn't offended because it was true—he did burn everything—but he also knew his daughter was just desperate to have Charlotte stay. Maybe as desperate as he was. There was a light in here now, and he wanted to cling to it. "We'd love it if you could stay. I mean, how am I going to repay you for making dinner too? At least eat with us and I can get you a glass of wine to go with dinner?"

Charlotte's mouth opened slightly, and it drew his attention to her full lips again. "Um, that's really nice of you guys, but I need to get going. This was really no trouble. I knew you were busy with work and I was here anyway," she said, scrambling to gather her notebooks and cramming them in her bag.

He shoved his hands in his pockets, her explanation reminding him of what she used to tell him about home. He could probably remember almost every conversation they'd had about their home lives. She cooked at home. She cooked to make life okay, easier, for her mom and dad. He quickly surveyed the kitchen, her expression, Sam's. Charlotte was doing the same thing here. She was cheering up his daughter, she was making his day easier. Hell. It made him feel like crap. He'd kept his distance. Or tried to. And she was here, opening herself up to Sam. He owed her more than dinner.

"Bye, Sam. I had a great time today," she said, flashing his daughter a big smile.

Sam gave her a forced smile, the light gone from her eyes. "Me too, Charlotte. I'll be here tomorrow," she said, insecurity lining her voice.

"Great. I'm looking forward to it," she said, before walking out of the room.

"Sam, I'm just going to walk Charlotte home. I'll lock the door behind me," he said.

"Sure," she said, picking up her phone.

He frowned, lingering in the doorway. It was his fault that Sam was disappointed and that Charlotte was leaving. "We'll have a good night. Maybe we can catch a Christmas movie and eat dinner in front of the TV," he said.

"Uh, sure," she said, shooting him a distracted smile.

Well, that wasn't too bad. He walked to the entrance only to find Charlotte ready to leave. "Hey, I'll walk you home."

"That's sweet, Wyatt, but I'm fine," she said, opening the door.

He shrugged into his jacket and boots. "Yeah, well, it bothered me the other night that I never walked you back to Ruby's. Please," he said, holding the door.

"Okay," she said, turning from him and stepping onto the porch.

After he locked up, he joined her outside. "Feels like snow," he said, trying to make conversation as they walked. It wasn't what he wanted to say, but it was better than awkward silence.

"I don't mind. I like your Christmas lights," she said, pulling her hat down a little further.

"Thanks. Sam and I usually put them up at the beginning of November. There's a lot of pressure being the house next to Ruby's," he said, shooting her a grin as they approached the end of the driveway. There wasn't a car in sight or a sound other than the wind, and it was such a far cry from where either of them came from.

"Very true," she said.

They walked in silence, and as they approached Ruby's house he knew he owed her more than he was giving her. Or maybe he owed himself too.

"Charlotte," he began, his voice sounding thick to his own ears, filled with the affection he'd always had for her.

She slowed, turning her head to him, those gorgeous eyes filled with the same quiet curiosity he remembered. She had always been easy to talk to, without judgment.

"Thank you for your help today. I can see that Sam really enjoyed spending time with you," he said, searching for the words he really wanted.

"She's a great kid, and it was my pleasure to help," she said, standing at the bottom step of Ruby's porch. This was all so formal, almost like they were strangers.

"When you made dinner it just brought back memories of our conversations and . . . how you always made dinner for your dad and—"

Her mouth dropped open. "What? That has nothing to do with it. I was there. Your daughter hadn't had dinner yet. That's all. Wow."

Shit. "No, I'm not . . . hell, I don't know what I'm saying or implying. Just never mind. Thank you," he said, taking a step back.

"I didn't think you remembered our conversations," she said, tilting her chin up, and he read the pride in her eyes. He knew then that he wasn't going to be able to pretend anymore, not to himself and not with her. He didn't quite know what to do about that yet, but he wasn't going to continue letting her think that she'd been insignificant and that their friendship hadn't mattered to him.

He took a step closer to her, drawn to her in the same way he'd always been. Her hair swayed gently in the wind and, for a second, under the twinkling stars and white lights of The Christmas House, he saw them both, the scared kids they were, and wished he could go back. He wished he could go back to that time where expressing his feelings with her had become second nature.

"I remember. I remember everything about you. I remember your smile when I'd hold the door open for you. I remember the look in your eyes when I'd tell you something about my dad. I remember the way I felt when I talked to you. I remember you were the only person I could ever talk to about my home life. You were a ray of sunshine in a dark time, Charlotte, and I'm sorry if I ever made you think that you weren't important."

His heart was pounding, and he had the inexplicable urge to reach out for her, to hug her and feel her in his arms. And it had so much more to do with how she made him feel than her just being an incredibly beautiful woman. She glanced away, but not before he caught the sheen in her eyes. "Thank you," she said softly.

He wanted her to stay and talk. He wanted her to say that he'd been just as important. Hell. He knew what all this meant. He didn't want to lose Charlotte a second time in his life. "It's the truth," he said, taking a step onto the porch.

She backed up a few steps. "I appreciate that . . . you told me that. You did the same for me. I'll see you later, Wyatt. Thanks for walking me home," she said, turning quickly and walking into the house.

He took a deep breath, trying to ease the tightness in his chest. He had wanted to believe that Charlotte being Ruby's granddaughter was a coincidence. That would have been easier. But as he stood on the steps of The Christmas House, he knew in his gut that Charlotte being in his life had never been just a coincidence.

CHAPTER EIGHT

JULY 30, 1969
SILVER SPRINGS

Ruby finished scrubbing the toilet and stood, wincing as her lower back protested. She forced herself to place all the cleaning items back under the sink and then washed her hands. The water ran over her soapy hands, and as she rubbed them together she noticed they didn't have the texture they used to. They were rougher now. She shut the taps and as she dried her hands on the linen hand towel she paused to gaze at her reflection.

The woman staring back at her in the mirror wasn't someone she knew, or really wanted to know. This woman made her anxious. The scarf tied around her head, which kept her hair securely off her face, was one she wore every Friday, cleaning day, so that she could focus on getting the house in pristine condition and never have Mrs. Pemberton doubt that she was capable of maintaining this house, even as her pregnancy advanced. Ruby touched her face, lightly running her finger over her cheek, noticing how full her face had become. She supposed it was normal, this close to childbirth. Her gaze wandered lower, taking in the obvious curves she now had, just the sight of her changing body making her uncomfortable. She clutched the side of the counter as a wave of heat washed over her—she'd come to recognize the feeling as humiliation. It had trailed behind her all this time after leaving Toronto; when she looked in the mirror, all she saw was shame.

Smoothing her hand over her rounded belly, a pang, a longing for her mother claimed her senses and for a moment she wanted to be a little girl again. She wanted to look up at her mother's face and ask her what to do, she wanted someone to solve this problem for her. She had thought that parental love was supposed to be unconditional. She would have unconditional love for this child. She would be better, do better, than the four grandparents who'd rejected this baby.

"Ruby dear, are you feeling all right?"

Ruby jolted and turned to see Mrs. Pemberton standing in the doorway. The elderly woman's forehead was deeply creased, and she was watching Ruby with worried eyes. Ruby forced a smile on her face.

"Oh yes, don't worry about me. I was just finishing up in here," she said, closing the cupboard, embarrassed to be caught daydreaming.

She owed this woman everything, and in the last few months had come to really think fondly of her. She was always making sure that Ruby rested at the end of the day, and she was never fussy about the food Ruby prepared. They ate every meal together and talked about things in the news or the weather or sometimes gossip about Mrs. Pemberton's friends. Her days here were full and busy, and she was thankful for that because it meant she didn't have time to feel sorry for herself or dwell on what had happened. In the quiet times at night, sometimes her thoughts would turn dark and she'd feel deep anger toward her family and Richard.

"Oh good, then how about we have a cup of tea together and some of those lemon cookies I baked yesterday?"

Ruby smiled and nodded. The older woman loved her tea, and Ruby pretended to like it just as much. Mrs. Pemberton had a sweet tooth and, on her better days, she liked to keep herself busy with baking. "That sounds perfect."

Mrs. Pemberton started walking and then paused. "Ruby, dear, there is something I've been meaning to ask you, but I'm afraid of offending you."

A pang of worry bloomed inside her. There were a thousand things that she could ask Ruby about and none of them were good. Of course, Sister Juliette had told her about Ruby's background, and the older woman had been so kind and nonjudgmental, but she also hadn't asked for any specifics about Ruby's circumstances. Maybe now she wanted answers. Maybe people in town were starting to talk about her. Ruby swallowed her pride and forced a smile on her face. She owed her everything, and she wouldn't say no to whatever this woman was asking.

"You don't have to be worried about that. Please, ask me whatever is on your mind."

Mrs. Pemberton bit her lower lip for a moment and then motioned for Ruby to follow her. She led Ruby to her large bedroom. It was the prettiest bedroom Ruby had ever seen and the first time she'd entered she couldn't believe how large it was, how beautiful the view was from up here. The large windows overlooked the forest and river below. Some early mornings Ruby had even seen deer. She focused her attention on

Mrs. Pemberton, who was looking inside her jewelry box. A moment later she turned around and extended her hand to Ruby.

Ruby was surprised to see her holding two rings. "Those are lovely rings," she said, not quite sure what Mrs. Pemberton was doing.

"Thank you. They were my mother's. Her engagement ring and wedding band. Sapphire with diamonds and gold. Ruby dear, I would like you to have them."

Ruby gasped. "I can't. Oh, it is so nice of you, but I could never."

Mrs. Pemberton tilted her head, her perfect curls swaying with the motion, her eyes shining. "I know the way the world is for young women without husbands. I know how people talk, and it isn't fair, dear. I want you to wear these and, if you're comfortable, you can tell people when they ask that you are a widow. You can keep them for as long as you wish."

Ruby's mouth dropped open and she stared at the rings and Mrs. Pemberton's eyes until her own vision blurred. The weight she'd been carrying for months felt like it had just become a little lighter, like she could breathe a little easier. She'd never brought herself to buy a ring, the need to hold onto her money in case of an emergency taking precedence. Yes, yes, she could just say she was a widow. "They're your mother's, though," she finally managed to whisper against the rawness in her throat.

"Well, they're just sitting in a box doing no good to anyone, aren't they? Take them, Ruby," she said, reaching out for Ruby's hand and dropping them in her palm.

Ruby stared at the sparkling rings. "Is it wrong? Is it wrong for me to lie?"

Mrs. Pemberton shook her head. "You aren't hurting anyone. He was your fiancé. You would have been married. You will give your child a much easier world like this," she whispered.

Ruby looked up from the rings. She was right. Maybe sometimes it was okay to hide. At the very least it was easier. Right now, easy was all she could handle.

"Thank you," she whispered.

* * *

"How's Olivia doing?" Charlotte asked her grandmother tentatively, while kneading the homemade pizza dough they were making. She thought it odd that Olivia hadn't been down for breakfast that morning.

Her grandmother placed a pan down in front of Charlotte. "Hiding. She's hiding from us, she's hiding from life. She said she slept in. But I'm not buying it. And she didn't eat a thing for breakfast—just black coffee. That girl is keeping something from us, and I'm worried about her. She's hurting and I hope that in a few days, once she's properly rested, she will confide in us," she said, wiping her hands on her tartan plaid apron.

Charlotte worked the dough so that it spread to all four corners of the pan that had already been drizzled with olive oil while she processed what her grandmother had said. She was rougher than necessary, now even more worried about Olivia. She used to love cooking with her grandmother in the big old country kitchen. It had been updated here and there through the years, but nothing major, and Charlotte was happy about that. Nostalgia clung to the vintage ornaments on the small tree in the corner of the eating area. Garlands sat atop the upper cabinets, and Christmas wreaths were hung in each of the four large windows.

She was worried about her sister. Maybe she should go and try and talk to her, even though it felt like Olivia should be the one to break the ice. But Charlotte thought her grandmother was right, that she might be hiding something. She battled with the dough a few times when it kept shrinking back until it looked stable enough to pass off to her grandmother to place the toppings.

"Maybe the smell of homemade pizza will lure her downstairs," Charlotte said.

"That's the plan, my dear." Her grandmother spread the sauce around, and Charlotte busied herself with tidying the kitchen.

"I'll be heading out to Wyatt and Sam's around three again today," Charlotte said, trying to keep her voice as natural as possible. Sadly, on the inside she was doing a teenage-type squeal.

I remember everything about you . . . You were a ray of sunshine in a dark time, Charlotte, and I'm sorry if I made you think that you weren't important. No man in her life had ever come close to eliciting the response inside her body Wyatt had, with just a few sentences, with the sound of his voice, or with the resolute gaze. She had wanted to run up to him and hug him, just as she had wanted to when she was twelve. But just because he'd said all that didn't mean . . . they would or could be anything more than friends for the holidays. She needed to stop thinking about him.

Easier said than done, of course. Even on her walk into town that morning, he'd been on her mind. She had managed to finish her Christmas shopping, with the exception of Sam. She'd have to get a little something for the girl now. Getting something for Wyatt would be silly. She didn't know anything about him. Not really.

"Smells good in here," Olivia said, standing in the doorway.

Charlotte turned to give her a big smile but struggled to hold it. Her sister looked better than she had the other day, but she still had those dark circles under her eyes. "Hi. We're making pizza and I was just about to put a pot of coffee on. Would you like a cup?"

"Uh, sure, that would be great," Olivia said, her voice strained and barely a smile on her face as she walked farther into the kitchen.

"Is that darling baby taking a nap?" Grandma Ruby asked while placing the pizza in the oven.

"She is," Olivia said, sitting down on one of the chairs at the butcher block island.

Charlotte paused, pretty sure she'd just heard a cry. "Did either of you hear that?"

Olivia sat up and frowned. "No, what?"

"I thought I heard Dawn crying."

"You sit yourself right down, Olivia," Grandma Ruby said when Olivia stood. "I'll go check on that sweet baby."

Olivia looked almost panicked, and Charlotte didn't know if it was because they'd be left alone in the kitchen or if she wanted to be the one to get Dawn. Either way, no one really ever argued with Grandma Ruby, so she sat back down as their grandmother marched out of the kitchen. Charlotte turned the coffee pot on and, when she heard the stairs creak, she walked over opposite Olivia at the island. She had to try and break the ice before she jumped into what she'd discovered in the basement. "So did Grandma tell you about the robberies?"

Olivia nodded.

"When I first got here, her neighbor—"

"The handsome sheriff Grandma keeps talking about?" Olivia said, raising an eyebrow. For a second it almost looked like she might smile. Charlotte glanced away, trying not to look guilty. She knew she should tell her it was Wyatt. She was pretty sure Olivia would remember him. But that would also mean Olivia bringing up Charlotte's crush on him and then making way too big a deal about this. And, perhaps selfishly, she didn't want to share her feelings with Liv because her sister had shut her out for so long. She didn't want to be vulnerable in front of her because at the end of the holidays if Liv walked out of here and their relationship wasn't back to normal, then she'd feel like an idiot. She had never shared the details of her life with anyone except Olivia. And she wanted to protect herself from getting hurt again.

"Right."

"The one you're helping?"

Charlotte frowned. She needed to stay on track. "That's beside the point. Anyway, Grandma thinks it's not a big deal, but I really worry about her being in this giant old house by herself—"

Olivia groaned as the sound of Dawn crying rang through the large house. Crap. Olivia stood and winced. Their grandmother seemed to be in better shape than her sister. "Char, I can barely keep it together. Just leave it with the sheriff to figure out. No one has ever been able to tell Grandma what to do anyway. I need to go and get Dawn. I'll . . . uh, I'll be back to grab my coffee later."

Charlotte tried to quell her disappointment, but the heaviness in her chest was unmistakable. It was the same one that had followed her whenever she thought about her sister the last two years. But now it felt as though the ache only grew because Olivia was shutting her out even when Will wasn't around. It's not like she'd said they could chat later. It felt like a real brush-off. She was so done with being the one who always got hurt. Olivia hadn't had a real conversation with her since she'd gotten married. Nothing. She knew nothing about her life anymore. This didn't feel good. It felt unhappy. Dysfunctional.

She walked over to pour herself a coffee, tension tightening between her shoulder blades. She needed a break from this, from being dismissed by her sister. She stared out the window, in the direction of Wyatt's house. Wrapping her hands around the mug, that pull toward him surfaced and she wasn't afraid of it. It was . . . hopeful. Everyone in this house had moved on with life except her. She had walked through life with full armor on, never letting anyone close because of her fear. Her father was long gone. Her childhood was over. Her relationship with her sister had deteriorated. But The Christmas House was still here. Grandma Ruby was still here. And Wyatt . . . had come back.

Maybe all of this was exactly as it should be. Maybe this was her chance to stop carrying the burden of her childhood and everyone's problems again. She was worried about her sister, about her grandmother, and she was dreading her mother's visit. It was stifling. She placed her mug down in the sink with a thud.

She wanted to escape. The long-forgotten feeling, the anticipation of walking out the door to see Wyatt hit her without warning. Pushing aside everything holding her back now, she surrendered to that twelve-year-old girl, buried deep inside, and grabbed her coat, smiling with anticipation at seeing Wyatt.

CHAPTER NINE

AUGUST 1969
SILVER SPRINGS

"'Come to me, all you that are weary and are carrying heavy burdens . . .'" Ruby recited the Bible verse repeatedly as she scrubbed the bathroom floor. Gasping out loud as another pain tore through her abdomen, she recited the verse out loud this time. She couldn't go into labor yet. She wasn't strong enough. She wasn't ready to be a mother.

But the pain grew in intensity, robbing her of her words, her hands digging into the rag she was using, holding her breath, willing the pain to subside. After a minute or so, the deep grip the pain had on her lessened, and she took a few long, deep breaths. She recited the Bible verse again and then finished cleaning the tile. Standing carefully, she glanced at herself in the mirror, worry growing, at the pallor in her face even though she was sweating. You are not going into labor. You are not going into labor.

She hurriedly placed her cleaning items in the bucket she was carrying and washed her hands. Now she needed to put away all the laundry and hopefully get to the ironing. She was careful not to disturb Mrs. Pemberton, who was sleeping. If the older woman found her like this she was going to insist Ruby rest while she called the midwife.

The reality of becoming a mother—a single mother—was hitting her hard this week. She hadn't slept a wink in the last two weeks. Between getting up to use the bathroom a few times every night and the ache in her back and the visions of everyone in her old life haunting her dreams, sleep was not for her. In fact, she'd been wallowing in self-pity during the night. But the deal she had made with herself was that, when daylight hit, she would not yearn for any of those people anymore.

Ruby gasped as another pain hit, and she clung to the side of the handrail, sitting on the top step of the grand staircase. The pains were too close together now. She knew what this meant. She squeezed her eyes shut and couldn't prevent the whimper that came from her mouth.

"'Come to me, all you that are weary and are carrying heavy burdens, and I will give you rest.'" She chanted those words, aware that she was speaking out loud now, as the awful pain gripped her.

"One of my favorite and most comforting verses," Mrs. Pemberton's sweet, soothing voice said. She rubbed Ruby's back. "Just breathe, child. You will be fine. You get through this contraction and then I will call the midwife," she said, rubbing Ruby's back in a circular motion. Ruby forced herself to concentrate on the motion, on the comfort Mrs. Pemberton was providing.

"I can't do this," she whispered out loud, hating that she was so weak, that she wasn't able to project the image of the hardworking, confident housekeeper.

"You are not alone, Ruby. I will be here with you," she said.

Ruby wanted her mother. She wanted her mother desperately. She let the tears she'd been holding onto for months fall, hoping Mrs. Pemberton would think it was all just pain.

"Ruby, you are a courageous young woman. A role model to others and to this child you will have," Mrs. Pemberton said, moving from behind her to take her hands. Ruby stared into her kind eyes and wondered how this woman who had known her less than a year could show her this much grace, this much love. As she held her hands, clutched her hands, she stopped wishing for her mother. She stopped wishing for Richard. And she started to love the woman in front of her.

"Thank you. I just . . . I wanted to finish cleaning first," Ruby sputtered out as the pain started to subside. Her greatest fear was that she wouldn't be as useful to Mrs. Pemberton and she'd be homeless with a new baby to support.

"There is a lifetime for cleaning. It's not every day that a house gets to host the birth of a child. My husband always used to say this was a house filled with magic and love and it brought people together. You are a part of the magic here, Ruby. I'm so happy to share this with you," she said.

The light shining in through the windows illuminated Mrs. Pemberton's head, and Ruby didn't know if she was starting to hallucinate, but it was almost as though there were a halo shining over her.

"I don't know what I ever did to deserve you," she said, completely humbled by this woman's generosity.

Mrs. Pemberton squeezed her hands. "How do you think you came here?"

"Sister Juliette," she choked.

"Grace led you to Sister Juliette and grace led you here. Grace will always lead you home. My husband and I always wanted a child. This

house was meant to be filled with children. But . . . I couldn't. I was never able to carry a baby to term. I have lost three precious babies, Ruby. But now you are here. You are a gift and your baby is a gift. You are a long-forgotten, now-answered prayer. We are family now, you are home," she said, leaning down and kissing the top of Ruby's head.

* * *

"Are you in seventh or eighth grade, Sam?" Charlotte asked, peering into Wyatt's fridge. Sam was sitting at the breakfast bar, chatting with her and doing homework.

"Seventh. But I can't wait for next year. I hate how grade eights lord their power over the rest of us," she said, making a face.

Charlotte let out a soft laugh and pulled out some prewashed lettuce. She joined Sam at the counter. "I remember that. I always thought it was so stupid, especially since we were only a year apart."

Sam nodded. "Exactly. Are you making dinner again?"

Charlotte paused, heat flooding her face as she remembered the last time. She was saved from coming up with an answer when Wyatt walked through the front door.

"Hey, guys," he called out as he approached the kitchen, as though this was a regular thing.

Charlotte's stomach fluttered as Wyatt walked into the room. His end-of-day look was impossibly handsome. His dark hair looked as though he'd run his hands through it multiple times, and stubble lined his strong jaw. He was wearing a navy T-shirt that emphasized his wide, strong shoulders and biceps and hung loosely over his flat stomach. His worn jeans fit his lean and athletic build perfectly, and Charlotte forced herself to glance away in case he noticed her staring. He was . . . he was beautiful and luckily not paying her any attention as he walked over to give Sam a kiss on the head and place a paper bag on the island. Sam peered inside.

"Hey, Charlotte," he said, with a smile that curled her toes.

"Hi," she said, smiling back, forcing herself to appear normal and not at all like she'd just been checking him out.

"I hope you like chicken and roast potatoes, Charlotte, because that's what Dad brought home," Sam said, placing the food on the island.

Charlotte's gaze went back and forth between Sam and Wyatt. "Oh, um, I was just going to head out. And you have to rush off to ballet—"

"Canceled. The snow is really coming down out there. We're in for a big storm," Wyatt said, coming to stand beside her at the island and washing his hands.

"Perfect! Do you want to stay, Charlotte?" Sam asked, leaning forward.

She couldn't say no to Sam again. She didn't want to, either. She smiled at her, pushing aside all the reasons she shouldn't. "Then I'd love to. I'll just finish this salad," she said.

"I'll set the table," Sam said, hopping off the bar stool and walking to the cupboards.

"Should we eat in the dining room since the table is filled up?" Sam asked, holding a stack of dishes and frowning at the table.

"Sounds good to me," Wyatt said.

"Sorry about that. I'll have that all sorted and put away tomorrow," Charlotte said, adding dried cranberries to the bowl filled with lettuce.

"No worries. Take your time. How about I get that bottle of wine? Do you like red? I think I have a bottle of merlot somewhere," he said, leaning over to check the built-in wine rack on the side of the island.

"Yeah, Dad's more of a beer drinker," Sam said wisely as she gathered the cutlery.

Charlotte swallowed her laugh and added walnuts to the bowl while Sam disappeared into the dining room again.

"You'll definitely need this after you dine with a tween," Wyatt said, in a hushed voice as he opened the bottle of wine.

Charlotte laughed. "She's lovely. Really. You have a great kid," she said softly.

He held her gaze and, for a second, it looked as though he was going to brush off the comment. "Thank you, I think she's pretty great too. There have been many days where I've wondered what I was doing, if I was screwing up along the way. With work and just everything, sometimes I felt like I wasn't going to make it. But she's my world. And her happiness is the most important thing to me. You remember what it was like . . . I wanted more for her," he said, his voice thick.

Charlotte swallowed hard, past the lump in her throat, past all those emotions and memories. He was opening up to her, just like he had when they were kids. "You make it look easy. Like you're a natural, and I can tell she knows she is very loved," she said softly.

His jaw clenched and he looked away. "Thanks," he said, holding out a glass of wine.

"Thank you," she said, taking the glass. Her fingertips brushed his and she knew, even before their fingers touched, that she'd feel a jolt of something. She knew because it had always been that way for her. She took a quick sip and she wondered if he'd experienced it as well. "This is nice," she said after putting the glass back on the island.

"Glad you like it. Can I help with that salad?" he asked as she tossed the lettuce.

"All done. I'll admit I was a little surprised that you had walnuts and dried cranberries . . . ," she said, looking at him over the rim of her glass.

He let out a short laugh. "Believe me, I'm just as surprised as you are. But actually, it was part of a gift basket my friend gave me," he said.

"Table is all set. Can I bring the salad in?" Sam asked, walking back into the kitchen.

"Sure, here you go," Charlotte said, sliding the bowl across the counter.

They both watched Sam pick up the bowl and walk back into the dining room humming "Winter Wonderland" under her breath.

"Let's go join Sam," Wyatt said, waiting for her to pass him in the doorway.

One of the things that had always surprised her about Wyatt was his manners. She knew he hadn't learned that at home. Charlotte sat beside Sam, and Wyatt took the seat opposite her. The dining room was cozy, with a bay window that overlooked the backyard. The large, dark wood table and upholstered parson chairs were the only furniture in the room.

"We should say grace," Sam said, and Charlotte caught the flicker of surprise that shot across Wyatt's face.

"Sure," he agreed, bowing his head while Charlotte did the same.

"This is so good," Sam said, a few moments later, taking an enthusiastic bite.

They ate in silence for a bit. Wyatt offered everyone seconds before helping himself to more chicken. Charlotte sat back in her seat, sipping her wine and listening to one of Sam's stories about the weird kids in her class.

"So how do you two know each other again?" Sam asked, looking back and forth between them.

Charlotte looked at Wyatt and raised her eyebrow. She'd let him take the lead since she had no idea how much he'd told his daughter about his childhood.

"We lived in the same apartment building in Toronto and went to the same school," he said.

"That's so cool. Did you go to high school together?"

Charlotte tensed, waiting for his reply.

He gave a quick shake of his head. "No. I, uh, left in eighth grade."

"What was my dad like, Charlotte?" Sam asked, turning to her with a big smile on her face.

Charlotte took a sip of wine and willed her face not to go red. Damn. She felt like they were being interrogated. "He was . . . nice. He was a really nice guy," she said, wishing she could expand without revealing her feelings.

"But I guess you felt sorry for him because he had no friends," Sam said, shooting Wyatt a teasing glance.

He barked out a laugh and picked up his own wine glass and leaned back in his chair.

Charlotte smiled. "Actually, your dad was really cool. Honestly, he was probably the coolest guy in school."

Sam's mouth dropped open. "I'm so shocked."

Wyatt coughed. "Thanks a lot, Sam."

Sam put her elbows on the table. "This is just so surprising to me. Were you guys like girlfriend and boyfriend?"

Charlotte choked on her wine.

"Uh, no. Because twelve- and thirteen-year-olds shouldn't have romantic relationships," Wyatt said, saving her from answering. She knew her face was all kinds of red at this point.

Sam rolled her eyes. "Fine, maybe in your century, but not mine."

Wyatt stood. "As long as you and I are in the same century, Sam, you have to go by my rules. Let's clear the table instead of scaring Charlotte off," he said, giving Sam a pointed stare.

"No worries, Dad, I'll do it. You can sit and relax a bit," Sam said, flashing him a smile before grabbing their plates.

"I should probably get going," Charlotte said, standing.

"No! You can stay," Sam said, appearing in the doorway.

Charlotte smiled. "Oh, hun, I'm sure you guys need to get on with your evening and you have homework and stuff. I'll be back tomorrow afternoon," she said, glancing over at Wyatt, who was silent.

"There's a snowstorm, it's the perfect time to watch a Christmas movie," Sam said, the longing in her voice making Charlotte's heart squeeze.

"We'd love the company, but if you have to get going we understand that too," Wyatt said, his hands in the front pockets of his jeans, a rare glimmer of vulnerability in his eyes.

"Please?" Sam said.

Charlotte couldn't walk away from them. And she didn't want to. "Okay, why not? I haven't watched a Christmas movie yet this year."

Sam continued cleaning up the kitchen while she and Wyatt walked into the large family room. The peaked ceiling overhung a large, stone, wood-burning fireplace and two large sofas. Wyatt rattled off the titles of different Christmas movies.

"Oh, will Sam like *It's a Wonderful Life*?" Charlotte asked.

Wyatt shrugged. "I have no idea. She's never wanted to watch it before, but she might like it. She does have an aversion to black and white, though."

They were standing side by side, close enough that she could smell his woodsy, fresh scent. Close enough that she could lean her head on his shoulder or touch his arms if she wanted to. She took a step back.

"All right, I've got popcorn for all. Let's watch!" Sam said, bursting into the room, popping the tension between them like a balloon.

* * *

A few hours later Charlotte was curled up on the sofa, sipping her second glass of wine very slowly and having the best night she'd had in a very long time. The fireplace made the room toasty, and its flickering lights were soothing—which was great because now that Sam had fallen asleep on the couch, things were awkward with just her and Wyatt. She kept her eyes glued to the large screen, pretending she was absorbed in it, even though she'd seen the movie five thousand times and her thoughts at that moment weren't about Jimmy Stewart and his problems, but her own.

Wyatt looked over at her as the movie ended, and she quickly jumped off the sofa like it had caught on fire. She was hyperaware of him, his every move, his every sound. "Well, I should really get going," she said, wishing the lights were on and it didn't feel so intimate in here.

"Thanks for, uh, staying and watching this with us," Wyatt said, standing. He had an easy, relaxed charm to him that seemed a contradiction to his physical appearance. He seemed like he should be tough and unapproachable, but he had a wit and a kindness to him that made her want to know more about the man he'd become.

"Why don't I help Sam up to bed and walk you home?" he said.

She waved a hand. "Oh, gosh no, don't worry about it. I'm fine."

His lips twitched. "Not this again. You know it's what we do, Char. We walk places together," he said, his voice thick and his eyes sparkling.

Warmth flooded her body. *It's what we do. Char.* "Okay. You're right. We have taken a lot of walks. What's one more?"

It was a walk and nothing more. In a few weeks she'd be back in Toronto. She was very happy with her life there. She liked her small condo in the city, she liked running her business, and she liked the simplicity of her everyday life. Having relationships meant that you were only fifty percent in control of your life. The other person, without warning, could completely change the trajectory of your life, and why would anyone want that? She knew kids and marriage weren't in the cards for her, and she was fine with that. Look at what had happened to the rest of the women in her family. *Tragic.* She had no intention of ruining her life. Why strive for something that could be amazing when her life was already . . . good? Why risk it all? She'd never understood that.

"Okay, I'll get Sam up to bed and meet you at the door," he said, walking over to Sam and crouching down.

Charlotte walked back into the kitchen, listening to Wyatt's deep voice speaking to Sam. She stood in the door and watched as he walked his daughter down the hall, his arm around her shoulders, and a warmth flooded her body as her throat tightened.

What was happening to her? Maybe she was becoming a sap like Olivia. It couldn't be the sight of the most gorgeous man she'd ever met, the perfectly masculine Wyatt, so thoughtfully taking care of his daughter, could it? He was clearly the real deal—a man who was strong and capable and loving.

He wasn't a man who would just walk out on a family . . . like her father had. Her father had been her hero. He had been there for her every morning and every night, until he wasn't. The sun rose and set with him and then he'd destroyed every sunrise and every sunset until she'd reclaimed them as an adult. Or she thought she had. But maybe the fact that she never let anyone get close meant that her father still held onto a piece of her heart that she wasn't giving away to anyone.

"Okay, ready to go?" Wyatt asked, appearing in the hallway.

She gave herself a mental shake, refusing to sit in a past that was steeped with pain. She shot him a smile. "Sure. Sam's all tucked in bed?"

He nodded, smiling. "She is. She knows I'm walking you home," he said, taking her coat from the closet and holding it out for her.

She could actually feel herself blushing as she put her arms into the sleeves. "Thank you," she said, cringing at her breathless voice. Why was she like this? Why couldn't she fake casual and cool? Because he was . . . he was more than any other man she'd ever been around.

A few minutes later they were walking down his driveway. The night air was brisk and cold and exactly what she needed to cool her overheated face.

"I always love the sky in Silver Springs," she said, looking up for a moment and pausing to take it all in. The stars were bright and copious and the moon so large that all the pines were almost completely illuminated as they swayed with the wind.

"I know. This view makes me happy we moved from the city," he said as they walked along the road, their boots crunching the snow.

She glanced over at him, her heart racing, and broke the silence as they walked up the path to the front porch of The Christmas House. "Where did you go that day?"

His jaw clenched and he didn't answer. There was a silence in the air as they kept walking, the kind that made her very aware of the intimacy of this moment. They stood at the door and light streamed through the transom windows. He glanced down for a moment and then up at her, his eyes filled with a pain that made her want to reach out and touch him.

"We had to leave. My, uh, my mom was in the hospital for a while and then we moved around a lot after that," he said, his voice thick.

She wanted to ask more but didn't want to push him. "I'm sorry," she said softly. She wanted to walk over to him and wrap her arms around him, around the boy he was, and make up for everything he'd lost. But they weren't the same people, and their lives were complicated now.

He shrugged and took a step back. "It was a long time ago."

She nodded. "So, I'll be by tomorrow," she said, her hand on the doorknob.

"Sure. Thanks again," he said, his deep voice slicing through the barriers she was so desperately trying to keep up.

"No problem," she said, turning the handle.

"Hey, Charlotte?"

She paused and turned to look at him. He was standing halfway down the long porch, his handsome face in the shadows. "Yes?"

"Thanks again for everything you're doing . . . and with Sam. I missed you," he said, his voice was thick with emotion.

She nodded, barely able to breathe normally, her words buried deep inside her chest, trapped. She wanted to tell him it was the best night she'd had in a long time. She had missed him too.

It had felt real and right and made her long for things that she'd forbidden herself to long for. But it was silly. These were silly little thoughts from a woman who had no experience with family and love. "Me too. Good night, Wyatt," she said, forcing herself to walk away from him.

The warmth from The Christmas House flooded her, and she leaned against the door, closing her eyes, and just as she suspected, the image of Wyatt was there, teasing her with the idea that there could be so much more out there for her, if she wanted it. She didn't want him to belong in her past anymore. She wanted him now. She just needed the courage to go for it.

CHAPTER TEN

CHRISTMAS EVE 1969
SILVER SPRINGS

"Merry Christmas. May you have the courage to go after all the dreams in your heart, baby Wendy," Sister Juliette said, raising her glass and toasting all of them.

Ruby's heart swelled, and it made it almost impossible to swallow the champagne in her mouth. But she did, as she looked around the dining room table. It was filled with the sisters from St. Michael's and of course her and Mrs. Pemberton, and baby Wendy, who was being passed around like pumpkin pie among all the women.

This was a room of dreams. Ruby had always thought it would be the perfect room for large families to gather and share in the joys of the holidays. Last Christmas Eve she had been a broken woman—just a girl, really. Now she was surrounded by new family, with a child of her own, with a knowledge of the world that she hadn't had before.

"Merry Christmas to all of you. There will never be enough words to express my gratitude to every one of you. But know that you have changed my life and Wendy's. One day I will find a way to make you all proud," she said, her voice wobbly as she forced her hand in the air triumphantly.

Everyone clinked glasses with hers. Ruby stood as the doorbell rang. "Why don't I get that? You all carry on with dinner," she said, placing her linen napkin down on her seat. She paused to kiss the top of sweet Wendy's bald head before leaving the room, the sound of animated chatter lingering and floating in the air.

Ruby opened the door to find Harry standing there, a handsome vision against the blustery snow swirling around him. "Merry Christmas, Ruby," he said, a slight smile on his face.

Ruby stepped out onto the porch, her heart pounding in her chest. "Merry Christmas, Harry! What are you doing here?"

He took off his hat, and that thick dark hair swayed slightly in the harsh wind. "Ruby . . . I . . . I came back to ask you one more time. I've met a great girl and . . . before I go any further, I want to know that this door is closed here with you."

She ignored the stab of jealousy that filled her. Whoever the girl was, she was a lucky one. She shook her head. "No, Harry. You go and live your life and get married to that great girl," she whispered softly, more softly than she intended. A part of her hoped the wind would carry away her words the moment she said them, but when his face fell she knew he'd heard her. She would never burden him like that. She would never be the woman he was forced to marry out of duty, no matter how lovely the idea of being his wife.

He looked away, and she studied his strong profile, the hard edges of his jaw, and waited for him to say something, wanting to hear that voice again. *"You're a great girl too, Ruby, and I think we could be happy together."*

"Harry, I'm not going to let you do that. I have a life here now, a healthy baby, a new start. I can't go back. I can't. It's too late." She didn't want to add that she didn't want to see his parents, that she would destroy his relationship with them. They would never forgive him for marrying her. And maybe, if she were a better person, she would be able to let go of the bitterness and resentment that was chained to her heart when she thought of them and her parents for tossing her aside like that. But she hadn't gotten over it still. It was something that burned inside her, that she hadn't shared with Sister Juliette because she knew how wrong it was. She needed to find a way to forgive, but she couldn't. She could never forget crying out for her mother, knowing her mother would never come to her again. Now she was a mother and she answered each of Wendy's cries, knowing she would give that child all her unconditional love.

Harry rubbed the back of his neck and then finally looked at her. *"If you ever need anything, I will always be there for you. But you should know that it's never too late for a happy ending, Ruby,"* he said, those words touching her heart, stroking her soul, even though she knew that, for her, it was too late.

"Thank you," she managed to whisper, refusing to cry.

He gave a nod in her direction. *"Merry Christmas, Ruby."*

"Merry Christmas, Harry," she whispered as he turned and walked down the long porch. She held her gaze on his strong, tall figure, knowing this would be the last time she saw him. He was on his way to start a life with another woman, and Ruby would never have a right to be a part of it. She would always be a part of his past. Looking back was a fruitless endeavor. It held nothing for any of them.

She walked back into the house, closer to the voices and laughter of the future that she was claiming. "Ruby, my dear, you look as though you've seen a ghost. Are you all right?" Mrs. Pemberton asked.

Everyone turned to look at Ruby, including Wendy. She forced a smile on her face. "Of course I am."

"Good, then it's my turn for a toast," Mrs. Pemberton said, leaning heavily on the side of the table as she stood. They waited as she coughed. The older woman had already warned Ruby that every winter she came down with bronchitis but not to worry. The sound of that cough did have everyone frowning, and just when Ruby was about to help her, she stopped and picked up her champagne glass. "This is to all of you, but especially Ruby and Wendy. You have made my dreams of seeing this dining room table filled with life and laughter and a new generation come true. Merry Christmas to us, this wonderful, unconventional mix of women. May the new year be filled with good health for us all!"

As they toasted and laughed, Ruby picked up Wendy and held her close, wishing that life could always be like this, that every Christmas could be filled with people like this and love like this. And she wished that Harry would find love and live a good life.

* * *

Wyatt knew he was in trouble the moment he entered the house and smelled baking. It evoked a feeling of comfort, warmth. He never baked. He probably *could* if he tried, he just didn't have the time. Sam had no interest. When he was growing up, there hadn't been a baked anything in his house. Aunt Mary had told him that his mother used to bake, but his father had basically destroyed all her happiness. He had never walked into a house with the smell of baking, had never known how the smell of vanilla and sugar could lull a person into thinking everything was going to be okay.

He shook off that sappiness as he hung his jacket, the anticipation of seeing Charlotte making it worth it. Christmas songs were playing again, and he smiled at the sound of laughter—Charlotte's and his daughter's. Something settled in his chest, a heaviness, a contentment he had never experienced. It was Charlotte.

The other night it had taken everything he had to not open up completely to Charlotte. But once they went down that road of sharing their pasts and their secrets, there would be no going back. He knew neither of them could get hurt again. Charlotte wore her trepidation on her sleeve, and he didn't want to risk anything hurting Sam.

He took off his boots and coat and made his way into the kitchen, stopping in the doorway, which had almost become like a new routine for him. He had never been the sentimental type, but it was too good a picture, too good a feeling to not want to savor. Charlotte was currently swearing under her breath and then covering her mouth as she burned herself on some sad-looking cookies, while his daughter looked delighted by the accidental swearing.

"Trouble?" he said, walking in.

They both looked up at him startled. "Charlotte and I burned the cookies," Sam said, not looking upset by it at all.

Charlotte winced, her face turning red. He didn't really care about the cookies. He cared about the feeling she managed to bring out in him. Two feelings actually—one of warmth and family, and then there were the other feelings . . . the not so platonic kind. Like, he couldn't ignore the immediate attraction he felt for her the second he saw her. Every damn time. He found himself wanting to reach out to kiss her or touch her. His eyes took in the curves that he knew he wanted to feel against him and the mouth that he wanted to taste.

"Those don't look too bad," he said, joining them at the island. He was contemplating trying one of the black cookies, despite their probable carcinogen rating, just so he could get his mind off kissing Charlotte.

"I wouldn't suggest it," Charlotte said, moving the tray.

"Don't worry, Dad, we have another tray ready to go in the oven. We got sidetracked and forgot the cookies because we finished all the kitchen organizing."

He didn't even know who his daughter was anymore. She was all smiles and amicability. There wasn't a scowl in sight. "Wow. That was fast. I can't wait to see what you've done," he said, turning to Charlotte.

She raised sparkling eyes to his and hell if he didn't actually feel himself getting pulled in. "We were motivated to finish because it meant we could eat cookies."

"And all the sugar is being counteracted by these," Sam said, holding up a green drink.

"Ugh. What is that?" He said, frowning.

Sam shoved the drink in his direction. "Dad, you have to try these smoothies from that new place in town."

He gently pushed it back. "Uh, no. I wish Mable's hadn't closed. Things aren't supposed to change in small towns. I don't need to try their smoothies."

"It's the pine energizer," Sam said, wriggling her eyebrows and sipping from the straw.

Charlotte laughed and shot him a look. "Sam warned me not to pick one up for you."

"Dad drinks a powder so he doesn't have to actually chew vegetables. Come to think of it, the only time he eats salad is when you're around."

Wyatt kept his head in the fridge a little longer, so that the heat hitting his face wouldn't be noticeable. Why was his daughter constantly trying to embarrass him? He forced himself to focus on the contents of the fridge and that's when he noticed . . . that he could actually see things. Like individual items. And the fruit and vegetables. All the ones he didn't eat. The shelves sparkled, and the doors of the fridge had neatly grouped bottles of condiments and his greens powders. "Wow. This looks like a brand new fridge," he said, shutting the door and turning around to Charlotte.

She smiled. "I'm glad you like it. Sam was a big help."

Sam pointed her awful drink to the pantry. "Open the pantry, Dad. You'll die."

"Great, exactly what I need to do," he said with a laugh as he followed her instructions.

Lo and behold, clear bins lined most shelves and like items were grouped together. The varieties of cereal were placed in tall, clear containers. Which was perfect since his daughter adored putting empty boxes of cereal back in the pantry and then complaining to him when they were out.

"What do you think, Dad? Don't spend the whole night in there, look at all the cupboards too. You know that pots and pans drawer you can never get to shut without swearing? It's all done too."

He cleared his throat and crossed the room to open the drawer. Pots were stacked and the damn lids that drove him nuts were all lined up in something that looked like a stainless steel file holder. "This is great, wow. Thank you, Charlotte."

"You're very welcome. But there was no way I could have gotten this done so quickly if it hadn't been for Sam," she said, shooting his daughter a smile. Sam beamed at her as though Charlotte had just given her the latest iPhone.

He glanced at his watch. He hated to have to leave. "Are you ready for ballet, Sam?"

"Nope. Almost. I'll go get dressed. I already ate dinner. A *delicious* salad. Oh, and I'm going with Cat and then sleeping at their house tonight."

"Does Scott know that?" he asked. He wasn't about to start thinking about the fact that his house was actually going to be empty and that Charlotte was here.

Sam rolled her eyes, and he felt a bit more comfortable knowing the daughter he remembered was actually still in there. "Of course. He promised we'd order pizza and get the TV in the family room."

"Sounds like he'll have a fun night," Wyatt said with a laugh, glancing over at Charlotte.

"I do make good salads, and I saved you some," she said.

He wanted to tell her that it wasn't her salads, that it was her. But that would be crossing a line and he'd rather never cross that line so that he could have her in their lives. This was the house he always wanted—as a kid, as an adult. One that was filled with teasing and laughter and love . . . he'd given up on that dream after Leanne had walked out. But now . . .

"I'm going to go pack," Sam said, racing by him and then stopping in the doorway. "Are those cookies going to be ready before I go, Char?"

Charlotte glanced at the oven. "Probably not, but I promise I'll have a stash just for you so your dad doesn't eat them."

"Hey, that's offensive," he said, reeling. This was the kind of conversation people had after months of knowing each other. Sam was even referring to her as "Char/"

"I might have told her about your issues with sugar," Sam said, laughing and running out of the room.

Suddenly the room felt small and quiet. Charlotte was washing her hands, getting ready to leave, and he didn't want her to go. He didn't want any of this to end. This house hadn't seen this kind of laughter or lightness in . . . forever. Maybe never, because when he and Sam had come here two years ago they were different people. Back in the city they were different people. When Sam's mom had been with them, they'd been different people. There had never been much laughter between him and his wife. There had been a lot of fights. A lot of shitty words spoken that made him uncomfortable now, looking back. He'd been younger. More of a hothead. He wasn't without blame in how their marriage ended. He regretted not doing better, not trying harder. But they'd been kids practically. Way too young to be parents, to be married. He understood that he had never loved Sam's mother the way he should because they were very different people, but maybe if he'd tried harder, then she would have had a role in Sam's life. He regretted not being able to give his daughter the mother she deserved. He regretted not being enough for his little girl.

"So, um, these will be done in ten minutes. You just have to pull them out of the oven when the timer goes off and then let them cool on the rack over here. Don't forget to use an oven mitt," she said, shooting him a smile.

He grinned. "Did you actually just remind me to use an oven mitt?"

Her face turned bright red, and she let out a choked laugh. "I guess I didn't need to mention that."

"You do know I've used an oven before?"

She crossed her arms, and he tried not to notice the way a hint of cleavage appeared above the top button of her red and green plaid shirt. This was getting more and more inconvenient. "Of course. It's just a habit."

"Sure. Or you could just stay and make sure I'm not that incompetent. I have wine. I mean, if you want to stay," he said, wondering at what point in his life he'd become such a wuss and backtracked on asking a woman to have a glass of wine. It wasn't his fault. It was the whole single-dad thing and the fact that Charlotte didn't really give off any vibes . . . he usually knew when a woman was into him. Sometimes he thought Charlotte was, but then she closed up and it was strictly platonic and he wondered if he'd imagined all of it.

"Oh . . . um." Her gaze darted around the room and he had no idea what she was looking for. "Uh, yeah, why don't I clean up first, then I'll leave?"

"What? No. I'm not asking you to stay so you can clean up my kitchen."

Her mouth dropped open slightly and he regretted his harsh tone. He didn't want to screw this up. Whatever it was. "Oh. Right. No, I just . . . I'm the one who thought we should bake. It's not fair that you have to clean up after a long day at work."

"We can actually have a conversation without a twelve-year-old listening in on us," he said with a smile.

Sam appeared in the doorway. "What am I not allowed to listen in on?"

Wyatt shut his eyes and pinched the bridge of his nose. He opened them just in time for Sam to reach up and give him a kiss on the cheek. As if that wasn't shocking enough, she gave Charlotte a hug and then a wave. "Scott's here. See you later! Bye, Char! I'll text you tonight, Dad."

"Sounds good," he said. He gave himself a mental shake. "I'll be right back," he said to Charlotte before leaving the room and following Sam to the door. He opened the door and waved to his friend as they pulled out of the driveway.

When he walked back into the kitchen, Charlotte was already wiping down the counters. "So what if I upped my invitation and we order pizza and have a glass of wine?"

She stopped wiping the counters and looked up at him, wincing. "I . . . I don't know. I should probably get back. My sister is in town and . . ."

She was letting him down. Easy. Awkwardly. "Sure, no, that's fine. I get it."

She bit her lower lip. "I just . . . I'm only in Silver Springs for a little while . . ."

"It's just pizza and wine," he said, softly.

She swallowed audibly. "Pizza and wine."

He tilted his head toward the oven. "And cookies."

Her gorgeous mouth curved into a smile that slammed him in the gut. "Right. Sure."

The tension left his shoulders, and anticipation coursed through him. He wanted this time with her. "Okay, I'm going to go change and order the pizza. I'll be right back. Don't clean up any more of this, I'll help when I come back. Oh, what do you like on your pizza?"

"Vegetarian."

Dear God, no. "Sure. Sounds great," he said politely and turned to leave.

She burst out laughing and he turned around. "I'm just joking. I don't really care. You could even get a meat lover's if you want. I'm not picky when it comes to pizza."

Her eyes were sparkling and he resisted the overwhelming urge to walk over there and capture a bit of that laugh, a taste of that mouth, of the woman that was making him want to rethink his opinion on doing life alone. He cleared his throat. "Thank God. I was thinking the whole vegetarian thing might end this relationship before it starts."

He left the room kicking himself for tossing the word relationship out there. They weren't in a relationship.

"Wait. Wyatt?" she called out as he walked out of the room.

"Yes?" he said, the tension in the room palpable, whatever it was glittering in her gorgeous blue eyes making him so glad he hadn't ignored his instincts about her.

She looked down at the counter for a moment before meeting his gaze, and he caught a flash of fear or trepidation across those deep, sapphire-colored eyes. "I'm just . . . Ugh . . . I don't know what to say. I don't do . . . relationships. I'm probably not the person you think I am, and I don't want anything to come between this friendship I have going on with Sam. I feel like she really needs a friend, and if things got weird between us, I'd hate to disappoint her," she said, her words gutting him. How could a woman who had been a stranger to his daughter a week ago now care enough about

Sam to put her needs first? The worst part was, that made him want her even more.

He cleared his throat. "Maybe we're just two old friends catching up and nothing more. There's nothing wrong with just being friends. The last thing I want is Sam getting hurt. I've been very careful about not introducing her to any women of my acquaintance. You sort of entered the picture thanks to Aunt Mary, but you're Sam's friend first. I wouldn't do anything to jeopardize that. So what's a glass of wine between two friends?"

She let out an audible sigh of relief, and he pushed aside his disappointment. Maybe it was for the best. Like him, Charlotte also hadn't had a great childhood. And if they got more involved it would mean sharing their pasts. He had never forgiven his father, he'd never forgotten. There was no way she would understand that. He had cut his father off, had shut the door in his face. That wasn't something he'd ever be able to share with Charlotte. Because as much as she understood family problems, he knew she still spoke to her mother. Charlotte would never have cut her family off the way he had. Her grandmother would never understand either.

Ruby Harris never shut the door on anyone.

CHAPTER ELEVEN

DECEMBER 24, 1974
SILVER SPRINGS

Ruby pressed Wendy's little thumb into the dough of a thumbprint cookie and was rewarded with her five-year-old's little peal of laughter. Mrs. Pemberton smiled weakly, but her eyes were still sparkling as she sat at the head of the table and watched them as they baked three dozen of her traditional Christmas cookies.

Ruby frowned as the elderly woman coughed, the sound deep and filled with congestion. "Did you finish the tea with honey and lemon?" Ruby asked, leaving Wendy to continue pressing her thumb into the neat rows of cookies, as Ruby rubbed Mrs. Pemberton's back and made sure her shawl was snug.

"Yes, dear, it was wonderful. I'm sure this annual bout of bronchitis is turning the corner and I will be well enough to have Christmas dinner in the dining room," she said, her voice wobbly and weak.

Ruby made a mental note to call Doctor Hiller in the morning and have him check in again. She didn't like the sound of that cough, and it didn't look like the bronchitis was close to clearing at all. Ruby had also noticed that the elderly woman's usually robust appetite hadn't returned either, and she was worried about her. The last five years together had made her like a mother figure, and Ruby had come to rely on their friendship. She had become family to Ruby and Wendy.

The doorbell rang and Ruby patted Mrs. Pemberton's hand gently. "I'll go answer that. Wendy, you be good," she said, pausing to give her daughter a kiss on the head before leaving the room. She walked quickly to the front door, almost positive that it might be the doctor stopping in after work.

Her stomach dropped and heat burned through her body when she saw her parents standing on the other side of the door. She drank in the sight of them, some kind of childlike happiness at seeing them overcoming her at first, until it was quickly replaced by the bitterness of adulthood, the image in her mind the one from Christmas Eve five years ago.

"Ruby, you're looking well," her father said. He still stood as proudly as he had her entire life, and she was somewhat disappointed to see that he hadn't lost that pride, that he still looked healthy, that he could still hold his head so high. His deep voice wasn't tinged with any regret or humility. Instead, it was stiff and formal.

Straightening her shoulders, she clutched the cold doorknob tightly, refusing to crumple in front of them like a rag doll, like she had done that awful night. She had been a child then. No longer. She now understood the way the world worked, how conditional love could be, how appearances were more important than blood. She knew how to stand on her own two feet.

"Hello."

"Ruby, we came to visit with you . . . and your child," her mother said, the tone in her voice making it sound as though they were doing Ruby a favor.

Ruby's heart raced uncomfortably inside her chest, too fast, too hard, too much. "How did you find me?"

"That doesn't matter. But we don't like how we left things," her father said.

Ruby's back stiffened at his dismissal of her question. After all these years and after the way they had treated her, this wasn't enough. She wasn't the same girl who had wept on their doorstep, alone and afraid. Where was the apology she had imagined late at night while lying in bed? It didn't sound like there was one coming at all.

"How we left things? You threw me out. In the winter. On Christmas. Pregnant. Without a dime to my name. I could have died. Your grand-child could have died. You're here, six years later. It took you six years to decide that you were ready to see me and what, you were just going to waltz in here and become a grandparent to a child you never met?"

Her father's jaw clenched. "That is not the way to speak to your parents, Ruby."

"I'm a parent too now. And I know that I would never leave my daughter to rot away at Christmas because she disappointed me. I would die for her. As a parent, I can now see how cruel you've been to me. Did you even miss me? Did you worry about me? Is there any part of you that regrets kicking me out like that?"

"Ruby, it was very hard for us to deal with all the rumors in our circle. We lost so many friends," her mother said, wringing her hands.

"Friends? You lost a daughter."

"Your fault. I'm not going to stand here and be blamed for your foolishness," her father said.

Ruby took a step forward, refusing to be intimidated. "I couldn't have been the first foolish teenager, surely. And what about Richard? He was to blame as well. Did his family hang their heads in shame or did they glorify him after his death?"

"This is not the way we wanted this conversation to go, Ruby. I would have hoped you matured," her mother said, her lips pinched.

Ruby's heart pounded painfully. "I have matured. But that small part of me who will always be your daughter had hoped you were here to tell me you loved me and that you were sorry for kicking me out, for letting so many years go by. I've built a life for myself now."

"As a maid? That's not a life, certainly nothing for you to boast about. Nor is being an unwed mother. If anything, you should be thanking us for wanting anything to do with you," her father said.

She recoiled. "I'm proud of what I've accomplished. I did it on my own and while pregnant. Everyone turned on me. Richard's family. You. I would think after everything you've done that you would at least have been contrite."

"Mama, who's at the door?"

Ruby inhaled sharply at the sound of Wendy's bubbly voice and quick little footsteps. She stared at her parents, watching as their eyes widened as Wendy appeared in the vestibule, the picture of health, her rosy cheeks matching her red velvet dress, her blue eyes large as she stared up at them. Ruby prayed for the strength to continue, to end this before they confused Wendy.

"These are just some people asking for directions. You can go back inside, sweetheart."

Her mother's face crumpled and her father's turned stony. Ruby glanced away, unwilling to let them break her resolve. Wendy scampered away, and Ruby took a step back from the doorway.

"This is my life now. I have changed. I hoped this could be more, that you could be more. I groveled at your feet. I apologized. I lived with shame for so long. Why did you even come here?"

For a moment, Ruby waited, foolishly waited for more from them. She wanted one of them to say they were sorry, that they hadn't slept in years wondering if she was alive, hating what they had done. She wanted them to beg for her and Wendy to be in their lives. But instead, this wall of pride stood between them, neither of them willing to climb over it. She'd swallowed her pride one too many times. She would never do it again. They had shut her out when she needed them the most.

"If you could just understand how hard this has been on us. Your foolish decisions have made us the object of so many rumors. We have lost friends."

Ruby choked on her anger. "You lost more than friends. You lost a daughter. A granddaughter. You haven't changed at all. I groveled. I apologized, and you turned me away. I don't know why you came here at all."

Her father straightened his shoulders, his jaw firm. "We wanted a relationship with our grandchild."

Ruby clutched the doorframe as hurt pummeled through her body. "But not me."

Her father lifted his chin. "You were always too proud, Ruby."

"Goodbye," she said, and slowly shut the door, reminding her of the door shut on her six years ago. But her parents weren't desperate. They had each other. They had a roof over their heads. She had been desperate. But no longer. She fought for control. She grasped onto it. She wanted to control the tears, the hurt, the disappointment. In her dreams it had never gone like this. In her dreams they had reconciled. They had been the people she'd always wanted them to be.

She shut her eyes and leaned her forehead on the cool door. She couldn't go back in the kitchen yet. After a few seconds she heard their footsteps slowly retreating on the porch and then from the corner of her eye, the headlights from the car. It was over. They were gone.

She had survived again. They had come here to discard her once again and use little Wendy to make themselves feel better. Until Wendy would make a mistake or talk back to them, and then they'd discard her as well, because they didn't have unconditional love. They didn't know the meaning of love.

She had vowed to never cry in front of them again, so she cried now, placing her hand on the door, as though she could still feel them on the other side, her last contact with them.

* * *

Charlotte decided she'd tell Wyatt about her Grandma Ruby theory once they'd eaten the pizza. Why was she hesitant to tell him? It was ridiculous. *She* was ridiculous. Or it was all her issues with trusting people. Grandma Ruby was so important to her, and talking about something that might be heartbreaking to . . . someone else was disconcerting.

"Okay, pizza is ordered. I have to thank you again. I know you think it was just part of the job, but what you did here in a few days was beyond what I expected. I'm sure it was beyond what my aunt bought as well," he said.

Charlotte wasn't exactly concerned about an hourly rate for organizational services. She didn't want this to be her last night here. "I feel bad because I'm not sure Sam knows this was my last night here."

He ran a hand through his hair. "I'll tell her. I'm sure it won't be the last time we'll see you."

She nodded a little too quickly to look casual. She was busy concentrating on the man standing in the doorway. Charlotte stared at him, knowing she needed to come up with something to say, but he took her breath away. He'd showered, and his dark hair was still damp, mussed up like he'd just run his hand through it instead of combing it. He was wearing a dark T-shirt and jeans that looked as though they'd been custom made for his athletic build. He was more mouthwatering than the entire batch of sugar cookies she'd made. He raked a hand through his hair, and the gesture sent the edge of his shirt slightly above the waist of his jeans, revealing taut abs. Heat flooded her body. She needed a life. This kind of thing wouldn't be a big deal if she had a life.

There was something very intimate in the air now that Sam was gone and she could smell whatever soap he'd used in the shower. She needed water. Then wine. Her mouth was parched.

She waved a hand. "It was my pleasure."

"Then there's Sam. I haven't seen her this happy since the tween years started," he said.

She smiled and shrugged. "We just hit it off."

"No, seriously. She doesn't open up to people easily."

"She seems so sweet and well-adjusted. She's way more put together than I was at twelve. That transition into full teen is awkward and painful," she said, scrunching up her nose.

"For me too. Nothing to make you question everything, until you raise a teenager," he said with a laugh.

"I can imagine," she said, feeling unqualified. He was a dad. He'd raised a child on his own. She had no experience with big kids, little kids, or anyone's kids. Her sister would know how to handle this conversation.

"Anyway, enough about parenting. Can I decorate some cookies?" he asked, approaching the island.

"You want to decorate cookies?"

"Is that a yes? Or a please get the hell away from my cookies?" he asked, coming to stand beside her.

She met his gaze and decided that it was a yes to everything. "Yes, sure. I'm just going to grab some water," she said, her voice sounding throaty to her ears. It was high time Charlotte Harris got a life. Clearly, everyone else in her family had their own life, so what was she doing? And besides, she was just having wine and pizza with a great guy. A handsome guy. A funny guy. A great dad. A hot man. The boy from her past.

"You okay?"

She was talking to herself. She flashed a smile that she hoped was normal and took a long drink of water before returning to the island. "Fine. Sorry. A little dehydrated. It's all coffee and no water over at Grandma Ruby's," she said, pulling out the icing.

He laughed. "She does make the best coffee. Okay, show me what to do."

"True. Okay, so I've been warned about your decorating slash baking skills," she said, not handing over the icing dispenser.

He leaned against the counter, folding his arms across his chest, and Charlotte had to force her eyes away from the biceps on display. "Let me guess, Sam?"

"I hate to betray her confidence," she said, slowly dispensing a perfect bead of white icing around the edge of a snowman-shaped cookie.

"I'm sure she'd have no problems with you telling me. In fact, I've probably already heard it," he said.

Charlotte swallowed a laugh and glanced up at him. "Direct quote?"

He let out a low, deep laugh that made her toes curl. She had no idea how he was able to go from hot man to almost boyish charm with one laugh. If they were an actual couple, or if she had an actual backbone, she'd have stood on her tiptoes and kissed him right then. But they weren't and she didn't. "That's the best kind. But I bet I can guess."

She raised an eyebrow and waited.

"Sam probably said I don't have any artistic talent and I'm better at eating cookies than I am at baking them."

Her mouth dropped open. "Well done. You know your daughter."

He gave her a wide smile. Very charming. Just the right amount of smug. "Well, she's right. But this isn't *actually* artistic. Don't you just squirt a bunch of icing all over the cookies?"

She inhaled sharply. "I can see the problem. Maybe I'll ice a couple of cookies, because I have a feeling you just really want a cookie with icing on it and don't actually care about the outcome."

He shrugged. "Guilty as charged. Fine, you ice the cookies and I'll clean up the kitchen."

"Deal," she said, getting the icing she'd already prepared ready.

The doorbell rang and Wyatt crossed the room. "I'll get the pizza. Do you still want that glass of wine?" he said as he walked out of the room.

Wine. With Wyatt. He was asking again, she knew, because of her awkward speech before. "That sounds great," she said as he came back in the room carrying a large box of pizza. He placed it on the island while she finished piping the rest of the snowmen cookies. The room suddenly felt way too small as he pulled out a bottle of wine and two glasses. It was also really quaint. Yes, Christmas music was still playing in the background, but there was a different kind of quiet. This was the kind that should have been filled with the two of them sharing their thoughts, but instead, they were holding back. Wyatt didn't seem to be the type to be shy or scared of speaking his mind, but all of a sudden with Sam gone, there was no one to hide behind.

"Here you go," he said, placing a glass of red wine in front of her on the island.

She picked up the glass and smiled, forcing herself to act like an adult who drank wine with hot men on a regular basis. "Thanks."

"Do you want to sit at the table and eat?"

She nodded. "Sure."

Once they were settled and they each had a slice of pizza, Charlotte took another sip of wine. She needed to loosen up. "Sam was telling me that you have vacation time coming up?"

He nodded and grabbed another slice of pizza. "Long overdue. I have a week off starting next week."

"That's great! Sam must be really excited," she said, finishing her piece of the very rich meat lover's pizza and taking another.

"Well, we'll see about that. But I am looking forward to getting some stuff done around here. And I'll have the night off for Candlelight Christmas, which will be a first. It'll allow me to enjoy *The Nutcracker.*"

She smiled. "I love Candlelight Christmas. My sister and I attended a few times with our grandmother. All the shops on the

Main Street were decorated and vendors set up on the corners selling roasted chestnuts, while Victorian carolers strolled the sidewalks."

He put down his pizza. "Would you like to go with me?"

She took a large bite of pizza, deciding that the humiliation of an overfull mouth was better than giving an answer she might regret. This shouldn't be a big deal. It was an evening out with . . . a friend . . . a friend from her adolescence. She should say yes. But she didn't really have friends. Especially not friends who might lead to more than friends. She'd be leaving Silver Springs in a few weeks and . . . She finished chewing and raised her eyes to his. His expression had changed, and she realized she had inadvertently hurt his feelings. The last thing she wanted to do to the person who was so kind to her. "I think I might be going with . . . my sister," she said.

Something flashed across his eyes, but he nodded politely. "Sure."

Charlotte toyed with her napkin and glanced at her wine glass, wondering how fast she could drink it without getting tipsy or how quickly she could leave without looking rude. She stood, grabbing her empty plate. "Well, I'd better finish icing those cookies and head back."

He stood a minute later and started cleaning up the kitchen while she iced the cookies in silence. She tried to get through them as quickly as possible while he cleaned up the kitchen. They kept conversation to the mundane, and she sensed a disappointment in him that she didn't know what to do with.

"Well, these are all done. I should get going. I have an early day tomorrow," she said, walking quickly out of the room.

"Right," he said, walking over to the closet to get his coat.

A trickle of mild panic rose inside her at the thought of walking back to her grandmother's with him again. "You don't have to walk me home, Wyatt," she said.

He opened the front door, his jaw clenched. It was probably the closest she'd ever seen him get to irritated. The fact that she'd managed to irritate him more than his twelve-year-old child said something. "I can't let you walk home by yourself."

She sighed and forced herself to be polite. "I do appreciate the gesture and the pizza and the wine," she said, stepping out into the cold night air.

"When did we get this formal, Char?" he asked, stopping once they reached the end of his walkway. He was standing close to the lamppost, and she could see the hurt in his brown eyes, so much so that she felt an urge to take a step back from the honesty he was about to give her.

She opened her mouth to tell him that she had no idea. She had no idea why she was pushing him away. She didn't want to. She wanted the opposite. She wanted to close that gap between them. She didn't want hands off. That was the problem; for the first time in her life she wanted *all* hands on deck. That terrified her. She was related to a bunch of women who'd been hurt by love, and she wasn't about to join their ranks. In a few weeks—if she could last that long—Wyatt and her attraction to him would be a distant memory.

She just needed to make it through Christmas and then get back to her condo in the city. "It's probably for the best," she said, walking away from the surprise and hurt that flashed across his handsome face.

"Right," he said, falling into step beside her. If he was angry with her, he did a great job of hiding it. The densely blanketed sky of stars held the same magic it had the night before. It was the kind of enchanted night you couldn't create anywhere but in the open country in the winter. Magic clung to the snow that sparkled under the moonlight, making it seem less dark out, the world not really that ominous. How could anything bad happen when there was this much beauty? But Charlotte had ditched her belief in fairy tales, or maybe she had never really believed in the first place. Maybe there was something wrong with her. They walked in silence and instead of feeling relieved that she had sort of ended any chance at having some kind of relationship with Wyatt, she felt a deep loneliness taking root inside her.

"Well, have a good night. Thanks again for all your help," Wyatt said once they reached her grandmother's front porch.

What had she done? His handsome face was closed off, and despite the twinkling white lights and the scent of cedar clinging to the air, there was nothing cheerful about this.

"Wait, Wyatt . . . ," she said. He stopped and turned around. His hands were shoved into the front pockets of his jeans, and his brown eyes were guarded, not twinkling like they usually were when they spoke. Now what? *Say something, Charlotte.*

"Yes?" he said a few seconds later, when she still hadn't come up with something to say.

"Um, I wanted to say thank you for trusting me with Sam," she said, blurting that out even though it wasn't at all what she wanted to say.

Something flickered across his eyes, but he gave her a formal nod. "I'm glad you two get along so well."

She took a step closer to him, because she already missed him even though that was crazy, even though she had no right because she had just made it clear that she didn't want a relationship. But if she did, it would be with someone like him. No, not someone like him. *Him.* She pulled her coat closer around her neck as an icy gust of wind circled around them.

She selfishly wanted to hear that caring note in his voice, that softness that, until just a moment ago, he'd used when speaking to her. But she'd blown it. She had stopped everything before it had started.

She forced a smile before turning to head into the house. There was no point in torturing herself out here. "Okay, thank you for dinner."

"Charlotte?"

She paused, her heart hammering in her chest as she waited for him to continue. "Yes?"

He gave her a long look and then shook his head. "Good night."

CHAPTER TWELVE

NOVEMBER 20, 1977
SILVER SPRINGS

Ruby held onto Mrs. Pemberton's hand, even though the elderly woman was sleeping. Her breathing seemed laborious, a wheezing, deep noise that scraped against Ruby's heart. She glanced over at Sister Juliette, who was on the other side of the bed. They had assumed last month, when her cough had started up, that it was just the bronchitis arriving early. But when the elderly woman had lost her appetite and started spitting up blood, Ruby had rushed her to the doctor.

"How did you and Mrs. Pemberton meet?" Ruby asked now, desperate to hear something besides the final labored breaths of the woman who'd been a lifeline and friend to her.

Sister Juliette smiled, deep lines forming around her mouth and her eyes misting over. "In the first grade. We became fast friends and were inseparable—until Donna started dating Charles, and I decided I wanted to give my life to Christ. But we stayed friends. Through it all. Through heartbreak. Donna did have her share of heartbreak, but you have been such a blessing to her, Ruby. You and Wendy. I haven't seen her this happy since Charles was alive."

Ruby blew her nose, and tears clogged her throat. "It doesn't seem like long enough, and yet I feel like I've known her for a lifetime. How is that possible? How is it possible to know someone for only ten years and feel like they've been family forever?"

Sister Juliette shook her head. "Donna has always been generous in heart, and I think you two were kindred spirits. She saw something in you, as I did," she whispered.

They both turned as Mrs. Pemberton squeezed their hands lightly and opened her eyes. Though they were clouded with pain, there was something else shining in them, a clarity that hadn't been present earlier that week, with the morphine the doctor had prescribed.

"My dear friends, I saw something in both of you. And I am so blessed to have had this time with you."

Ruby shook her head. "There can still be more time," she whispered, frantically, desperately because this wasn't enough time. Logically she knew, they all knew. The doctor had confirmed that the lung cancer had reached the final stages, and since Mrs. Pemberton had refused any more treatment, the end was near. But Ruby wasn't ready for that. She wasn't ready to say another goodbye.

Mrs. Pemberton squeezed her hand harder this time, looking deep into her eyes. "Ruby, you were brought to me for a reason. You were the daughter I always yearned for, and Wendy was the granddaughter that I was never given. The two of you filled this big old house with joy and laughter and you made my final years the happiest since my Charles was alive. But I don't ever want you to leave here. I want this to be your home—you and Wendy."

A ragged breath seeped from Ruby's mouth, and she shook her head. "No, no, I can't. First you need to stay here with us, and it's too much. It's . . . not ours. I can't," she said, this time the sob she'd been holding onto breaking free as she lowered her head to kiss her dear friend's hand. Her weathered hand grazed Ruby's hair, slowly stroking it, giving her that affection, that comfort that her own mother had denied her. Each stroke reverberated inside her, a warm balm on her weary soul.

"Yes, Ruby. Make a life here. Fill that dining room table with people every Christmas. Please don't be afraid to love again. Please open yourself up to all the world has to offer you."

Ruby clung to her side, not caring that she was acting like a child, needing her friend to just stay with them a little while longer. One more Christmas.

The three of them stayed there in silence. The slow rhythm of Mrs. Pemberton's hand stroking her head, confirmation that she was still alive. The sound of Sister Juliette's softly spoken prayers a warm blanket. As day escaped them and night seeped in, the shadows playing against the wall, Ruby noticed that Mrs. Pemberton's hand had stopped moving; instead, it was lying heavily on top of her head.

Ruby squeezed her eyes shut and cried for the woman who had taken her in and given her a new life. She cried for their years together, for the girl she was when she had first come here, for the woman she was now, just before Christmas, and feeling so lost.

Open yourself up to love again. *Ruby had already lied to her. She knew there was no way she could open herself up to love again. It hurt too deeply. She thought of Harry and knew she had done the right thing. She didn't need that kind of love ever again.*

* * *

Charlotte shut her laptop after placing an impromptu Christmas gift order for Samantha. She was hoping she'd like it. It was amazing to her how much she found herself thinking about Sam . . . and Wyatt. She was still worried that Sam would think she was coming over after school that day.

Since her epic stupidity the previous night, she hadn't managed to get Wyatt off her mind. She didn't know why she had shut him down. She wanted him. She was attracted to him on every level, but she couldn't make herself just take that next step.

She'd never had trouble keeping her distance from people. But those two had managed to fill her heart with something she hadn't known it needed. She had thought that by just putting up boundaries her problem would be solved. But when they'd stood outside together, the longing she'd felt for him had been something she'd never experienced before. She had wanted to take everything back. Except she hadn't. Instead, her rejection had hung between them.

She looked up from her calendar and planning items sprawled on the bed as a knock sounded on her door. She was already wearing her skating penguin pajamas despite it being only six o'clock in the evening. "Come in."

Outside the door stood Olivia, looking a little more rested. Her hair was shiny again and pulled up into a top knot, and she was wearing a red sweatshirt with the words *Let It Snow* in gold lettering scrawled across the front, paired with black leggings. She looked like the Olivia Charlotte remembered. But that almost hurt more somehow, because she desperately wanted that Olivia back. "I'm sorry for being such a crappy sister, Char. I know you're probably on the verge of hating me and never wanting to see me again, but I just want you to know that it wasn't you. You didn't do anything. It was me. I screwed up badly, and if you can ever forgive me . . . I would love that and would do whatever it takes to have you back."

Charlotte choked out a sob as Olivia ran across the room, and she opened her arms to hug her little sister. Her heart swelled to the point she thought it would burst with happiness. She hadn't expected this. She had thought it was her. That there was something inherently wrong with her that made people able to detach themselves from her. She had thought Liv was gone forever. "It's okay, Liv," she said as her sister burst into tears.

"I'm such a wreck," Olivia said, pulling back and sitting cross-legged on the bed beside her.

Charlotte reached for the Kleenex box on the nightstand and handed her one. "What is going on with you?" she said gently after blowing her own nose and regaining composure.

"I can't do this, Char," Olivia said, running—more like yanking—her hands through her hair.

Alarm rang through Charlotte at the abrupt change in her sister. "What?"

"I hate my life. I hate myself. I hate Will. I hate everything. Except Dawn, but I've already screwed everything up with her too."

Charlotte watched in shock as her sister burst into tears. She leaned forward and wrapped her arms around her. "It can't be that bad, Liv. You haven't screwed anything up. You are an amazing mom."

Olivia drew back and shook her head. "I left Will because he's a total dipshit," she said, crying even louder.

Charlotte's mouth dropped open. Now it all made sense. Her heart sank. It was true. The man *was* a dipshit, and she'd known right from the moment she met him. But she'd rather cut her arm off or have someone steal all her organizational products than tell her sister that. "Why, what happened?"

Olivia waved a hand in front of her face and then wiped her eyes on her sleeve. "It's so bad, Char. I should have known. I don't know why I ignored all the signs—oh, yes, I remember—because I was desperate. I was desperate for a family of my own and a husband and the white picket fence. I wanted my Barbie life to be my real life, and I feel so, so stupid," she said, flopping backward on the bed and covering her face. Charlotte tried to gently pull her planner and markers from under Olivia, without having any of the pages creased.

"You can't blame yourself for what he did," she said.

"I'm an idiot," she said, staring up at the ceiling.

Charlotte's eyes welled with tears for her sister, the ache in her chest making it hard to speak. She lay down beside her, feeling like the big sister again, the one who would do anything to protect her. It was true. Olivia had been the idealistic dreamer, and she should have had her happy ending. She deserved it. They both did. The only difference was that Charlotte knew the truth about people—you couldn't trust them. They might start out okay, then turn on you when the going got tough. But she wasn't going to tell her sister that. She needed to lift her up. Olivia had the most important job in the world—she was a mother. "Okay, listen to me. Whatever Will did is on Will. That's not your fault."

Olivia lifted dead eyes to her. "Did you ever like Will?"

153

Charlotte shifted. "Well . . . you know me, Liv, I'm kind of . . . um,"

"Smart?"

"What? No. I mean, I just don't trust people, but that hasn't really gotten me anywhere, has it? I mean, I'm like closer to thirty than twenty now, with no significant anyone who isn't a blood relative in my life. I have issues. Trust issues. Control issues. What has it gotten me? Great stationery products and organizational bins for my pantry and closets?"

Olivia stared her down. "Wyatt?"

She gasped out loud and she felt guilty for not telling Olivia sooner. "You heard?"

"It's *the* Wyatt?"

Charlotte nodded.

"And he turned out even more gorgeous than we could have possibly imagined?"

Charlotte nodded again.

Olivia smiled. "You know this isn't a coincidence, right?"

"You've been spending way too much time with Grandma. It's a total fluke. A total coincidence. And Wyatt . . . he's just a . . ."

"A hot man who wants you?"

She swallowed hard. "Did Grandma say that too?"

"Well, in a more dignified way. I think she said he was strikingly handsome to be exact. Something about providence. Then when we were in town getting Dawn's picture taken with Santa, Grandma spotted him across the road. She pointed him out, and I almost smashed the stroller into Santa's sleigh. I mean, Char, this is not the kind of man one comes across every day. Sheriff—"

"Deputy—"

Olivia shot her a look and she shrugged, crossing her arms.

"Devoted father—"

"Single dad."

Olivia rolled her eyes. "I should hope he's single, for your sake."

"Okay, what's your point?" she snapped, softening the attitude with a forced smile.

Olivia laughed out loud. "My point is that you could have a life if you wanted one."

She was not going to fill her sister in on how she'd just destroyed her chance of a life last night. "We've always just been friends. It's way too soon to be talking about a life."

"It's the uniform, isn't it?" Olivia said with a sad smile.

Charlotte grabbed a pillow and held it close to her chest, oddly comforted that her sister knew. "That's stupid . . . but maybe it's back there, buried inside. I hate thinking of Dad, I hate that he can still have an impact on my life," she whispered.

Olivia nodded. "I know. It kind of sneaks up on you, right? Dawn smiled and looked at me the other day and for a second I could have sworn it was Dad's smile."

Charlotte ran her hands through her hair, refusing to get emotional about this. "Ugh. We're supposed to be talking about you and your problems. Not mine. Tell me what happened with Will. Maybe it's salvageable," she said.

She shook her head. "Let's open a bottle of wine. I haven't had wine in so long because I'm always home with Dawn at night and I'm too paranoid to drink in case I have to rush to the hospital or something. And then what would I do? Arrive in a cab, fumbling with my baby into the ER? Then what if they called child services and took Dawn away?" Olivia said.

Charlotte didn't even know where to begin with that. "Why would you need to go to the hospital?"

Olivia waved a hand. "I don't know. It's just scary being a single parent. And a first-time parent. Babies are scary. Very unpredictable."

Charlotte's chest felt heavy. "Okay. Let's have wine. Also, I think if we're having wine we should pair it with that peppermint white chocolate popcorn I spotted in the pantry this afternoon."

Olivia's eyes widened, and she scrambled into a sitting position. "Yes. We can plan all the things. How you're going to get a life, how I'm going to get a life."

Charlotte laughed. "Fine. Who's going to the cold cellar to get the wine?"

Olivia straightened her shoulders and stood. "I'm doing this, because I gave birth, so therefore I'm strong enough to walk across a crusty cement floor and through a basement filled with potential danger at every turn . . . and I owe you big time for everything you ever did for me as a big sister," she said, her voice cracking.

"Okay. But the giving birth part is just showing off. Let's go quietly and make sure we don't wake Grandma.," she said, walking over to the door.

Olivia's mouth dropped open. "Okay, I'll meet you in the TV room," she whispered.

They snuck down the stairs, and suddenly it felt like they were kids again, sneaking into Grandma's pantry at night for cookies and secrets. For a second she wished she could go back to their childhood. She wished she could tell those young girls that they would be okay, but she wished she could tell them . . . she wished she could tell Olivia to be strong and not hold onto the first man who came along, that true love was waiting out there for her. And she wished she could tell herself not to live in fear. She wished she could go back and warn them that their relationship would be tested, but that they were each other's greatest ally and to never lose sight of that. As Olivia disappeared into the basement, Charlotte tiptoed into the kitchen, a lightness to her spirit, to her body. It was as though the magic of Christmas had finally arrived.

"Hello, my dear."

Charlotte let out a little scream. Grandma Ruby was standing by the pantry in her red velour robe with a smile on her face. "Grandma, you scared me!" Charlotte laughed.

"I'm glad to see you and your sister haven't forgotten how to have fun—and how to sneak snacks from the pantry," she said, opening the door for her.

Charlotte's eyes widened. "You knew?"

Grandma Ruby smiled and gave her that stare that made Charlotte wonder how her grandmother had become so wise. "Why do you think I always made sure there were fresh treats in there? Nothing beats girl talk and treats. Watching you and Olivia grow up together was one of my greatest blessings. I'm so happy that it seems she's coming around," Grandma Ruby said, reaching up and grabbing the bag of popcorn.

Charlotte accepted the bag, not even asking how she knew this was what they were after. "Thank you, Grandma. Do you want to join us?"

Grandma Ruby shook her head and walked out of the pantry. "Thank you, but I'm ready to settle down and read for a while before I turn in early. You girls have fun," she said, patting Charlotte on the shoulder before walking out of the room. Charlotte watched her retreat, taking in the way she moved, noticing that she was walking a little slower tonight. Even though Grandma Ruby always appeared to have it together, Charlotte knew these years were coming to an end and she was desperate to hold onto all of it. If she could keep them all close, huddle the time and memories near her heart, she would.

She blinked as the sound of feet clomping heavily up the basement steps pulled her from her nostalgia. Olivia appeared at the top of the stairs a moment later. "I just avoided death by a thousand spiders," she said, marching into the kitchen and raising the bottle of wine in the air like a trophy.

Charlotte burst out laughing. "You get the wine glasses and I'll get a bowl," she said, somehow knowing she was going to find the white bowl with the holly pattern waiting for her on the island.

A few minutes later they were seated side by side on the forest-green sofa, and she poured the popcorn into the bowl while Olivia opened the wine and filled their glasses.

"Now, as soon as I have a long swig of wine, I will tell you the tale of how I found out my douchebag husband was a disgusting, lying cheater."

Charlotte shut her eyes as rage and pity swam through her. "Oh, Liv," she whispered as her sister drank half the glass in one long drink.

Olivia waved a hand. "It's okay. Really. I'm totally fine. Also, we have our two glass limit, so I really will be okay. I've never gone back on that rule," she said, her eyes misting over.

Charlotte nodded. "Me too," she said softly, remembering the night they had promised each other they would never become dependent like their mother.

"Here. Have some." Charlotte shoved the bowl of popcorn at her, hoping the mix of sugar and chocolate might help lighten the mood.

Olivia dug her hand into the bowl. "I may as well. I'm going to eat everything while I'm here. Then on January first, it's going to be a new me. Pretty cliché, huh?"

The half-smile she shot Charlotte was filled with self-loathing and made Charlotte cringe. "Well, I think the Liv sitting beside me right now is pretty awesome."

Olivia took another drink of wine. "You're the best and I treated you like crap. I'm so sorry, Char."

"I don't want to talk about that again. Okay? Tell me about Will," she said, shoving a handful of popcorn into her mouth. The white chocolate and peppermint melted decadently while she waited for her sister to speak.

"I should have known. It was all the classic telltale signs—late nights at work all of a sudden. Business trips when he never used to have business trips. He was always on his phone. He was also . . . he never, like, wanted me anymore. I'm surprised we even conceived Dawn. I mean, like it was basically a miracle, and she is. I mean, I have no regrets because that would mean she wasn't in the world. But I wanted to be a better example to her," she said, staring ahead at the Christmas tree and blindly shoving her hand into the bowl of popcorn.

"You're not the one who cheated," Charlotte said, her voice shaking with anger. She topped up both their glasses, because she didn't know what to do with herself.

"I blame myself for not seeing it . . . and then not leaving right away. He . . . he tried to justify it. I figured it out when I was seven months pregnant. He told me I had become fat and undesirable and—"

"What?" Charlotte hissed.

Olivia rolled her eyes and nodded. "Great guy, right?"

"I'm going to hunt him down and hurt him."

Olivia laughed and turned to her. "Do you know I thought he was right? And I'd stand there and look at myself in the mirror from all these different angles and just hate myself. I hated my kankles. I hated the fuller face. The bigger boobs. The stomach. Everything. And then I hated myself for thinking all those things because one of my friends is struggling with infertility, and I thought what kind of person am I to be so superficial and hate all these changes that are true blessings? What that woman next door to me would give to have the kankles and all the stuff that goes with it. And there I was, sad about it because my douchebag husband didn't like the way I looked?"

"Omigosh, I feel so bad you went through all this alone," Charlotte whispered.

"I didn't leave him then. Stupid, right? I told him I thought we should work on our marriage and that after I had the baby, I'd lose all the baby weight and we could get back to where we were. I don't know how stupid I could have been. I just know that I was vulnerable and weak and I didn't want to be a single mom."

"What did he say?" Charlotte asked, ditching the popcorn and relying solely on the wine now.

"He reluctantly agreed, and the rest of the pregnancy was awful. I was depressed and lonely and kept eating because I had no one. When I finally went into labor, he was there and left halfway through the birth. I remember the nurse and the OB-GYN giving each other looks, and I knew, after I gave birth to that baby girl, that I was gone. He missed her birth. He missed her birth because he was sexting his lover," she said, before downing the rest of her wine.

"I'm going to smash things," Charlotte whispered, her voice coming out in a hiss, before she gulped down a giant swig of wine.

"It's okay. I kicked him out of the house and he didn't even care, because he went to live with her. I filed for divorce. I have full custody. I have everything I could ever want. Oh, I even lost twenty of the fifty pounds I put on," she said, and then burst into tears.

Charlotte put her arm around her, just like when they were little. "Everything is going to be okay, Liv. I promise. You have a beautiful baby girl, and you are doing a great job as a mom. I'm here for you. Whatever you need, okay?"

"I need to get my shit together, Char. I need a fresh start. I want something of my own. I don't want to live off his money. I want the day to come where I don't need a dime of his. I want to do it on my own," she said.

"Then you will. You are talented and smart. You can do anything you want."

"Yeah, except I haven't worked in a couple of years because I wanted to be the 'perfect wife' and gave up on everything else."

"Then work for me. With me. I'm doing great, business is going well. We could totally partner," she said.

Olivia smiled. "You're the best big sister. But not partners. I'm not going to join in on something you created from scratch. But I will take any job you give me. But I have to find my own way. Do you remember when I took dance?"

Charlotte nodded. "Grandma Ruby got us the gift certificate to the dance studio near our house. I sucked, but you were great."

Olivia let out a sad laugh. "I always thought that I'd grow up to be this prima ballerina. So that didn't happen, but maybe I could teach dance and one day have my own studio."

"That's a great idea. Why don't you use this time to research that? You have all of us around to help with Dawn. Do it now. Then start a business plan—I can help you with that."

"Is that crazy though? How would I even start a studio?"

"Do you own the house?"

Olivia nodded slowly.

"Well . . . with real estate prices the way they are in the city . . . you could sell it. Move here. Live with Grandma and use that money toward starting a studio. I know Wyatt's daughter, Samantha, goes to the long-standing studio in town, so maybe in the next town over? They might not have a studio. You don't need a big place to start, Liv."

"Wow. How did you come up with that so fast?"

She shrugged. "I'm not saying it'll work. Like, obviously, you'll have to do your research. And I think Grandma needs someone here with her now."

"What about you? Would you consider moving here?"

Charlotte took a deep breath. "I've thought about it, every now and then, but I don't know. It's too early to be thinking about that. Let's focus on you for a while. You need it. I can figure me out."

Olivia looked down. "I need to get back into shape, Char. It's not so much the weight, but it's the feeling of not being able to run and stretch and use my body like I used to. I haven't worked out in like nine months. First because I had the worst morning sickness when I was pregnant. Whoever said it was morning sickness was a liar. It was all day and all night. So I never ran. I just stopped. I stopped doing barre workouts, and those at least kept me feeling like I had my foot in the door with dance. I can't even imagine dancing, and I certainly don't think I can even stretch enough to touch my toes at this point."

"Okay, so listen. Here's what we do—we walk. Every morning. If Dawn isn't napping, we bring her with us. Actually, we should plan it for when she's awake so that you can use her naptime for work time. Shoot, I feel like we need a planner down here or something," she said, looking around.

"You're the best, I'm already feeling better," she said.

Charlotte pulled out her phone and started making notes. "Okay, here's what we do. Naptime is when you start your business plan. Exercise during awake time. She gets fresh air and you get a workout. Then you need to download a barre app. I did once because I had this idea that maybe it would be good for me to increase flexibility, but as you know, I'm very tightly wound and it wasn't pretty. I stick with jogging so that I can get my anger out."

Olivia burst out laughing. "Omigosh, I missed you so much. I'm so sorry, Char. I'm sorry for shutting you out. I knew you didn't like him, and he didn't want any of you around. That set off major alarm bells, but I didn't know what to do. I wanted my marriage to work. I think he wanted to isolate me from all of you so that he could make me into who he wanted me to be—his doormat. I was . . . embarrassed. I was embarrassed to be married to someone like him and to confide in you. You've always had it all together. I'm the needy one, and I screwed up so badly."

Charlotte held a hand to her chest, the ache there making it hard to breathe. She had been wrong. She had assumed Olivia had pushed her away for different reasons. "I don't have it all together. Underneath the color coordination is a hot mess."

Olivia almost laughed. "Not true. But thanks. I convinced myself things would get better after the baby. I was embarrassed to admit any of this, and now that the wine has worked its magic I can also admit that I was embarrassed to see you."

"What do you mean?"

She shrugged. "I started putting on the weight really fast and Will was a jerk about it. I had a hard time looking in the mirror and I didn't want other people who knew me before my pregnancy to see me."

Charlotte's throat tightened at Olivia's words. Just the thought of Will leaving the room while Olivia was in labor was enough to make her want to scream. But she had to deal with that on her own time, the fact that she would have dropped everything to be there to support her sister, but that hadn't been an option. She wasn't going to ever say anything to Olivia about that. What was done was done, and her sister had made the best decisions at the time—she had tried to save her marriage, and she had had faith in a man who didn't deserve it.

"Dawn . . . did you choose that name?" Charlotte asked, the name clicking only now.

Olivia nodded. "It was . . . Dawn. And it was a new beginning."

Tears welled up in Charlotte's eyes. "I believe in you. I always have. You may think you screwed everything up, but I think you're on the cusp of a whole new life, Liv. Maybe this was all meant to be. There are better things, better people, waiting out there for you."

"Hello! Everyone, I'm here! Let the holidays begin!"

They both gasped and turned to the door as their mother's voice reverberated through the quiet house.

CHAPTER THIRTEEN

FEBRUARY 1, 1978
SILVER SPRINGS

Ruby would not lose Mrs. Pemberton's house.

She sat down with her mug of coffee at the last available table at Mable's Bakery with a huff. Wasting no time, she pulled her notebook and pen out of her purse. She had one hour before it was time to pick Wendy up from school, and she couldn't waste it. She needed to brainstorm ways to make enough money to keep up with the maintenance of that home and have enough left over to live off of. While she'd inherited the home and a small amount of money, Mrs. Pemberton had donated the rest to various charities, along with a large sum for the Sisters of St. Michael's. Mrs. Pemberton had also been collecting her husband's pension for years. Once Ruby had done the calculations, she quickly realized that there was no way she'd be able to stay afloat in that house, since she was now also out of a job. She knew that the home required continuous upkeep—even just maintaining the grounds cost a small fortune every year.

Taking a sip of coffee, she stared at the blank notepad, panic slowly filling her as the reality of her current situation sank in. She had no education, no formal job training, and a massive home that if she sold would be able to provide for her and Wendy for life—except she couldn't do that. It was Mrs. Pemberton's legacy and she wouldn't go back on her promise. Ruby owed her everything.

She should have done this months ago, but the grief of losing her friend had made it impossible to think clearly. She'd been focused on getting through the day to day and on helping Wendy cope with the loss of a woman who'd been a grandmother to her. The only grandmother she had.

Picking up the pen, Ruby became aware of the woman standing close to her table, holding a coffee. She made eye contact with the young woman and smiled. She looked familiar.

"Hi, um, do you mind if I sit at your table? There isn't another one available. I'll move as soon as one comes up, though," she said, walking over to Ruby's table.

Ruby didn't want to appear rude, even though she didn't have time to make small talk today. She needed to get her life in order—again. "Of course, no problem," she said, gesturing to the empty chair.

"Thanks so much. You're Ruby, right?"

Ruby nodded, smiling.

"My name is Mary, I think I recognize you from church. You have a little girl, right? And you live in the big house on the hill?"

"Wow, that about sums me up. Yes, all correct. Nice to meet you, Mary. I thought you looked familiar. Have you been in Silver Springs long?"

The woman shook her head and took a sip of coffee. "My parents and younger sister live here. I'm on my way out of town. I'm going to spend the year traveling. I plan on coming back, though."

Ruby was struck by a stab of envy. To travel the world. A server brought over a slice of chocolate cake "Thank you," Mary said.

"That looks great," Ruby said.

"Would you like to split it with me?"

"Oh no, but thank you. I love baking, and I still haven't walked off all the Christmas treats," she said with a laugh.

Mary sliced into the cake and waved her fork. "I wish I was more of a baker, but I never had the patience to be so precise with all those measurements. Cooking is more my thing. I hope I'm not interrupting your work," she said, pointing to the pen and notepad.

Ruby took a sip of coffee, contemplating whether or not she should tell this woman her troubles. There was something about Mary that made her feel relaxed. "I'm happy for the company, but yes, I came here to try and brainstorm some ideas. I was a housekeeper for years to a lovely woman. She died a little while ago and left me her house. But I need to earn an income in order to keep it running, because it's a huge historical property, and I don't really have any kind of experience in anything or even an education beyond high school."

Mary leaned forward and nodded as Ruby spoke. "I'm sorry for your loss"

"Thank you," Ruby said.

"Maybe I can help you brainstorm," she said, taking another bite of her cake.

They sat in silence for the next few minutes and the conversation from the table next to them drifted over. The couple were complaining about how there were no vacancies in town and the only inn was always booked up during the holidays. A ridiculous idea popped into Ruby's head, but then she made eye contact with her new friend and realized the notion might not be so ridiculous after all.

"A bed and breakfast," Ruby whispered, leaning forward.

Mary's eyes sparkled and she pushed her empty plate to the side. "It's perfect. I think there might only be one other bed and breakfast in town, and it's very modest."

Ruby nodded, tapping her pen against the table with a nervous energy. She could do this. She knew how to cook, how to clean, she knew enough about finances and spending because she had even taken that over for Mrs. Pemberton the last few years. Excitement flowed through her veins. This could be the next chapter of her life. "Yes. The house has six bedrooms that aren't being used . . . I'd be able to stay at home for my daughter still, and Lord knows I can keep house."

Mary leaned forward. "You need something. Some spin, something that makes your place stand out."

Ruby sat back in her chair, taking her mug of coffee and wrapping her hands around it. "You're right," she said, staring out the window, thinking.

"Was there ever anything special about the house, anything that stood out?"

A shiver crept down Ruby's spine and, for a moment, it was as though the reflection in the window changed and she saw herself on that cold winter's night, pregnant and alone, and she remembered how she always thought that the house would be magical at Christmas. And she had spent her best Christmases there. Mrs. Pemberton had always wanted Christmas dinner with a table full of guests . . . Ruby's mind was spinning and her heart was full with purpose as she turned her gaze to her new friend.

"I have it. I know what I'll call it, I know what I'll make it . . . it'll be The Christmas House."

She sat there for the next hour mapping out how she would give back to the world, to people who had been alone and hopeless like her, and a friendship with Mary blossomed in the process. When she stood with her new friend, she caught her reflection again and remembered looking into the mirror at Mrs. Pemberton's, fearful and afraid of becoming a single mother. And now she was here, making her way in a world which she had thought far too big and scary for someone like her.

* * *

Wyatt looked up from his desk to see Aunt Mary walking into the station; it wasn't a new sight, but judging from the spring in her step and the smile on her face, it was about a certain someone. He stood before she could announce to the entire department that he was getting married to Charlotte Harris.

"Do you have time for a late dinner with your dear aunt?" she said, as he approached.

He grinned and gave her a kiss on the cheek. "I do, and you have perfect timing because I'm starving and my shift is over. Scott is taking Sam to ballet so I have about an hour before I have to get home," he said, waving to a few officers as he left. It was also a welcome distraction because his house was going to feel extra empty without Charlotte in it.

"Good. How about we try the new Greens on Queen? Everyone is talking about it. Though I'm sad Mable's Bakery is gone, I am curious to try this place. There are smoothies and salads and everything is vegetarian," she said as he held open the door for her.

He grimaced. That place again. "I was thinking more along the lines of a burger at the Dairy Bar."

She gasped. "You can't eat like that now, Wyatt."

"Why? What's now?" he asked as they headed down Main Street. The sidewalks were plowed, but every now and then he grabbed his aunt's elbow when he spotted a patch of ice. She'd been known to talk fast and walk even faster, and had fallen once each winter for the past five years.

"Because you have to keep that flat stomach of yours if you want to keep Ruby's granddaughter interested."

Hell. There were so many things wrong with this conversation he didn't even know where to begin. "Aunt Mary," he began, with a resigned sigh as he held the door open for her. The little restaurant was bustling, for sure. He wasn't aware there were so many health-conscious people in Silver Springs, considering how busy the usual greasy-spoon restaurants were.

"Don't worry, I'll make sure we finish this conversation when we find a table," she said as they stood in line and read the large blackboard menu mounted behind the cash counter.

Wyatt's gaze wandered the new restaurant and he could see the appeal. It was younger and trendier than a lot of the establishments in town. The tables were white, marble-topped with some kind of wicker or rattan chairs that looked marginally comfortable. The large windows that fronted onto Main Street were lined with twinkling white lights. Overall, it was a nice setup. He focused his attention back to the menu when his aunt gave him a nudge.

Right. So far the main contenders were a grilled vegetable sandwich with a vegetable soup or a salad with more grilled vegetables and cheese on top. So. Many. Vegetables. A young woman took their order, and soon they were looking for an empty table.

"Do you know what I like about going out with you, Wyatt?"

"That I'm a very witty and charming companion?" he asked with a smile as they found a table near the window that had just been freed.

She laughed and patted his hand. "That we get a lot of looks when people recognize who you are. Sometimes it makes me feel like a celebrity," she said, taking a sip of her green tea.

He laughed. "I'm glad I can make you feel like a celebrity."

Her face grew serious and she toyed with the corner of her napkin. "Did I ever tell you this is where I met Ruby Harris, back when this was Mable's Bakery?"

He smiled, remembering the story fondly. "Yes, you did. You played an instrumental role in the start of The Christmas House if I recall."

She waved a hand. "She did it all herself. A force to be reckoned with, that Ruby. I'm glad her family is all coming for the holidays. She deserves that."

He nodded, bracing himself for where he knew this conversation was inevitably headed. "She does."

"This is a very nice spot to sit, don't you think? I love that we can see the old post office from here. That antique Santa sleigh they put out every year is so charming," she said, staring out the window.

He didn't need to look to know what she was talking about. He just had no idea what was taking her so long to make her point, which was unusual for her because his aunt usually had no issues speaking her mind. A server brought their meals and, even though the presentation was impressive—as impressive as a sandwich without meat can be—he had no raging desire to eat it. "Aunt Mary, are you upset or worried about something?"

His aunt lifted her brown eyes and he put his sandwich down as her eyes glistened with emotion. "I . . . I worry about you, Wyatt."

He leaned forward, lowering his voice. This was a shock—if anything, he worried about her, living in that old little house all by herself. He'd asked her to move in with him and Sam many times, but she always declared she was an independent woman who needed her space. "Me? Why?"

"I know life has handed you some hard blows, and sometimes I wish I hadn't been such a free spirit in my younger days. I should have been around and more aware of what was going on with my sister and how you were being raised. Even this childish aversion to vegetables that you have—it was probably because of how you were raised."

His mouth dropped open, but he actually contemplated what she was saying. That couldn't actually be true, could it? He looked down at the vegetables on his plate and wracked his brain for one of those memories he kept hidden away. There hadn't been fresh anything when he was a kid. There had been bottles of booze. There had been needles. There had been trash. His throat constricted painfully, and he took a bite of the sandwich, telling himself it was delicious. See, he could eat vegetables. No lasting childhood scars here.

"Oh, for crying out loud, you are the most stubborn man I have ever met, Wyatt. I didn't say that to make you prove you could eat vegetables," she said, leaning forward.

He shrugged and swallowed the somewhat edible food. "I'm just proving to you that I can eat vegetables."

She shook her head and leaned forward. "You don't understand. I blame myself. I'm sorry. I'm sorry I wasn't there for you when you were young. I could have gotten you out of there earlier, I could have convinced Betty to leave before it was too late."

His stomach churned and what minuscule amount of appetite he had for the meal was now nonexistent at the mention of his childhood—and even worse, that his aunt felt guilt over it. There were things that he'd figured out along the way to adulthood that had enabled him to succeed—one being that you don't dwell on a past that you can't change. So he rarely thought of his childhood or his parents. He cleared his throat. "It wasn't your responsibility to look after me or to get Mom to make the right decisions. You can't blame yourself. Ever. You didn't know. I'm over it. I've made peace with it. You have been there for me . . . in so many ways, and I'll never be able to repay that favor. Where is this coming from all of a sudden?"

She sniffled and shrugged. "Christmas makes me nostalgic. I can't help but look back on all the past Christmases, and I have a lot of regrets. I've been thinking about what your Christmases were like."

Hell. They were hell, but that was like any other day of the year with his abusive, addict father. While his mother hadn't been abusive, she'd been a junkie like him. "Why on earth would you waste your time thinking about that? Aunt Mary, I'm living a great life."

She wrapped her thin hands around her cup of tea and raised a brow.

He couldn't handle tension, and he avoided his past more than he avoided vegetarian restaurants. "Seriously. I think the problem is that you're regretting not ordering coffee and you're stuck drinking that sour tea and a bunch of vegetables you don't really want."

A small bubble of laughter escaped her mouth. "Oh, Wyatt. What would I do without you? When you and Sam moved to Silver Springs, I thought I'd be helping you, but it turns out you've helped me just as much. Sam is like a granddaughter to me, and you're like the child I never had. I want you to be happy."

He frowned. "I *am* happy."

"I know you're *happy*, but not the kind of happy that comes from being in love, finding your soul mate."

He should have guessed. "There are plenty of people living their lives alone, I'm one of them. As long as Sam is happy, then I'm fine. Besides, what about you then? You're alone."

She put her cup down and leaned forward. "I've lived a full life. I met my soul mate a long time ago, and the time we spent was treasured. But that's me and I'm old . . . *er* . . . than you."

"I'm happy," he insisted.

Her eyes twinkled. "But maybe you'd be happier if you had someone special in your life . . . like, oh, I don't know . . . Charlotte?"

He ignored the unexpected lurch his stomach did, as if he was a teenager talking about his girlfriend. Which was ridiculous, of course. He was well past innocent days of crushes. "Clearly you've forced her into my life with that early Christmas gift," he said, barely able to keep a straight face.

"Wyatt, I would think as deputy you'd know that gift was a sham and I wanted to set you up with Ruby's wonderful granddaughter," she said, her eyes wide.

He choked on his coffee and couldn't help but laugh at his aunt's antics. "Right. Well, thanks." She *was* wonderful. He wasn't too embarrassed to admit to himself that he hadn't stopped think-ing about her since she'd come to town. He felt as connected to Charlotte as he had when they were kids.

"You're very welcome. And how is the organizing going?"

"Great. As thrilling as cleaning out a cupboard could possibly be. Nothing says love like finding moldy cheese in the back of the fridge and then wiping it down," he said, because it was just too easy to tease his aunt.

She placed her head in her hands and moaned theatrically. "I should have come over and cleaned up before Charlotte arrived."

"Better finish this before it gets cold. And don't worry, I was joking about the moldy cheese. I actually had a giant basket of fresh cheese in there, which I heard you were responsible for as well," Wyatt said, smiling as his aunt's cheeks turned red.

"Dealing with you and Scott has become a full-time job for me," she said with a huff.

He laughed, opening the top of his sandwich to peer inside at the vegetables again.

"Delicious," his aunt said as she ate a forkful of her food.

He had to agree as he chewed his sandwich again. The vegeta-bles were grilled to about as perfect as a vegetable could be grilled, and there was some kind of creamy sauce that made all the flavors meld together well. It was better the second time around. "It's actu-ally not bad," he agreed.

"Wonderful. So now, back to our conversation about Charlotte, the mysterious woman from your past who just happens to be my best friend's granddaughter."

He rolled his eyes.

Aunt Mary nodded. "She's very kind. Ruby said she's taken her sister under her wing and is helping nonstop with the baby. I'm sure she's busy spoiling Ruby with gifts while she's here."

He washed the sandwich down with a large swig of coffee, hoping this conversation would be over soon. "I'm sure she is. So are you still planning your annual shopping trip and sleepover with Sam?"

She unfolded her napkin and blotted the corners of her perfectly clean mouth. "Spoken like a man trying to escape where I'm delicately trying to lead this conversation. And of course I'm still doing our girls' trip to the city. I wouldn't miss it for the world. So, back to you and Charlotte. I saw those sparks at Ruby's house."

"We *were* sitting in the same room, weren't we?"

She huffed and set her napkin down with a thud. "Wyatt, I'm going to be blunt. You are a good man who deserves a good woman. So much so that I had to resort to purchasing a gift certificate to get that woman over to your house. And that daughter of yours deserves a good female influence in her life too. Just because you married the wrong woman once—and I do take partial responsibility for that because I am a keen judge of character and, had I met her before you married, I would have warned you off of her—doesn't mean it will happen again. You're too young, too good-looking, too wonderful to be by yourself. Believe me, these are your best years. It's all wrinkles and type 2 diabetes after this."

Hell. "I love that you think so highly of me, but I am happy. It's hard as hell raising an almost teenager, and my job is crazy, with different hours every week, but I *am* happy."

She pursed her lips. "Sam called me last week and, dear, I hate to judge, but the poor girl said she was embarrassed by the state of the kitchen. But besides all that, she seemed so happy when she talked about Charlotte. And happy for you too."

A pang hit him in the chest, and it had nothing to do with the cheese basket. He put down the rest of his sandwich and looked out the window. Hearing about his daughter even calling Aunt Mary privately was . . . sad. Had she really wanted a woman in the house? Or was it Charlotte she wanted? He sighed and turned back to his aunt, who was still staring at him with a bit of hope lighting her eyes. "I know I'm not enough for Sam. I know she misses having a mom, but I can't jump into a relationship for Sam, and I also can't let Sam's heart get broken all over again. When Leanne left us . . . no one got over it. She destroyed the family we'd built. Yes, we didn't have the perfect marriage, but it was *okay*. It was okay enough that she could have stuck it out, or she could have had a relationship with Sam. How could I ever convince Sam to trust another mother figure if her own mom ran out on her? I'm not doing it, Aunt Mary. I'm not risking what I've built with Sam."

Aunt Mary reached across the table and took his hand, her eyes filled with sympathy, the lines around her mouth pronounced. "Of course. Of course. Wyatt, you are doing a wonderful job. Forgive me for being so opinionated. I just don't want you to settle for good when you could have great. Is there any chance you might hear from Leanne this Christmas?"

He sat back in his chair and tossed the napkin on the table. "Of course not. When she said she was leaving, she meant it. Five years is a long time. She left and never looked back. As far as I'm concerned, Sam doesn't have a mother. But that doesn't mean I can't give her a good Christmas."

Aunt Mary nodded, the weak smile she gave him making him doubt it himself. How the hell had their lives gone from fine to complicated in two weeks?

Charlotte Harris. That's how.

* * *

"Well, now, let me see my grandbaby," their mother said, standing in the hallway as though she hadn't been MIA forever.

Grandma Ruby walked down the stairs to join them, her smile strained. She was the only one smiling besides their mother. Charlotte didn't want to upset their grandmother, but she was furious with their mother. Charlotte knew she hadn't been around for Olivia. This is what their mother always did, and Charlotte couldn't help feeling protective over her sister, just as she had growing up. Grandma Ruby gave her a stern gaze, and Charlotte squirmed. This was why she avoided the holidays here. There were so many unresolved feelings. So many memories of their mother checking out emotionally or physically. Sure, she'd gotten better over the years, but Charlotte vividly remembered the times they had been simply dropped off at their grandmother's. That feeling of being an inconvenience had taken root inside her. She knew Olivia didn't remember all those times, but Charlotte did. Maybe she'd never forgiven their mother for it.

Charlotte rolled her eyes. "She's actually away at university," she said, unable to keep the sarcasm from her tone.

Olivia laughed, but Grandma Ruby patted Charlotte's shoulder—it was a warning, she knew.

Her mother rolled her eyes. "You were always sarcastic, Charlotte dear. You grew up too fast."

Charlotte bit her tongue until it hurt. It was good that they'd consumed so much wine, because this was painful, and their mother hadn't even been here for ten full minutes.

Her mother's gaze darted around the entrance. "So, where's this granddaughter of mine?"

"Mom, it's nine. She's sleeping," Olivia said, crossing her arms.

"I don't think it's too much to ask to go and wake her up, it's a special occasion," their mother said, taking off her bright green coat and unraveling her scarf from her neck.

"It shouldn't be a special occasion. A grandmother should have already seen her granddaughter by now," Grandma Ruby piped up, cinching the belt of her burgundy velour robe.

Her mother let out a huff. "Oh, right, I forgot I'm the black sheep. Wow, what a nice Christmas welcome. The censure in the room is suffocating. If I'm not wanted, then I'll just leave right now," she said, making no move to put her coat back on.

Charlotte looked away, knowing one of them should pipe up and say, no, no, of course they wanted her to stay. She glanced over at Olivia, who was removing some imaginary lint from her shirt.

Grandma Ruby sighed deeply. "No one wants you to leave, Wendy. Just try to be more aware of the things you say."

Her mother threw her arms in the air. "Fine. If we can't speak like a real family, let's keep to the safe topics. How are you all?"

"Good," Charlotte said, looking down at her feet.

"Good," Olivia echoed, glancing up the stairs.

"I'm really tired, actually," Charlotte said, faking a yawn.

"Oh, me too," Olivia said. "I was just on my way up to bed. Dawn really is an early riser, No, um, pun intended," she said, smiling sheepishly.

Charlotte almost laughed before they awkwardly ran up the stairs. Charlotte held her breath, hoping they'd be able to make it to their rooms and that would be the end of the evening run-in with their mother. Now that she'd arrived, things were going to be tense and awkward.

"Well, all right. If you must," their mother said with a tight smile.

Charlotte glanced over at Grandma Ruby. She felt bad for ditching her. She had no idea how her grandmother could have so much patience with her mother; they were such opposites.

"Wendy, how about I make you a cup of tea? I have your room all set up," Grandma Ruby said.

"Okay, you get the tea while I check my phone for messages," she heard their mother say while the two sisters stood listening quietly outside Charlotte's bedroom door.

Charlotte and Olivia frowned at each other. Charlotte bit her tongue, not wanting to interfere and say that maybe for once her mother could make the tea, maybe for once someone else could sit down and relax.

Charlotte peered over the railing and saw Grandma Ruby walking to the kitchen, and she stared at her retreating figure, the pang of sympathy for her grandmother making her keep silent. She wouldn't want Charlotte to cause a fuss. She glanced over at her mother, who was busy texting someone.

"I guess the Christmas fun starts now," Olivia whispered.

"Come to my room," Charlotte said, tugging on her sweater.

They quickly shut the door and sat on the bed. "We're in for some drama," Olivia said, grabbing the throw at the bottom of the bed and wrapping herself in it.

Charlotte nodded, deciding to bring up what she'd discovered in the basement now before they got sidetracked again by another interruption. "Hey, I wanted to tell you something about Grandma. I found a box stashed in that creepy hole in the wall in the basement. There was Mom's stuff from when she was born . . . and I don't think Grandma was married. She was listed as Miss Ruby Harris and there was no father's name."

"No way. What does all this mean?" Olivia whispered.

"I have no idea," Charlotte said, lying down on the bed with a sigh.

"Do we ask Mom or Grandma?" Olivia said.

Charlotte shrugged. "Maybe we should just bring it up at dinner or something. When Mom is there too. Maybe it's nothing and we're just being dramatic. Like, maybe it was too painful for Grandma to list his name."

"But they were married."

"I know. It doesn't make sense. Maybe they were divorced and Grandma didn't want anyone to know?"

Olivia nodded. "Maybe. But why wouldn't they have told us? All these years? Okay. Tomorrow night we ask."

"Perfect. So that's sorted out. And tomorrow morning we are walking and then planning your new life, right?"

Olivia beamed. "Yup. I can't wait. Let's walk and then stop for giant coffees at that new café."

Charlotte nodded. "It's a great little place. Okay, I'll bring all my note-taking supplies," she said, thinking she now knew what to order her sister for Christmas—planning supplies.

"Can't wait," Olivia said, her eyes sparkling for the first time since she'd arrived. Charlotte was relieved. She'd help Olivia get her life back on track. Right now, helping Olivia get her life back on track sounded much easier than figuring out her own. Her thoughts ran between helping her sister and Wyatt, that uncomfortable feeling that she'd somehow hurt him making her wonder just how involved they were really getting. She didn't really have a reason to go over there tomorrow. A pang of regret hit her. She didn't want it to be over. She wanted to keep seeing Sam, and she worried whether she'd made it clear to Sam that she wouldn't be coming back. And she wanted more time with Wyatt.

Time for going to Candlelight Christmas and *The Nutcracker* and all the things that he'd promised with his eyes; all the things she'd said no to.

Time to figure out what she really wanted from life.

Time to figure out if Wyatt was worth the risk.

CHAPTER FOURTEEN

AUGUST 3, 1985
SILVER SPRINGS

"Wendy, is that you?" Ruby called out from the vestibule. She hoped so. She had been so worried about her this year.

It was almost midnight and Wendy had gone out with her friends. She was three hours past her curfew and Ruby could hear giggling on the other side of the door. She peeked through the glass and relief swept over her to see Wendy on the other side. Ruby quickly unlocked the door and Wendy stumbled in laughing and reeking of alcohol.

Ruby grabbed her arm to steady her. "What have you been drinking?"

Wendy rolled her eyes and leaned back against the door, her shoulders limp as a rag doll. "Mom, you're so old-fashioned. What do you think kids my age do?"

Ruby heart sank. "You told me you were going to the movies."

"We did. Then we drank," she said, shoving herself off the door and walking past Ruby as though she were worthless.

"Just a minute, young lady. If you think this behavior is acceptable, you're in for a rude awakening. You are now grounded for a month. No phone. Nothing. Until you can figure out what you did wrong," Ruby said, trying to keep her voice low. The last few years with Wendy had been trying. She seemed to have issues with everyone—her teachers, school, Ruby. She was never happy.

"No way!" she exploded.

"Keep your voice down! Guests are sleeping!" Ruby hissed.

"I hate your stupid guests and your cheesy decorations and I hate this stupid house. I want a house where there aren't any strangers eating breakfast or wandering around in their gross pajamas," Wendy said, far too loud.

Insecurity rippled through Ruby. She knew this wasn't a conventional way to grow up, but it had so many perks too. "I'm trying my best, Wendy. There are worse things in life than growing up in a beautiful home. I'm here for you whenever you need me."

Wendy rolled her eyes. "Right. Just you. No dad."

Ruby winced. "I can't change the past. Your father is dead, but you have a mother. We can either look at all the things that are wrong with our lives or we can focus on the things that are right."

Wendy shook her head and stumbled up the stairs. "Great talk, Mom. Can't wait to have Christmas Eve dinner with all the losers in town again," she said, walking away.

Ruby watched her daughter's retreating figure, worry and shame taking root deep inside her. She had failed Wendy. Somewhere along the way she had done something wrong. She had tried her best. When she had come up with the idea for the Christmas Eve dinner for those in *need, she'd thought she would be setting an example for her daughter. To open her heart, especially at Christmas.*

She had so many regrets. So many things she would do over again if she could.

She had wanted the very best for Wendy. She blinked back tears, refusing to give up. She would never give up on herself or her daughter.

* * *

Wyatt was having one of those days where he wished he understood his daughter. He had worried more about her this year than he could ever remember doing in the past, even when she was a baby. But she was his life, his entire life, and he'd do anything to make sure his mistakes didn't ruin her.

At first he thought she was just angry because Charlotte wasn't there. The house was quiet today after school and that pang of emptiness at Charlotte's absence took him by surprise. It was shocking to admit that someone who had been in their lives for a little more than a week could be so deeply missed. But she was.

He missed her. He missed her laugh and her smile. He missed the way she seemed to dodge everything personal, just like he did. He had missed Charlotte before, and he missed her again now. She made him uncomfortable in the best kind of way. He wanted more time with her. Because he knew, deep in his gut, that her walking into his life again wasn't an accident.

After her brush-off, he'd replayed their conversations and moments together and knew he hadn't imagined the spark between them. He wasn't sure what to do about his feelings for Charlotte. The attraction had been instant and undeniable, but it was the other stuff there that lingered between them. Unspoken words and glances.

He'd never had the need to share his thoughts with other people before. He had always found it difficult, and it had been one of the things his ex had nagged him about. But he'd grown up never trusting anyone, never speaking out. The hostility and threat of violence wasn't something that he could hide from daily. It had loomed like dark clouds and rumbling thunder, every day. It hung over their home, ready to be unleashed, unapologetically, without warning, without an end in sight some days.

He had gone into a profession that was filled with men and women who made it their mission to keep people safe, especially the most vulnerable. At one time he'd been the vulnerable one. He'd been the one seeking out a savior, and one had never appeared. Everything in their house had been either a yell or a whisper, and it seemed to him like all those in between tones were the happy ones, the ones he heard in other people's houses.

So he'd become his own hero. He'd wanted to become his mother's hero, but she hadn't wanted one. She'd wanted her husband and had been willing to die for him.

He scrubbed a hand down his face, pushing away those thoughts, because he had sworn, when he found out that he and Leanne were expecting a baby, that these thoughts, these emotions, the anger and resentment that had never fully healed, wouldn't ever come to light in their house.

But he'd screwed up his marriage too, and he'd be damned if he'd screw up his daughter's life as well. So when people like Charlotte . . . people who wore their hurt on their sleeves, he felt a connection to her. Except it was so much more than a hard past that they shared. She had this way about her that made him want to believe that there might be more for him out there. That maybe *this* wasn't it. As grateful as he was for this life he'd been given with Sam, maybe there was a place that was filled with laughter and love and intimacy. True intimacy. Not the kind that could be had after a night at a bar. But the kind that started like a wildfire and kept burning, could flicker in the darkest of times, could simmer during long winters, and would last forever.

He glanced over at Sam, who was sitting at the island on her phone, with schoolbooks strewn about, not even looking up at him when he greeted her. He tried to sympathize but irritation rose inside him.

"I said, 'Hi, how was your day?' If you don't lift your head and make eye contact with me in three seconds, I'm taking your phone and chucking it out the window into a pile of wet snow."

She let out a theatrical sigh and lifted her head. His gut clenched. Her eyes were rimmed with red and her face was pale. *Oh, hell.* "Are you okay?"

She frowned and put her head back down so quickly it was like she had no muscles in her neck to keep it up.

"Hey," he said, crouching down beside her. "I asked if you were okay."

"I'm fine. I just want to be alone."

His muscles tightened. "Well, not going to happen. First off, you're in the kitchen and that's a public space. Second, I can tell you've been crying, so now I'll just bug you all night until you tell me what's wrong."

She leaned back in her chair and tossed her phone on her math textbook. "Charlotte didn't come over."

He should have prepared her. "Is that what's bothering you?"

She shrugged. "It was a crappy day at school, and I was looking forward to spending the afternoon with her, but she texted to say that her job was done here and she'd see me soon."

Some of the tension left his shoulders. He appreciated that Charlotte had reached out to Sam. "Well, maybe we can set something up. But you know, I'm here, and I happen to be cool." He knew that remark wouldn't go over well.

She gave him a wobbly smile, and that was ten thousand times better than an eye roll, so he'd take that as a win. "I think Charlotte just made that up about you being cool."

He let out a laugh. "Maybe. So, what made school crappy?" he asked, walking over to the fridge and looking for the ingredients to re-create the salad Charlotte had made. He stopped to roll his shoulders, trying to shake the tension from them instead of reaching for a beer.

"It's just stupid school crap. I hate this school."

He piled the ingredients in his arms and fought the urge to tell her to stop complaining, that he'd had it much worse, but he didn't. She needed someone to talk to, and he wasn't going to shut her down. "I know you don't like it here, Sam. But you have a best friend, which is more than lots of people have," he said, dumping the ingredients on the counter and searching for a bowl. He also contemplated a beer, again.

"You're missing the cranberries," she said, joining him and opening the container of mixed greens.

"Thanks. I thought there was something missing," he said, and then stood in the middle of the kitchen. "Do you know where those would be?"

She nodded, smiling and pointing to the pantry. "They're on the shelf with the baking items. Beside the nuts you also forgot."

"Great," he said, opening the pantry door, amazed again at how nice it was to have it so organized. It was weird because it was nothing he would have ever thought of. It was survival mode over here and he'd never been the best at getting things organized. But having things lined up in a row, neatly labeled, had a calming effect he hadn't expected.

He pulled out the cranberries and walnuts and added them to the salad bowl that Sam had already filled. "So, do you have a lot of homework?"

She scrunched up her nose. "Some stupid project for socials that I'm not going to do."

That was it. He was getting a beer. The doorbell rang, and he was so happy for the interruption because he was close to losing his temper. There were only so many lectures he could give on the importance of homework.

"Maybe it's Charlotte!" Sam called out from the kitchen.

He couldn't ignore that small ripple of hope he'd felt too. He couldn't tell his daughter that he'd blown it with Charlotte. "Don't get your hopes up. It's probably some kid selling chocolates."

He swung open the door and Charlotte was standing there with a red dish in her hands and a gorgeous smile on her face. If his daughter hadn't been sitting in the kitchen, or maybe even standing in the doorway watching, he'd have pulled Charlotte into his arms and kissed her the way he had wanted to from the first day she'd walked back into his life again.

From that very first time they'd stood on The Christmas House porch and she'd whispered, asking him where he'd gone. He'd tell her. He'd tell her everything if it meant a chance with her.

He held the door open wider. She was here. Despite the way their last night had ended, she was here. He didn't know what made him want her more—the fact that she might be here for him or for Sam. Or maybe, in his wildest dreams, for both of them.

"Hi . . . this is the best surprise," he said, smiling and shoving a hand in his front pocket.

She held his gaze, surprising him. "I, um, I missed you guys," she said softly, sending a crazy ripple of emotion through him. He hadn't been wrong about his instincts.

"The feeling is mutual," he said, closing the door behind her.

"I also have this casserole that needs a home. Apparently it's your favorite, according to my grandmother," she said, holding up the red dish.

He grinned. "Your grandmother does spoil us. But I don't think we can eat that unless you join us."

"Char?" Sam shrieked, appearing in the hallway.

Charlotte's eyes darted to Sam, and he knew they had her hooked. There was no way she was going to say no to that enthusiasm. The fact that his daughter responded like this to her . . . warmed his heart and made him hopeful that maybe she really could be happy again. Charlotte smiled at Sam. "You guys . . ."

"You *have* to stay for dinner. Dad was trying to make that salad you made the other night and it was so sad. You got here just in time, because he was going to attempt the dressing next."

Wyatt rolled his eyes. "Thanks, Sam."

Charlotte laughed and handed him the casserole dish while she took off her coat. He looked away quickly because he knew he had no business admiring those curves, and being around Charlotte was becoming an exercise in self-discipline and cruel torture.

"I'm sure he would have done a fine job, Sam," she said, walking past him with a twinkle in her eye and maybe a smug smile on her face.

"No, he just pulled out maple syrup instead of honey and white vinegar instead of balsamic."

He wanted to defend himself, but the truth was, he didn't even know they had more than one kind of vinegar. They seemed to be having fun laughing, though, and that was a sound he wanted more of in this house.

"Should I put this in the oven?" he asked as he walked into the kitchen. Sam was leaning against the island, hanging on Charlotte's every word.

"Sure. Not for too long because it was already warm. It might have just cooled slightly while I walked over. Take off the aluminum foil," she said, as she pulled out a jar of honey, looking as though she belonged here.

"Sam, honey, you should take your homework and spread it out on the dining room table or in your room," Charlotte said.

Wyatt didn't say anything and pretended he was taking a while to set the oven temperature, because he was curious how Sam was going to reply to that. She gave him grief with any minor instruction.

"Sure, Charlotte. I'd put it in my room, but it's such a disaster and so disorganized. I never even use my desk," she said, gathering her things.

Wyatt turned around and stared at her in disbelief. He didn't even know who she was anymore. She quickly packed up her books and pens in her school bag and swung it over her shoulder. "Do you want help with your room?" Charlotte asked as she drizzled olive oil over the salad.

"Really?" Sam asked, her face lighting up as though Charlotte had just told her she could use makeup and however much she wanted and could go out with whoever she chose.

He cleared his throat, hating to be the bad guy again. "Sam, I don't think that's a good idea."

Charlotte's face turned red. "Omigosh, I'm sorry. Sam, I totally should have asked your dad. That was really overstepping."

He shook his head. "What? No, no. Not at all. That was really generous of you. I just mean that you're here visiting family and you organize all the time. You're on vacation." He was shocked that Charlotte would want to do that for his daughter.

Sam's face fell. "Right. Dad's right."

Charlotte gave Sam's shoulder a squeeze. "If your dad doesn't mind, then I'd love to help you organize your room," she said, her eyes darting to his.

"Maybe you should look at her room before you actually agree to do this," he said with a wry smile.

Sam's eyes widened. "Dad!"

He held up his hands. "It's only fair. Last time I was in there, I almost fell on my face because of all the stuff you have on the floor."

His daughter's face actually went red. "I'll clean it up before you start, Charlotte. Then we just have to actually organize it."

Hell, he had no idea what was even happening anymore.

"That's perfect. While you're doing that, why don't you spend some time thinking about how you'd like your room to look? Maybe we can do some small stylizing too?"

Sam beamed. "I'd love that! Okay, I'm going to bring all this stuff to my room and start cleaning. Let me know when dinner's ready!" she shouted as she bounded out of the room.

Suddenly the room felt way too hot, too uncomfortable without Sam. "The only way I'm letting this happen is if you charge me for this."

"What? No way. I'm helping my friend. I love what I do, and I'm more than happy to help her out. Also, I'm kind of going crazy at my grandmother's house. My mother just arrived, and suddenly six thousand square feet feels way too small," she said, with a laugh that was slightly strained.

"Ah, family and the holidays. It always seems like such a good idea until it actually happens," he said, taking down three plates.

She smiled, tossing the salad. "No, I already knew it was a bad idea, but unavoidable I guess. It does make you wish for those perfect Christmases that you see on TV, though, doesn't it?"

He joined her at the island, leaving the dishes next to the oven. "I guess."

"Do you have any family that visits for the holidays?"

He gazed into her expressive blue eyes and wanted to tell her the whole thing. But he never talked about his childhood . . . she knew bits and pieces, but not everything. He would tell her, but not with Sam around. "Both my parents are gone."

Surprise flickered across her eyes. He supposed he was young to have both his parents gone. "It was a car accident," he said, his voice sounding a little harsher than he intended.

"I'm sorry," she said softly.

"Thank you. We're happy to have my Aunt Mary, though. She's taken on the role of grandmother to Sam," he said, relieved that he could at least say that truthfully. His Aunt Mary had been like a beacon in a storm. She'd always been tough as nails on the outside, rising to any occasion, but a soft place to fall. She was the only other person in the world who knew about his childhood, and she'd been to hell and back trying to save her sister. She had never given up on her, until it was time to focus her attention onto him. When there was nothing left to do except say goodbye.

Maybe once a year or so, during the holidays, he and Aunt Mary would have a drink by the fire at her old house, and she'd bring up her childhood with his mother. How much fun they'd had together, how wonderful their parents had been. And inevitably she'd shed a tear or two, wondering how his mother could have fallen for someone like his father. Usually he'd down the rest of whatever it was he was drinking because he knew he didn't have the heart to ask her to stop talking. She had suffered too, and he knew she didn't talk about it to anyone. Abuse fanned out to everyone in the family until no one was unscathed. The survivors kept going, but always with a part of them missing.

Aunt Mary had lost a sister to someone who didn't deserve her. Someone he was ashamed to call a father. At the end of the conversation, she'd always look at him, with that rare show of vulnerability, and tell him she wished she'd known earlier, she wished that she could have raised him. He'd reach across and kiss her cheek and tell her that he knew that, but that everything had worked out in the end. Then he'd get up and leave, because his memory lane was paved with horrible memories and there was only so much he could take.

"That's nice. She's sweet. A lot like my grandmother," she said, finishing the salad and looking around.

It was that tension again, the one that was easier to hide when Sam was in the room. "Should I get that casserole out?" he asked.

She nodded. "I'm sure it's ready."

He pulled it out of the oven and placed it on the trivets he kept on the table and then poked his head out into the hallway and called for Sam. She walked into the kitchen just as they were sitting down, looking winded. "Wow, who knew I could clean up a room so fast?"

"When I ask you to clean up your room you take an entire day," he said, taking the salad that Charlotte passed over to him.

"Well, I'm motivated," Sam said, helping herself to a giant piece of casserole.

Charlotte let out a muffled laugh. "Did you give any thought to the decorating?"

Sam nodded vigorously. "Yes. I think it can look so cool. And I have ideas for how to organize my closet and desk too. You're the expert, though, so you tell me what you think is best."

He resisted the urge to roll his eyes because he really was happy she was so enthusiastic . . . and happy. "Sure. Maybe I'll have a quick peek after dinner and take some measurements and notes so the next time I come over we can get started?"

"That'd be great!"

He quashed any hurt he felt that he hadn't been able to reach his daughter in this way after everything they'd been through. But he'd heard it said many times that parenting was a thankless job. It wasn't lost on him that Charlotte offered something he couldn't. In some ways, Sam was like the Charlotte he remembered. Maybe they had a connection too. He wasn't even going to start worrying about what would happen when the holidays were over and Charlotte went back to her regular life in the city. He was going to take this one day at a time.

CHAPTER FIFTEEN

OCTOBER 1988
SILVER SPRINGS

"Hi, Mrs. Harris."

Ruby held the door open for Mac. She knew that he was coming over. Wendy had talked nonstop about the young man for the entire summer. Ruby had to admit, he was very handsome; tall with dark hair and lean features. He was a summer student who'd been looking for work and Ruby had hired him to repaint all the shutters and the porch. He'd been a hard worker and had taken his job very seriously. But she'd have to be a fool not to have noticed the looks Mac and Wendy had exchanged. Wendy had chattered on about him every night at dinner and had brought him iced tea a few times as well. Then she had started pestering Ruby for details about the legend of the house helping people find love. Ruby had brushed her off, telling her that it was all old myths and none of it based on reality. She had even gone so far as to mention how she'd lived here for so long now and had not dated one man. Clearly, it was not a house where people found love.

"Hello, Mac."

He gave her a nod, and Ruby caught the insecurity that flitted across his features as he smiled and extended his hand. She shook it, firmly, and gestured to the living room.

"You have a beautiful home," he said as he sat across from her.

"Thank you," she replied, keeping her eyes trained on him. She wanted to project the image of a tough mother, for a moment wishing there was a man here to intimidate him a little. But Ruby had it on good authority that she could be intimidating too, so she made sure not to look away.

"I, um, I wanted to ask your permission to go out with Wendy on a date," he said, rubbing his hands down the front of his jeans.

Ruby had been expecting this. She did think it was rather charming of him to formally come in and ask her. It was also a good sign that he was so nervous. She knew no one really did that these days, but she saw it as a sign of respect for both her and her daughter. "I like you, Mac, and I know that you're a hard worker. You've managed to restore those shutters and the porch beautifully. What were your plans for your date?"

"I was thinking of taking Wendy out for dinner and then a movie."

Ruby folded her hands. "That sounds fine. I don't think I've met your parents at all, have I?"

His cheeks flushed slightly and averted his gaze. "Uh, no, they don't live in town."

She knew enough, through the gossip mill that was forever running in Silver Springs, that his family had come to town a few years ago and kept to themselves for the most part. "I see. Well, maybe one day we can meet."

He gave her a nod and then looked down quickly. "Ms. Harris, we aren't like you and Wendy. This house you have and all its grandeur. My parents are pretty, um, well, not wealthy. My mom works in a coffee shop in the next town over, and my dad is a mechanic."

Ruby's heart squeezed. "Oh, Mac. I don't come from a long line of millionaires, and I'm the last person to judge someone else. All I care about is whether you're a good man who will treat my daughter right."

He let out a deep breath and stood. "Thank you."

Ruby stood and held out her hand. "I like you, Mac. If you are the man I think you are, and you treat my daughter with kindness and respect, then I think we'll get along just fine."

*   *   *

"I'm so tired of having to live up to your impossible standards!" Wendy's voice echoed from the kitchen, down the hallway, and into the family room where Charlotte and Olivia were enjoying a Hallmark movie bingefest the next night.

Charlotte looked over at Olivia, who rolled her eyes and shook her head. She was holding the TV remote in her hand. The spread in front of them had been half eaten—a lavish display of holiday gluttony that neither of them felt guilty about, especially since they'd been putting in long brisk walks as planned. "Should I mute this?" Olivia whispered.

"That depends on whether or not we're prepared to break our two glass of wine limit," Charlotte said, leaning over and picking up her wine glass with this new turn of events, instead of the peppermint and white-chocolate-drizzled popcorn.

"Good point. Okay, so let's just keep watching and living vicariously through the people on TV," she said with a laugh, propping her feet, in their Rudolph slippers, on the coffee table.

"I do not have impossible standards. If you grew up and got your act together, you would know that. Instead, you just want to blame everyone else for your problems. It's never your fault, is it, Wendy?" their grandmother bellowed, with the strength of a much younger woman.

"Point one to Grandma," Olivia said, raising her glass.

"Oh, that's good. Maybe we should have a drink every time Grandma gets a point," Charlotte said, desperately trying to make light of this situation. She had already known her mother coming would result in way too much drama and the reopening of very old wounds.

"Oh, right. Having a husband walk out on me and ditch me is my fault, is that what you're saying?" their mother yelled back.

The humor was sucked out of the room, like a powerful vacuum, and was replaced with a weighty blanket of memories.

"I didn't say that. Of course that was never the right thing to do. Ever. But have you really reflected on the type of mother and wife you were? You have two daughters in this house and do you know anything about what's going on in their lives? You have poor, sweet Olivia, who has always tried to please everyone and keep everyone smiling, on the brink of a breakdown."

Charlotte didn't even look at her sister, she just passed her the box of Kleenex, and then pulled one out for herself, just as Olivia blew her nose loudly.

She stared at the screen, with the happy couple paused in Hallmark-land. They had been searching for the perfect Christmas tree and were smiling and happy, and their biggest problem was that one of them was from the city and didn't celebrate Christmas. If only it were so easy.

"It's not my fault Olivia is that way. That's just her personality."

"Then you have Charlotte, who has been so hurt by you and Mac that she can't stop organizing—bordering on OCD in my opinion— because she was raised in a house with so much disorder that she uses it as a way to control her life. That little girl was trying to keep your marriage together by keeping the house together. She hasn't had a relationship her entire adult life. Do you really think that's healthy, Wendy? Oh, I suppose you're not to blame for any of this?"

Charlotte squeezed her eyes shut and choked on the sob in her chest. "Grandma's killing me. Did you know there was this much wrong with us? I thought I just liked color-coding," she managed to strangle out. She grabbed a few Kleenexes from the box Olivia was holding for her.

"Oh, so basically everything is my fault."

"Fix it. Be a mother now. It's not too late."

"I really don't need advice from someone who was so perfect that their fiancé killed himself," their mother said.

Charlotte's body froze, and she and Olivia slowly turned to face each other. "What did she just say?" Charlotte whispered.

Olivia clutched Charlotte's arm. "This is so bad. I have no idea what Mom is talking about. I think we need to say something."

"How dare you, Wendy? How dare you speak to me like that, about one of the most horrific things in my life?"

"What is happening?" Olivia whispered.

"He was a weak man," Grandma Ruby said, an uncharacteristic break in her voice.

"Oh, that's rich. Now you're even insulting my dead father. You're better than my dead father. Thanks a lot, Mom."

"Wendy, I've had enough. Yes, yes, I made mistakes, and I faced them. Choices I can never take back, but at least I faced them. Alone. I didn't wallow and pout and blame the world for my problems. You've always had me. I didn't have a soul until those nuns took me in. I was on the street with not a dime to my name and no husband attached to the baby in my womb. Don't you go comparing your life to mine."

"Now it's all making sense," Charlotte whispered, her stomach churning with wine and popcorn and family secrets.

Olivia nodded, dropping her hand, her eyes as wide as the holly-rimmed china saucers on the table.

"Oh, so sorry. I'm not going to play the game of who had a worse life, Mom. But you should really stop and think of what my life was like, being raised by someone like you. So high and mighty—"

"Oh, Wendy. High and mighty? I cleaned toilets, I scrubbed these floors on my hands and knees. All the while taking care of a newborn baby. How dare you? How dare you? All the stupid things you've done—I've never turned you away. Don't compare yourself to me. My parents shut the door in my pregnant, innocent face and left me to freeze in the Toronto winter. I'm not babying you anymore. You want to turn your life around? Then be a real mother and a real grandmother. If you're looking for me to hold your hand and tell you how difficult your life has been and listen to you talk about all the people you want to blame, then go somewhere else."

There was silence then, and Charlotte and Olivia stared at each other, mouths open, the moment so similar to ones they'd had as children as they had listened to their parents arguing. "We have to go in there and break this up. I'm worried for Grandma," Charlotte said standing.

"I agree. Let's go together," Olivia said, already making a beeline for the door.

"Should we ask about what they were fighting about?" Olivia said, pausing.

Charlotte shook her head. "No. Not tonight. Maybe when things calm down."

Olivia nodded and they walked out of the room. This was what Charlotte had been avoiding for so long. The fighting. The secrets. The emotional toll it all took. The arguments reminded her of her childhood—the disruption, the chaos, the insecurity. But they weren't kids anymore, and this shouldn't bother her. In a couple of weeks, she'd be back in the city. She'd be able to walk into her calm and peaceful condo every night, never having to worry about an argument.

The scene in the hallway was not good. Their mother was pretending to pack her already packed purse while Grandma Ruby was standing there with a fierce frown. "Why don't we just agree to disagree tonight and wake up tomorrow refreshed?" Olivia said, with a valiant attempt at sounding cheerful.

Their mother flung her red scarf over her neck, the image suddenly reminding Charlotte of Snoopy the Flying Ace that she had watched relentlessly when she was a kid. She stifled a giggle, then coughed when everyone looked at her. Olivia's eyes were comically wide. "Sorry, too much wine."

Grandma Ruby's eyes filled with tears, and Charlotte regretted the callousness of her remark. "I'm sorry, Grandma. Don't worry. Olivia and I have a two glass limit pact and we've never broken it."

Their mother let out a strangled noise and marched to the door. "Well, I guess I'm the only one who's imperfect!"

Charlotte rolled her eyes and spoke the words she really didn't want to say, but she did it for the grandmother who had always put them first. She deserved a great Christmas. And Charlotte knew that, for her, it meant having them all there under one roof. "Mom, we all love you, and no one is trying to make you feel bad. Why don't we take Liv's suggestion and start over again tomorrow?"

Wendy crossed her arms, and her shoulders relaxed slightly.

"When Charlotte and I go on our walk tomorrow, I can leave Dawn here and the two of you can have some bonding time," Olivia said with a strained smile.

Their mother gave them a wobbly smile. "That sounds nice. Okay. Let's try again," she said, extending her arms. She and Olivia hugged her.

"You too, Mom," she said, motioning to Grandma Ruby.

Grandma Ruby came over, and they wrapped their arms around her too.

The four of them stood there and Charlotte knew this should be a happy moment, but she didn't feel happiness. She felt agitated. She'd had hugs from her mother before, and they meant nothing. This was all temporary. Everything with her parents had been temporary. She was happy for her grandmother, she was happy that Olivia was looking better, but it wasn't enough. There was something missing. Something for her. Someone for her.

"Well, I'd better go to bed. Dawn usually wakes up at least once during the night," Olivia said, pulling back.

"That's wise, dear. I think I'll head off to bed as well," Grandma Ruby said.

"Me too, I'm wiped," their mother said and the three of them walked up the stairs.

Charlotte couldn't bring herself to move yet. "I'll clean up the family room," she called out after their retreating figures.

Olivia paused. "Oh shoot. I'll help."

Charlotte waved her off. "No, no. It'll only take me a minute. Go to bed," she said, giving her sister a smile and walking to the family room before Olivia could argue.

She piled all their things into the empty bowl, her thoughts on the argument they'd overheard. What had her mother been talking about? A part of her didn't even want to know. Then there was Grandma's analysis of her and Olivia; as much as it made her uncomfortable, she was right. Grandma Ruby was always right.

None of them were living their best lives—maybe her most of all. She had been on the sidelines, proud that she had remained unscathed, but it was a lie too. She had been fooling herself that she was really living.

She loaded the dishwasher and glanced at the time on the oven. It wasn't that late.

Not questioning the pull, the deep yearning, she quickly put her coat and hat on and walked out the back door into the night.

*　　*　　*

Wyatt opened his front door, grateful that Sam was sleeping over at his aunt's house that night for their yearly girls' shopping and bonding trip. The timing couldn't be better, because it would get her mind off Charlotte. Unintentionally, it had worked out perfectly for him too, because he couldn't see his daughter right now. He needed to be alone and decompress for a little bit. Thank God he was officially on vacation because he needed it.

There were days when he loved his job with everything he had, when he made a difference in someone's life, and then there were days that made him want to hand in his badge. Usually on those days, he didn't come home straightaway if Sam would be here, because he'd need to detox and get his head screwed on straight first. Tonight was one of those nights. He didn't bother taking off his jacket or boots; he headed straight for his liquor cabinet and poured himself a double shot of scotch and then marched out to the back deck. He swung back a healthy dose and then took a deep breath, the cold air a blistering contrast to the heat of the alcohol in his mouth.

He squeezed his eyes shut and gripped the snow-lined wood railing with one gloved hand. One of his most detested parts of his job were things involving some kind of crime against a woman or a child. As a father, as a nephew, as a son, as a decent man in general, it made it hard for him to stay professional and to keep his heart out of it. But as a victim and witness of abuse, it made it damn near impossible to not take an involuntary trip down memory lane.

When Mary Beth Chalmers's son called 911 tonight, Wyatt had already known it was going to be a grim situation. He'd been going to that house for years and, just like always, Mary Beth refused to leave her husband. Even when he knocked her down the stairs unconscious and her kid had to witness it all. That's when it made it very hard for him to just be a man in uniform. That's when he just wanted to be a friend, when he wanted to beat the shit out of her husband, and take her and her little boy and put them in a shelter for women and kids. He wanted to tell that little boy to stay strong, that one day he would grow up and he didn't have to be the kind of man his father was. He swung back the rest of whiskey and hung his head back, staring at the sky. There were some nights he stayed awake worrying about all the things that could happen to Sam; he would go through all the what-if scenarios, and he'd wish he could just keep her safe.

As much as the whole sarcastic, preteen thing drove him nuts, a part of him liked Sam's sarcasm—it showed that she wasn't afraid of him. He would have never even dreamed of speaking to his dad like that without risking a brutally violent reaction. He was proud, knowing that even if he was screwing up at this parenting thing, at the very least he'd done better than his parents. His daughter knew that when he raised a hand, it was for a hug, never for violence.

He stared up at the sky. There were days and nights he searched for signs, signs that there was more. Up until a couple of weeks ago, the world he knew was filled with lonely people and messed-up lives, and sometimes it was pretty damn lonely to be raising a girl alone. Sometimes it was too damn hard to always be strong, to always have his shit together, to always be brave. He had gotten over his childhood, the crap that he'd been through, but nights like tonight brought it all out in a blizzard of haphazard memories he'd rather avoid. Tonight he identified with that little boy more than his parents.

He wished he was a man who could just believe in something so much greater and more powerful than him, but there were days . . . there were days he looked for it and came up empty. There were so many lonely days and nights where he wished he had a partner to talk it out with. Like Charlotte.

"Wyatt?"

Her voice cut through the night air and through the stillness of the night. She was here. Unplanned. Like she somehow knew. She had always been that light in the darkness for him. He couldn't turn her away. He could never reject Charlotte. He turned around, somewhere in his gut knowing that she was the last woman he wanted to see in this condition, but she was also the *only* woman, the only person, he wanted to see.

She was standing there in that cute red hat with the pom-pom and the cranberry-colored coat and matching lipstick, and he wanted nothing more than to walk over and kiss her until neither one of them could remember the way the world had screwed them over, until all they were in the moment was more than enough.

He stood still, not knowing what to do with his emotions, not wanting to tell her to go away, but not having the words for polite conversation. But she was here at this hour of the night for a reason. He didn't want to hope. Hope was for fools. He held her gaze, her beautiful face illuminated by the moon. The uncertainty in her eyes changed to something else as her gaze flickered over to him and she took a step forward.

"Are you okay?" she asked softly.

He gave her a nod, not knowing if he'd be able to speak without telling her what was really on his mind. But he didn't want to scare her off, he didn't want to jeopardize this friendship they were building. He knew she had her own baggage and her own insecurities, and the last thing he wanted to be was a man who reminded her of a father who couldn't keep his shit together and fell apart.

He wanted to show her that he was strong, that he could hold it all together for the people he loved. This was just a bad day and nothing more. He didn't want to lose the first woman to ever make him wish for miracles and happily-ever-afters. He cleared his throat and looked down. "Fine. Just a long day," he finally managed to force out, cringing because his voice sounded rough.

Charlotte walked toward him, silent, her gaze locked onto his, until she was maybe an inch or two from him, and it felt like she had always been within an inch or two of him. Charlotte had always been there, just slightly beyond his reach.

He didn't know if he had the words he thought she needed to hear, or if he'd ruin the moment by speaking, but somewhere in his gut he knew that Charlotte needed more than the little he had left tonight.

"It's pretty late," he said, wanting to know if it was there, hidden under all those gorgeous layers of vulnerability and kindness. He wanted to know if that pull that he felt existed inside her too, or if he was just delusional, dreaming about a woman who didn't feel the same way.

She crossed her arms and looked down, kicking at a tuft of snow. "My mom and grandmother got into a fight and it was just . . . it was old family stuff and I didn't want to deal with it, you know? Whenever I'm here . . . with you . . . I can forget all of it. I just wanted to see you. Just like I used to look forward to seeing you every morning before school."

And there it was, that honesty she'd always given him, when she trusted him back then. Wyatt stood motionless, conflicting emotions tangling their way through his body as he processed Charlotte's words. Laced ever so gently throughout her voice was an honesty that touched him and reached the part of him that no one ever had. Charlotte made him want things—things he'd told himself and everyone around him he didn't want. But it wasn't just a woman he wanted, or just a mom for his daughter, it was Charlotte. He wanted her. Physically, emotionally.

His throat felt raw, tight, but he needed to tell her how much she meant to him. "It was the same for me. You were the same for me. You were sunshine. Your smile would lift me out of the hell I was living in, Charlotte. And now . . . now you're here on a dark day, and you're this ray of light. Again. I don't know how it happened, how we found each other again, but I know in my gut that you and I have never been a coincidence."

She ran her teeth across her lower lip, her eyes glistening. The image of him, gently pulling, tugging on that lip with his own mouth crossed his mind, and he pushed aside the thought. In that half second, he reached for her and she walked right into his arms. Her soft curves pressed against his body and she held onto him like she couldn't let go, and he let the emotion reach the part of himself that he kept locked away.

He brushed his lips across the top of her head, because he wanted, needed more. He didn't know if he could still pretend that he was fine with just friendship. She slowly pulled her head from his chest but didn't pull away from him. Instead, she leaned back and stared up at him, those blue eyes filled with the same hunger he felt, and that was all he needed. Maybe she was all he needed to get out of the place he was sitting in right now, that hell between work and real life. Maybe she was the one who could bring him right back home, like she had always done, like he'd done for her.

"I missed you so damn much," he whispered roughly, his hands gently framing her face before he leaned down to finally kiss Charlotte.

Maybe he'd waited a lifetime for her, for this moment. Charlotte's soft lips opened under his and he kissed her, unable to get enough of her, unable to remember all the reasons they were supposed to not be doing this. But this was Charlotte, the girl that had reached him when no one else could, the last good memory of his childhood. Now she was here, in his arms, filling him with a desire he'd never experienced.

He left his one hand on the side of her face while the other traced the curves on the side of her body, and she made a sound that seemed to reverberate through all his nerve endings. Her hands went inside his jacket and found his waist, scrunching a bunch of his shirt in her hand. He kissed the impossibly soft, fragrant skin below her ear and tucked her into his body as he felt her knees wobble. "I missed you so damn much," he said as he trailed kisses under her ear to her jaw line.

"God, me too, Wyatt. I used to dream about you," she said, raising her mouth to his again.

"Really?" he said, wanting to talk but not wanting to.

"I had the biggest crush on you," she said, sliding her hands up his chest in a torturously good, slow motion.

"You're kidding," he said, in between kisses.

"Yup, the cool thing wasn't a lie," she said.

He laughed as he kissed her, a first for him. "I guess I shouldn't be surprised. I *was* cool."

She punched him playfully, laughing along with him, until she pulled back slightly. "When you disappeared, I felt this huge hole in my life. I'd stop outside your apartment door, waiting to see if I'd hear you guys. For weeks. But it was like you just vanished," she whispered.

He held onto her waist, forcing himself not to back away, knowing the only way to get closer to Charlotte was to give her what he'd never given anyone else, to talk to her like he never talked to anyone else, to trust her with all of the truth. "You remember . . . the arguing in my house," he said, his voice sounding choppy and harsh to his ears.

She nodded, her eyes filled with empathy.

"It wasn't just arguing. My dad was an addict, and my mom became one too eventually. Maybe to cope with him, maybe because he wanted her to, as a way to control her. He was brutally violent when he wasn't using. He would knock her down. Would knock me down. He'd use whatever was around—a chair, a bottle, his fist. That day . . . he'd been forced to take her to the ER because she wasn't waking up. He'd given her a concussion. Someone from our school was there and he panicked, thinking he'd get reported. So we took off. Again."

She leaned forward and kissed him softly, her hand on his jaw, and the tears he felt against his face were almost his undoing. He hadn't known what it would feel like to have Charlotte's sympathy, her heart. It was the best damn feeling. He had never wanted pity, so he never talked about his past. But he knew it wasn't pity from her—it was understanding.

"What happened?"

He pulled her close. "I grew. Larger than him, stronger than him, and I begged my mom to come with me, to leave him. I told her I'd help her, we'd go to Mary, I'd support her. I told her I could protect her, that I was going to be a cop."

She hugged him tighter when his voice broke, like she already knew.

"She refused to leave him. So I had to. It almost killed me to leave her there, but I did. I tried to explain it to her—that I wouldn't survive if I stayed, that I was so damn afraid I was going to turn into him or that I'd kill him. But she didn't get it. She hated me for leaving. But I hated him more. I hated him with every breath I took. I was consumed by it until I didn't know who I was anymore." He stopped speaking abruptly, his voice raw. He held his breath, waiting for signs of judgment, for a flicker of censure across her expressive eyes.

It didn't come. Instead, she raised her hand and placed it over his heart, unknowingly making him fall in love with her just a little bit more. "You could never be like him. I knew you the moment I met you. Who you are in here."

He blinked back moisture in his eyes, fighting to keep going, to trust her with all of it because he never wanted to talk about this again. "Char, I never contacted them again. I left my mother and cut her off from my life and if I had to do it all over again, I would. I would, because then Sam came along and that's when I fully realized that I would do whatever it took to keep her safe and happy. And if that meant keeping hate and anger out of my life, I would. It made me realize how unfair it is for people like my parents to demand the loyalty they demanded. They never asked for forgiveness, no one repented. They never thought there was anything wrong with it. But I know. I know because I'd cut my own arm off before I hit my child. I had to break the chain of violence. Having them out of my life was the only way I knew how."

"You offered your mother a way out, Wyatt. She didn't take it. You didn't just walk out on her. You have a right to live your own life, to make your own decisions. You had a right to draw a line in the sand. You didn't want violence in your life, in your little girl's life, and I . . . I think so much more of you for it."

He bit down hard on his back teeth and tore his gaze from hers, the empathy in them, the emotion in them, more than he could have ever hoped for. Her faith in him was humbling. "I felt guilty for a long time. I was her defender. I would have taken care of her, Char."

She reached for his hand. "I know you would have."

"A couple of years later they both died in a car crash. Tonight . . . there are some nights that my job makes me think about how I grew up. I hate thinking about those days. Or how scary the world can be out there, for women especially, and I think of Sam and all the horrible things that could happen to her one day and I . . . I don't know. I shut down. I get scared that I've already screwed it all up. For so long, I worried that I was too damaged to be the dad Sam needed me to be.

"I have a lot of regrets. I'll never group Sam into that pile; she's the best thing that's ever happened to me. But I do still blame myself for the role I played in the pain in her life. I should have known that my ex wouldn't be able to deal with parenthood. I should have known she wasn't the type to take the role seriously."

"You can't predict other people's behavior," she said.

He shrugged. "No, but there are clues. And we were too young. But I was also a dreamer in some ways. I had convinced myself that we could make it work. I wanted what I saw in friends' homes—the family, the love that was always missing for me. We were eighteen and having a kid. But I wasn't afraid of hard work. I wanted to be a dad, maybe I wanted to prove that I could be a better dad than the one who raised me. I wanted to be a husband, and I think that maybe I imposed that on her. She wasn't thrilled to find out she was pregnant. I thought maybe she'd come around, that she was just surprised. But she grew more and more distant as the pregnancy progressed. I was the one making the doctor's appointments, the ultrasounds, all that. I was the one putting the picture on the fridge. I think she hated me for it."

Charlotte cupped his face and looked deep into his eyes, finding that place that only she knew. "How were you supposed to know that? You were there for her, and that's more than a lot of people get."

He held her gaze. "It wasn't enough. I would have stayed. I would have stayed in that relationship for Sam," he said, hating to admit that. "Without love. I would have stayed without being in love with her."

Charlotte tore her eyes from his and stared out into the darkness. "I'm sorry you were in that position," she whispered, finally, taking a step back.

Damn. He shouldn't have gotten into his relationship with his ex. It was too soon. "I'm sorry. I completely unloaded all this on you. This is the last thing I want to be talking about. I don't know how this happened," he said, running his hands through his hair.

"Don't be," she said, with a wave of her hand, and it was like the intimacy of their conversation vanished with the motion, with the distance between them now.

His phone vibrated, and for a second he didn't move, but autopilot took over and he pulled his phone out of his pocket and stared at the screen. "Sam, of course. I've got to pick her up, she's not feeling well. I hate to end this now."

She squeezed his hand. "Don't apologize. Thank you for telling me. I think it's pretty amazing. What you've done. What you've been through—how selfless you are. I think that if you weren't so hard on yourself you'd see what I see—a hardworking, loving man, doing his best for his daughter. Sam is your priority—as she should be. As you should have been to your parents. You did it, Wyatt. You broke the chain."

CHAPTER SIXTEEN

JANUARY 2, 1989
SILVER SPRINGS

"Why can't you just be happy for me, Mom?"

Ruby stared at Wendy, who was sitting on the edge of her bed, holding her left hand out and moving it from side to side, as the sunlight caught the sparkle of the small diamond. No, she wasn't happy. Not by a long shot. But she knew enough about Wendy and enough about life to keep that to herself. Ruby put her hairbrush down and leaned against the large dresser, determined not to have this conversation end in an argument.

"You know I love Mac. I think he's a great guy. I think the two of you could have a wonderful life together, but I just think you're too young. I think you're giving up a lot of opportunities."

Wendy rolled her eyes and crossed one leg over the other. She was twenty and naïve and idealistic, and that was the problem. "I can go to school any time. Even after we're married."

"Of course you can, but will you?"

"What's wrong with just getting a job in a store or something and being his wife? We want kids, and I want to stay at home with them."

Ruby clasped her hands together in an effort to keep her mouth shut for a moment longer as she chose her words carefully. She didn't want to transpose her own fears and beliefs onto Wendy, but she did need to protect her. *"There is nothing wrong with that . . . in an ideal world. Life isn't always ideal though, Wendy. What if Mac can't work anymore? Would you be making enough money to support the two of you? What if once you have children you feel you need more? You will have no education to fall back on. All I'm saying is, take some time, go to college, and get some security."*

Wendy sat up straighter and she could already tell by the tilt of her daughter's chin this conversation was pointless. *"Just because life didn't go as planned for you doesn't mean that will happen to me. Besides, it all worked out for you anyway. You landed this job and this big house. You're practically famous in this town now, with your Christmas Eve Open House dinner."*

Ruby took a deep breath, refusing to explode with anger at the glossing over of her life. *"That's not exactly how I got here, Wendy. I still remember what it felt like to be alone in the world with not a dime to my name or an education or job prospect. I scrubbed toilets and washed floors on my hands and knees while I was pregnant with you. Did my life turn out in the end? Yes. But there were hard days, weeks, and months. I'm trying to spare you that. What if your relationship doesn't work out and you become a single mom? How will you support yourself and your children?"*

Wendy let out a sound and stood up. *"Gee, thanks a lot. You're basically saying we're going to get divorced before we're even married!*

And let's just say that you're right. Mac isn't the type of guy who would just leave us with nothing. He would never do that."

"First off, I'm not saying you're doomed to divorce, but when making life decisions you have to look at all possibilities. Second, yes, I agree, I don't think Mac would ever up and leave you with nothing, but he's going to be a police officer. It's a dangerous job, Wendy . . ."

Wendy shrugged. "This is just stupid. It's so negative. Mac and I are getting married this summer. It's not that big a deal. I'll get a job, he already has a job. We want to have the wedding here."

"At least take some courses after you're married. You like hair, why don't you go to beauty school? You would even be able to take clients in your home and make some money on the side, even with children," she said, forcing a smile and an upbeat tone to her voice.

Wendy rolled her eyes. "I like doing hair, but my hair. I don't want to touch other people's heads."

Ruby knew she was going to lose it. She stared at her daughter, taking in her pretty features, her long, shiny dark hair. She had given the world for this girl. Wendy had been her whole life for so long. But they were different people. Maybe it was Ruby's fault. Maybe she had indulged her too much, sheltered her from the ugliness out there. Wendy had never wanted for anything . . . except a father. All Ruby had ever told her was that he had died before she was born. To protect her. So that she would never think that she was responsible for her father taking his own life. But now, Wendy had grown up into this beautiful woman with no idea how hard it was out there in the world. She was going to place all her faith in a man, and that had been Ruby's downfall eighteen years ago.

"Wendy, to be a true adult you have to be able to support yourself. As your mother, before I let you move out of this house, I need to know that you are prepared for the real world and can support yourself."

Wendy threw her arms in the air. "I can always come back here. It's not like I'm going to be left homeless. Besides, remember how Mrs. Pemberton always said this house was magic? That it brought people together? That she met her husband here when her car had broken down outside the house and he helped her? The same is true for me and Mac. We met here when you hired him."

Ruby shook her head. "Oh, Wendy, you can't possibly believe these things. The house had nothing to do with it."

Wendy walked to the door, tossing her dark hair over her shoulders, and Ruby's advice along with it.

* * *

Coming over to Wyatt and Sam's had become something Charlotte didn't question anymore. It was like she'd finally found that piece that had been missing from her life. She'd always said she didn't want to get involved with a man, that marriage and kids were out of the question—not worth the risk.

And then that evening with Wyatt had happened. He'd let her in. He'd kissed her until she couldn't stand. Her heart had broken for him, and all the missing pieces had come together like a tragic puzzle. But in the midst of all that heartache, she'd experienced the absolute sheer bliss of connecting with him, with his thoughts. Being held by him had made her feel safe and alive and like a different person. The person she thought might exist somewhere inside.

She wanted more. More of the people in this house. She and Wyatt were more than friends . . . yet they weren't. There was a simmering, delicious tension between them, which left her breathless when she thought about it. She wanted more time alone with him, and when he'd answered the door tonight she knew he did too, she could read it in his eyes. But Sam was home, and neither of them wanted to confuse her.

He was sweet and sincere, and the fact that he was taking things so slow proved what she already knew about him. Her relationship with Sam had grown and if she didn't worry too much about what all this meant, she could admit to herself that she was the happiest she'd been. Ever. In her life. They were only one night away from Candlelight Christmas and *The Nutcracker*, and then after that would be Christmas Eve. She had already told Wyatt she would love to go with him.

Even things at The Christmas House were going as smoothly as possible. Her mother was actually helping Grandma Ruby get ready for Christmas Eve, and Olivia was getting stronger every day. It all actually filled Charlotte with a hope she hadn't had since she was little.

She and Wyatt were loading the dishwasher after Sam had run off to her room to finish her homework.

A loud crash followed by Sam stomping through the hallway had them both glancing at each other. "Everything okay?" Wyatt called out.

"Where's my mom?" Sam said, bursting into the room, her face red, holding up a piece of paper in her hands as she stood in the doorway.

Charlotte glanced over at Wyatt, whose face had frozen. "Pardon?"

"For this stupid assignment. I need to know where my mom is so that I can ask her about my family tree on her side of the family. I can't exactly just answer that I was a mistake and my parents got married because my dad got my mom pregnant even though they didn't love each other and then my mom took off," she said, her eyes filling with tears even though her words were angry and harsh.

Charlotte's eyes blurred, and her chest ached, as Wyatt walked around the island, his face drawn, his eyes on his daughter. "Hey, hey, Sam, my God, that isn't what happened at all," he said, his voice thick as he placed his hands on her shoulders.

"Right. Sure. Well, I'm doing my homework now, and I kept putting it off because I didn't want to deal with it. But now it's due tomorrow and I don't know what to do!" she said, the panic in her voice hard to listen to.

Charlotte's chest ached for both of them. She knew their pain. More than they thought. "Um, I should probably get going and give you some privacy," she said, gently.

"You don't have to go. Maybe you already know the answer to this, and I'm the only one who doesn't know anything around here," Sam said, looking back and forth between Charlotte and Wyatt.

Charlotte glanced at Wyatt, who still hadn't moved.

"No. I haven't lied to you, Sam. Ever. But you're so wrong about you being a mistake. That is never, ever, how I saw you. God. That kills me. Samantha, you weren't planned, but that doesn't mean you were a mistake. You are my biggest blessing, and I'm so privileged that I get to be your dad. I will be here for you for as long as I'm alive. I am here for you. I will always have your back. You need to know that you actually saved me—you're the reason I'm here, you're the reason I wake up in the morning, the reason I kept going after your mom left. Since the day you entered the world, Sam, I loved you in a way that I didn't understand. That moment . . . that moment I held you, I knew my purpose and I was a changed man," he said, wiping his eyes with the base of his palm.

Charlotte stood there, clutching the island like a lifeline and watched as Sam threw her arms around Wyatt. Maybe it was that moment, Wyatt's words, his love for his daughter, when Charlotte realized that she was in love with him. That she had always loved him. He had lived up to every single fantasy about the boy she thought he was and the man she wanted him to be now. He was hard and fearless, but incredibly tender and noble at the same time. She stood on the sidelines where she'd always been comfortable and safe, and it didn't feel right anymore. Watching Wyatt and Sam, in what they saw as an imperfect family, she saw perfection, because of the profound love between them.

"I love you, Dad," Sam said, crying as she held onto her dad. "Sometimes I feel like it was all my fault, that if I were a better kid or cuter, she would have stayed."

Charlotte tried to take a deep breath against the tightness in her chest, but she felt this girl's pain right down to her core, and it dug out every single thought and memory she'd carefully tucked away for so long.

"God, no. It was never your fault. It was her fault. You know I will never talk about her cruelly, but it was her fault. Her fault for leaving. Something inside her couldn't cope with this life, and it had nothing to do with you. I know that because there is nothing you could ever do to make me leave," he said, kissing the top of her head.

"Promise?" she whispered, love shining in her eyes as she stared up at her dad.

He nodded and made an "X" over his heart.

Sam turned to Charlotte and her face turned red. "Sorry, Charlotte. You must think I'm such a brat."

Charlotte shook her head rapidly, knowing what she wanted to say, feeling like she was here at this moment for a reason. "I know how you feel, Sam. I get it. My dad walked out on us when I was twelve."

Wyatt turned to her sharply. She knew he must be doing the math. When they knew each other, she'd had a dad at home. She dragged her gaze from his and turned her attention back to Sam, ready to lay it all out there. The truth was tucked away inside, and she had carried it around with her like an old scar that she kept hidden under the makeup of a perfectly organized life. Now she'd just removed it all and let them see the real her. But she had to. After what Wyatt had revealed to her . . . she owed him. She owed herself.

"Really?" Sam said, sitting down.

"Really."

"He just left?" Sam whispered, the anger in her eyes disappearing.

"Without warning. He was my hero. He was . . . a cop. He was the nicest, strongest, best dad I could have ever asked for," she said, stopping when her voice cracked, unsure what to do with this emotion she was so used to keeping under wraps.

But this . . . this sucked. She blinked back tears as she stared at the girl who needed to hear this story so badly. She saw herself in Sam, saw the reflection she'd forgotten. She saw the vulnerability stamped so proudly on her face. She saw the insecurity. The self-blame. She saw the anger. The fear. The fear that her other parent would leave.

"The last morning I saw him, he was supposed to come to school for career day."

Wyatt made a noise and ran a hand over his jaw. He knew. The day *he* had disappeared, so had her father.

"What happened?"

Charlotte leaned against the island, not feeling as awkward anymore or as vulnerable. Words tumbling out without the road-blocks. "I stood in front of the entire school and introduced him even though he wasn't even there. But I was so sure he'd show up. I was also sure that I'd get the cool kids to like me once they saw how awesome he was."

Sam cringed.

"Yeah . . . so clearly that plan was an epic fail," she said with a laugh, glancing up at Wyatt.

He didn't share her smile. His gorgeous brown eyes were glistening and his jaw was clenched, his hands in his pockets. She knew neither of them were going to tell Sam that was the day he'd disappeared from her life, but it hung there between them, another bond they shared.

"Did you . . . did you ever see him again?" Sam asked, her lower lip trembling.

Charlotte shook her head. "I looked for him . . . for a long time," she said softly. "In the grocery store, at the mall, at the coffee shop he used to go to. Outside work. Then I stopped looking. One day I just sort of gave up, because I realized that maybe I didn't want someone like him in my life. Because for a long time I blamed myself." She stopped speaking for a moment, trying to take a breath against the weight in her chest. She had looked for Wyatt too on occasion. On her walks home with Olivia. Her days had been bleak, then, without Wyatt to listen to her.

"You did?" Sam whispered.

Charlotte nodded. "I thought maybe if I just helped out more around the house, or maybe if I'd just done a better job of taking care of my little sister, or maybe if I'd been able to make my mom happier he wouldn't have left. But that was wrong. It took me so many years to realize that there was nothing any of us could have done to keep him. Because it wasn't in him. Some people walk, not because of the life they are given, but because of something in them that makes them decide they can't deal anymore."

Sam's face was white. "Do you miss him?"

Charlotte looked away for a moment, staring at the clock on the oven, searching for words that she didn't know she had, searching for an answer to somehow give this girl some comfort, to let her know that her entire life wouldn't be filled with this ache every day. "I did miss him for a long time. His memory slowly faded, and I know that sounds kind of sad, but it doesn't have to be. In some ways it helped me. I was angry for a long time. Then I was sad. Then angry again," she said with a little laugh, relieved to see that Sam almost smiled. "But I also appreciated the people in my life who helped me. I . . . I will never be able to repay my grandma for being a constant source of support. I don't know what we would have done without her. My mom wasn't exactly the most stable person, and a lot of times she wasn't able to take care of us. We knew that we could always rely on Grandma Ruby. So I learned to look at the people who were in my life differently. It made me love my grandma even more. Your dad is strong. He's so trustworthy and he loves you more than anything," she said.

Sam's gaze went from Charlotte to Wyatt. "I know. Thanks," she whispered.

"You're welcome. You can talk to me about this anytime. Any questions, or if you just want to talk about how you're feeling. I know there will be days it sucks and days you'll be able to be just fine. But you have your dad and having someone like him on your side is . . , everything." she said, not even thinking twice about her words.

Sam walked over to her and threw her arms around her. Charlotte held on tight, an unexpected wave of maternal affection, love, flowing through her.

Sam pulled back suddenly, looking almost back to normal. "I'm sorry your dad took off on you, Charlotte. And thanks for talking about it with me."

"Thanks, and you're so welcome," Charlotte said.

Sam turned to Wyatt. "So, Dad, maybe I can get out of this assignment with a note from my dad? You can make it like dramatic or something. Or maybe official police business?" she said with a charming smile.

Wyatt gave a short laugh. "I'll see what I can do. Don't worry about this."

She left the paper on the kitchen table. "I'm, um, going to finish the rest of my homework. Thanks, Charlotte. Are you still coming to *The Nutcracker*?"

Charlotte smiled. "Wouldn't miss it for the world."

Sam broke out into a huge smile that made Charlotte's heart squeeze before Sam ran out of the room.

"Hey," Wyatt said, his deep voice gruff, as he crossed the room to stand in front of her. He grasped her arms gently and she looked up at him and she wanted to stay there forever. She wondered if this was the moment that she'd remember forever. Because what was shining in his eyes was something she'd never seen before from anyone.

"I'm sorry, Char. I'm sorry I wasn't there that day your dad didn't show. I'm sorry I wasn't there to walk you home," he said, raising his hand and gently cupping one side of her face.

All those old memories and that vulnerability seemed to wash away as a ripple of awareness, of need for him, tore through her. Her breath caught in her throat as her gaze wandered over his hard features, and he leaned down to kiss her, slowly, softly, innocently, almost like the kind of kiss she had imagined at twelve. She ran her fingers over his stubble and stood on her tiptoes, threading her hands in his thick hair. He made a noise deep in his throat that sent desire pooling in her abdomen. Wyatt could be everything at once to her, he could be strong and hard and tender and sweet and she didn't know what she liked best. Maybe it was him, like this, all walls down like her, that she liked best. He backed her up against the island, his body hard against hers and then lifted her onto the counter. His hands were tangled in her hair and she forgot all about self-preservation.

"Aren't you glad Charlotte made you clean up the kitchen?"

They both froze, and Charlotte stared at Wyatt in horror as he slowly pulled back from her to look at Sam. She was standing in the doorway looking like it was Christmas morning. She sauntered in, clearly pleased with their discomfort, and grabbed her backpack. "Carry on, kids," she said, before skipping out of the room.

Once she left, Wyatt turned back to look at her, his eyes sparkling. "So much for not letting her know," he choked, lifted her off the island and giving her a quick kiss.

Charlotte let out a small laugh, trying to hide the sudden jolt of panic she felt at Sam seeing them together like that. Sam had obviously been thrilled.

But this was dangerous . . . letting her get excited about a relationship that might not be here when Christmas was over.

*   *   *

"Why don't you borrow something? I just bought three different dresses and they arrived already," Charlotte said, reaching under the bed and pulling out the box. She didn't want to add that the reason she'd bought three new dresses was because she was going to see *The Nutcracker* with Wyatt. Or spend the holidays with Wyatt. That had a nice ring to it. But she didn't want to look so chipper in front of Olivia.

Olivia's eyes twinkled and she sat on the bed. "Oh, because of that hot cop you're dating?"

Charlotte couldn't help the . . . *giggle* that escaped her mouth. It occurred to her that she didn't think she'd ever *giggled*. In her entire life. Just the word giggle sounded so out of character for her. There had never really been a point in her life or her childhood that she'd ever been filled with such hope. Like, being with Wyatt . . . and Sam, made her feel like maybe she could belong to a family of her own, one where she could make traditions and be loved and give love. One that wasn't filled with selfish people trying to steal her joy or relying on her to keep it all together. Sure, Grandma Ruby had never done that to her, but Grandma Ruby did come with ties, because of her mother. Coming here at Christmas meant dealing with her mother, and some Christmases she just couldn't do that. She had thought that she and Olivia would have their own

Christmases forever and that eventually this would extend to their own families . . . but Olivia had shut her out the last two Christmases, and Charlotte had been on her own in the city. She'd just sat in her small condo and worked. She glanced over at Olivia now and noticed her face had fallen.

"What's wrong?"

Olivia's eyes filled with tears and her chin wobbled. "Ugh. I'm sorry. I'm sorry for being a shitty sister, Char. I pushed you away for two years and now you're offering me your dresses like I didn't act like an idiot."

Charlotte shook her head, despite the heaviness in her heart, despite the deep hurt that had taken root, which had made it even harder to trust people because Olivia had been the last person she'd ever expected to turn her away. But she wasn't a shitty sister, and she knew that. She was a product of crappy parents and a crappy husband and she'd made a mistake. She didn't need Charlotte stomping on her when she was down. "That again. You haven't been. You've got to move on, we already went over this. Stop torturing yourself," she whispered.

Olivia curled her legs up and wiped her eyes with her sleeve. "I have. I shut you out, even at Christmas. I know it's too late, and it can't take away the hurt you must have felt, but I want you to know that they were the worst Christmases I ever had," she said, her voice breaking.

Charlotte wrapped her arms around herself, hating that a part of her was happy that she hadn't been the only one hurting.

"I felt awful. And I hated Will for pushing me away from you, and then I hated myself even more for letting him. Char, all I ever wanted was the perfect little family and I was willing to throw anyone under the bus in order to get it. You know, the perfect couple, the perfect house, and the perfect kids. I wanted the Williams Sonoma table top with the Christmas dishes, the girls in red dresses with big red bows, the boys with little suits and red bow ties, the perfect tree, the stockings for Santa. I was willing to throw everything away for that Instagram life. I don't need that. I just need to have you back in my life again," she said.

Charlotte blew her nose and then reached across to hug her sister and held on tight. "I love you so much. And I don't blame you. I get it. I wanted that too. I've been collecting Christmas dishes from Pottery Barn every year after Christmas when they go on sale. I have this stash in my storage locker of Christmas things for when I have . . . I don't know what. I don't know why because I always said I never wanted a family and yet, I collect this stuff . . ."

"Maybe now you can use it with Wyatt and Sam," Olivia said with a smile.

"It's almost too scary to dream about, Liv. Like, all that stuff, if I imagine taking it out of the boxes and setting that table . . . what if it never happens? Or what if it happens and then it's gone? It's almost easier to not have it at all because I think having it and then having it disappear would be so much harder."

Olivia shook her head. "I don't want to stop believing that we can have our happily-ever-afters. I was an idiot with Will. A total idiot. But Wyatt isn't Will. Look at the way he shows up for Sam. I always imagined us sharing Christmas with our families. One of us could host Christmas Eve, one of us could host Christmas Day. And we could force Grandma Ruby to join us."

"What about Mom?"

Olivia rolled her eyes. "I hadn't let myself think that far."

Charlotte took a deep breath. "Yeah. Okay, enough about this stuff. It's too depressing. How about you pick a dress? I have three to choose from."

Olivia looked at the box and sighed. "They're your dresses, you should have first pick. Also, I don't think we're the same size anymore. Unless they have stretch in them," she said, wistfully opening the box.

"They all do, and one of them is a sweater dress. You could go up or down a size in most of them," she said, unfolding the deep burgundy velvet stretch dress.

"Wow, that's gorgeous," Olivia said.

"Then try it on!" She shoved the dress at Oliva.

"Okay," she said, looking a little more hopeful as she stood up. I'll just go over here," she said, opening the closet door and basically hiding inside it. A pang of sympathy shot through Charlotte at her sister's new insecurity. Olivia had never been insecure before. Charlotte was going to have to help her get through this. She was fully prepared to boost her sister's self-esteem. A minute later, she emerged from the closet and looked in the mirror and burst into tears as she stared at her reflection.

"I hate myself," she said, and slammed the door shut.

"What? No, you look fantastic! Liv, you had a baby like six months ago. You look amazing," she said, standing up and walking across the room.

They turned at the sudden gasp from the doorway. Charlotte stiffened as their mother stood there, wide-eyed. "Oh dear. Dawn has done something to your stomach," she said as she stared at Olivia.

Charlotte's mouth dropped open but Olivia just stood there in silent agreement, shame shining from her eyes.

Charlotte stood up, her hands balled into fists. "How dare you say that to your own daughter? How about telling her that she looks beautiful! That you're so proud of what she's trying to do with her life and what a good mother she is?"

Their mother placed her hand over her chest. "Stop making me sound like a bad mother."

"I don't have to! You do it to yourself!" Charlotte said, trying to keep her rage and resentment under control, even though it was starting to hiss out of her like a wild, uncontrolled balloon losing air.

"What is going on in here?" Grandma Ruby said, appearing behind Wendy. She glanced at Olivia. "Oh, my dear, don't you look lovely."

Charlotte crossed her arms and smiled at her mother. "Like that. Take some notes."

Their mother turned in a huff and stomped out of the room.

"I'm glad everyone is filled with the spirit of the season," Grandma Ruby said, before slowly turning and leaving the room, her shoulders hunched slightly, her gait slower than usual.

Charlotte had the urge to just run out of the room. Sympathy for her grandmother flooded her—she didn't deserve to have a daughter who was so self-absorbed and miserable. She'd had such a hard life and she was so the opposite of their mother. And her sister . . . who was currently scrambling out of that dress as though she'd been told it was filled with fleas. She didn't want to deal with any of this. She wanted to run out of the house . . . down the street to Wyatt's. For the first time in years, she didn't want to be alone. She wanted to be with . . . him. But she wouldn't do that to her sister.

"Hey, don't listen to mom," she said, when Olivia had wrapped herself in her robe again.

"She's right. My stomach is a disaster. It's like a deflated balloon with some air still stuck inside that refuses to come out."

"Seriously, enough. That's crap. You gave birth to an eight-pound—"

Olivia winced. "Almost ten-pound—"

Charlotte shuddered. "See, right there? You should be proud of that! I'd be curled up in a ball in the corner, still reliving the horrors or childbirth."

Olivia almost laughed. "It *was* really bad, Char."

Charlotte nodded. "Yeah . . . so instead of listening to Mom, who has to be the center of attention at all times, listen to me. You're a gorgeous woman and you've always been gorgeous. So your body isn't the same as it used to be, that's not a bad thing."

Olivia nodded. "I know you're right. I know I'm supposed to be grateful. I know that there are so many women out there who are struggling with infertility and would slap me if they could for being so superficial. But I can't help feeling . . . uncomfortable in this body. I was, all through my pregnancy too. The boobs. The hips. All of it. I just feel self-conscious."

Charlotte nodded. "I know I don't know what you're feeling, and I can't give you wise words from someone who's had a baby. But I can tell you that you look great. You don't have to look like you did before Dawn to still be beautiful."

Olivia nodded. "Or I can buy SPANX."

"They do solve a lot of problems for all of us. Baby or not," Charlotte said with a smile.

"I missed you, Char."

Charlotte reached down to hug her sister. "Me too."

CHAPTER SEVENTEEN

SEPTEMBER 1995
TORONTO

"Wendy, are you home?" Ruby frowned, worry running through her when she knocked on her daughter's apartment door for the third time. She knew she had to be home. They had confirmed this time, and she was supposed to babysit her adorable granddaughter, Charlotte, today.

When she heard Charlotte crying she tried the doorknob, knowing she'd break the door down if she had to. The door opened and she sighed with momentary relief when she spotted little Charlotte running down the hallway and straight into her arms.

"Grammy, Mama's sleeping," she said. The panic in her voice told her that it wasn't good. Ruby swooped the precious three-year-old into her arms and marched through the apartment, frantic to find Wendy, panic rising in her throat at the absolute disarray in the home.

Dread filled her when she spotted Wendy on the couch, one arm loosely dangling over the side, her hand on a bottle of some kind of alcohol. Relief flooded her when she could see that she was breathing. That relief gave way to a mix of rage and worry, a combination of emotions that she had become sadly accustomed to with her daughter.

"Wendy!" she said, shaking her daughter, relieved to see her open her eyes. She swallowed down the rage bubbling inside her, knowing she couldn't frighten Charlotte any further.

"Mom?" Wendy said, her words slurred as she rubbed her eyes.

"Get yourself together," she hissed, before turning away to look at Charlotte. Her heart squeezed at the sight of the little girl, watching her with wide eyes.

"Come, Charlotte. Grandma is going to get you some food and get you all dressed and you can watch a show, okay?"

Charlotte's perfect little rosebud mouth turned up in a wobbly smile, and she raised her arms. Ruby gladly lifted the precious babe and carefully stepped around the scattered toys and newspapers on the floor and made her way to Charlotte's bedroom. Once she had changed and cleaned her, they went to the kitchen where Ruby sliced an apple into bite-sized pieces alongside small pieces of cheese. She filled up Charlotte's sippy cup with water and sat her in front of the television. "Grandma is going to do some clean up. You sit here and enjoy your snack and show, okay, dear?"

Charlotte looked up and grinned. Ruby leaned down and kissed the top of her head, determined to put on a cheerful face even though her stomach was churning. She could hear the water running in the bathroom.

She began picking up the litany of odds and ends scattered around the apartment while Big Bird was rattling off a list of his favorite letters in the background. In ten minutes she'd managed to make the main living area presentable and then turned her sights on the filthy kitchen. She glanced back at Charlotte every few minutes while she scrubbed the pile of dishes in the sink and then focused on cleaning the counters. By the time Wendy joined her in the kitchen she put a pot of coffee on and looked at the daughter she was so worried about . . . and so disappointed in.

Wendy held up her hand. "Before you start lecturing me, you should know that it's been a really rough week. Mac has been working double shifts, and we've been arguing nonstop."

Ruby folded the dish towel and searched for words that could help this situation instead of pushing Wendy into a deeper hole. The coffee percolated, the sound louder than that of the rain drumming against the windows. How she wished this was just a normal visit, that her daughter had found happiness and was living a happy life as a wife and mother. She wiped dry two mugs that she'd just cleaned and poured the coffee. She walked over to the table and joined her daughter, choosing the seat that would allow her to keep an eye on Charlotte. It didn't go unnoticed that Wendy hadn't even bothered to say a word to her daughter or give her any kind of affection as she walked by her.

"I'm not here to lecture you, Wendy. I know how hard life can get, but you can't just check out and do what you want when you're a mother."

Anger flashed in Wendy's eyes before she took a sip of the black coffee. "This is where you start with your high-handed lectures about how rough your life was, right?"

Ruby sat back in the chair and folded one leg over the other, determined not to lose her temper. "Don't make this about me, it's not. I'm just trying to show you that I'm not judging you, that I get it."

"Well, you don't get it, because you never had a husband."

Ruby wrapped her hands around the hot mug. Yes, Wendy had pointed that out to her dozens of times growing up, and it never failed to make Ruby feel inadequate. Maybe she'd even spoiled Wendy out of guilt for not having a father in her life. The image of Harry popped into her mind and, not for the first time, she wondered what life would have been like with him. Maybe all this could have been avoided. Maybe her daughter would have been able to cope with life more easily. "I can listen. I may not have had a husband, but I had different challenges, and if I'd decided to just ignore my responsibilities then we wouldn't have had a roof over our heads or food in our mouths. And I was young. What's your excuse? You and Mac were married for over five years before you decided to have a baby. You two have had your fun. It's time to grow up. Why don't you tell me what's really bothering you instead of trying to turn the tables and make this about your childhood?"

Wendy rolled her eyes. "Right. Of course, nothing is ever your fault, is it?"

Ruby leaned forward, ready to dish it out harshly in order to make her point. "It doesn't matter. It doesn't matter that your childhood may have been less than perfect or that you didn't have a father. What matters is right now. You are an adult. You take responsibility for your own actions. You get to decide the type of mother you want to be. Blaming me for your problems won't make your problems go away. Only you can make your problems go away. So either take my offer to help you or I will take that little girl and raise her myself."

"Fine. I hate my life. I hate motherhood."

"Well, that's a start. I think many people feel that way at times. Maybe you have no balance here. What about an outside hobby? A job? Maybe you need to get out of this apartment more."

Wendy toyed with the red handle on the mug, tracing it with her finger. "Mac has crazy hours, and I don't know how we'd swing that. I don't even know what I'd want to do."

"Have you told Mac how you feel?"

She shrugged, turning her gaze to the rain-smeared window. "He has his own issues with work. A few months ago something pretty awful happened, and he hasn't been the same."

"How often have you been drinking like this?"

Wendy shrugged. "Not that often."

"Wendy."

Wendy put her face in her hands. "Lately it's been a few times a week. I thought Mac was going to be home today, that's why I drank last night."

"You can't do that again. You're a mother. Before anything else, Charlotte's safety comes first."

Wendy nodded, closing her eyes.

Ruby reached across the table, determined to find a solution. "Why don't I bring Charlotte back to The Christmas House? She loves all the decorations. I can keep her for the week. Maybe you can have a breather. Take some time to regroup. You and Mac can have some alone time too."

Wendy nodded. "That would be nice."

Ruby took a deep breath, relieved that she had come up with a solution, but the heavy burden of knowing her daughter was not coping well still sat in her stomach like rocks. "Okay. Go and pack a bag for Charlotte."

Wendy nodded and stood.

Ruby took their empty mugs of coffee and placed them in the sparkling sink, suddenly feeling older than her years. Wendy's childhood *and teen years played across her mind, and Ruby frantically thought of all the ways she hadn't been a good enough mother. She needed Wendy to pull it together.*

"Gamma?"

Ruby jumped and looked down at Charlotte who was standing beside her. "Yes, sweetie?"

"TV wif me, Gamma?"

Ruby reached down and scooped Charlotte in her arms, giving her a giant hug. "I'm going to do even better. You can come and stay with Grandma and sleep over. We can bake treats together and read stories and maybe fly a kite. Does that sound fun?"

Charlotte's eyes were wide and she nodded, smiling at Ruby before throwing her arms around her and cuddling her tightly. Ruby held onto her darling granddaughter, promising she would do better, that she wouldn't give up on any of the people in this home. Charlotte held onto her, and Ruby prayed over her, prayed that she would get out of this childhood without her heart being broken.

*   *   *

"Dad, do you want to do my bun?" Sam asked, poking her head into Wyatt's room.

Hell, if his heart didn't squeeze, reminding him what a sap he was. He stood there, across the room from the girl who had been his entire life for so long, and images of her raced across his mind like clips from an old movie. They'd been to hell and back. And on his worst days, she'd been his only reason to keep going. Her sweet little smile, her bubbly laugh, her unlimited hugs. What she'd needed, he'd been able to give. She'd made him into a better man. And somehow, when the days had seemed to drag on forever, they'd turned into years, years he wished he could erase only to live again, to have one more shot at doing it better, at getting to be a dad to that amazing little girl.

He'd give anything to hear her say "Daddy" again. But "Dad" was his new name, as of last year, and it made him want to hold onto these years even more tightly, despite her need to grow.

He cleared his throat and blinked a few times, the image of his six-year-old ballerina giving way to the beautiful young woman in front of him now. A bun? He'd take it, any day.

"Sure, have a seat on the chair," he said, pointing to the chair in the corner beside the window. "I hope I still remember how to do this," he said, taking the pins, brush, and spray bottle from her hands and placing them on the side table.

"I'm sure you will. You turned into a real pro. Cat says Scott never really mastered it and that she has to secretly add more bobby pins after he finishes her buns," she said as he brushed her hair into a smooth ponytail.

He laughed. "Well, this isn't easy. I just make it look easy," he said.

"Ha. Funny. Are you wearing that tonight?" she asked, shifting slightly to look him up and down.

He frowned. "Why, what's wrong with this?"

She shrugged, and he paused as he twisted the ponytail. "It's okay. But if you really want to impress Charlotte you should wear one of those suit jacket things over your shirt."

"Really?" he said, carefully adding pins as he made her hair into a bun and glancing at himself in the mirror.

"It's impressive. You look good when you dress up," she said.

Huh. "Well, I'll put one on then."

She nodded. "Sure. So, no offense, but one of the teachers will do my makeup for the show. I don't really trust you with a makeup brush."

He stifled a laugh. "Good, because I don't trust myself either."

She hopped out of the chair and leapt across the room. He had no idea where she got her grace from. His chest swelled with pride as he watched. She stopped at the door and stared at him for a moment, looking like a child for the briefest of seconds, reminding him of all their conversations about life and love and whatever it was she was thinking about. Being her father, her only parent, had forced him to deal with his own past as best he could, in order to give her what she needed. At night he'd lie awake, especially after a difficult parenting day and wonder if he'd ever be enough. If he'd ever have the right answers, if he'd ever be able to give her enough love, if he'd ever be able to fill the hole that her mother had left behind. His biggest fear would be that she grew up and looked back on her childhood with sadness. He knew that pain, and he knew it was the kind of pain that could stop him without notice as a memory barreled into him without warning. He wanted Sam to be able to look back and have all the good memories be greater than the bad; he hoped that her happiness would shine through the sorrow.

"Are you and Charlotte coming backstage after the show?" she asked, pausing in the doorway.

"Of course. You'll do great, Sam," he said. He'd already picked out a dozen yellow roses for her, and the bouquet was waiting in the trunk of his car so he could surprise her.

She smiled. "Thanks, Dad."

* * *

243

"Hold on," Charlotte said, stopping at the edge of the downtown core. "I need a moment to soak this all in."

Each store had fresh evergreen boughs draped across their storefronts, with red bows and twinkling white lights. Each lamppost had a lit boxwood wreath, and the sidewalks were filled with shoppers carrying packages and bags. Victorian carolers strolled the sidewalks, and the smell of roasting chestnuts filled the air. Soft tufts of feathery snow tumbled from the sky. It was straight out of a Hallmark Christmas movie.

Or maybe it was being with Wyatt that made it feel so special. Maybe if everything was removed and it was just her and him, she'd have the exact same feeling. He'd picked her up and they had driven into town, planning on wandering through the shops before they went to watch *The Nutcracker*. Something had felt different the moment he'd picked her up. That barrier she had tried to keep up had been lifted, and she wasn't afraid anymore.

"So where else should we go?" she asked, as they walked down Main Street.

Wyatt reached for her hand as they strolled. "Are you hungry?"

She shook her head, heady with the warmth and excitement of holding onto him. "Not really, but if you are I don't mind stopping. There's this nonstop supply of baked goods at my grandmother's, especially this close to Christmas. I think I may have eaten a dozen cookies today alone," she said with a laugh.

"I can't wait to have some. Your grandmother's baking is legendary," he said as they turned down one of the quieter side streets. There was a small park with a skating rink. Multicolored lights were strung around the rink, and it was bustling with skaters and people buying hot chocolate.

"How long do we have before we head to *The Nutcracker*?"

He glanced at his watch. "Half an hour. If we're walking we could slowly start over there," he said.

She nodded. "Okay, let's walk over. It's a gorgeous night," she said, not wanting any of this to end. It was a snow globe moment, and it had come to life for her.

They strolled and took in all the window displays, and Charlotte didn't think she'd ever been this happy. She swallowed past the lump of emotion in her throat and looked up at the man partly responsible for making her feel this way. They were headed somewhere she'd never been and she didn't want to stop it. She didn't want tonight to end.

If she were a dreamer, she'd imagine doing this every year with Wyatt, holding hands, lightly swinging between them as they walked past the shops. She would have looked forward to their evening after the shopping, maybe sitting by the fire, drinking a glass of wine . . . instead, she was almost fearful of where this was all going. He wasn't sixteen, and neither was she. He was on his second phase of life, and she hadn't even really lived her first phase.

"I think I forgot how magical this town was," she said, shooting him a smile.

"How's your sister doing?" he asked as they approached the end of downtown.

She took a deep breath of the fresh air. "Good. Much better than before. I think she has a bit of a challenging road ahead as a single parent, but she can handle it."

He gave a short laugh. "Yeah, it's a bit of a rude awakening for most. Then there are those really irritating people who fall into it naturally and make it look so easy."

She laughed. "You make it look pretty easy. I'd say you're one of them."

He stopped, his eyes growing serious. "Thank you. But it wasn't always like this. And I don't ever feel like it comes naturally to me. It's been a rough year with Sam. There are days when I wonder if I'm screwing it all up, if I'll ever be enough for her, if I'll ever be able to repair the damage that's been done," he said, his voice gruff, a flash of vulnerability softening his otherwise hard features.

A lump formed in her throat. "I think that, even though her mother left and that's something that will always bring her pain, having such a devoted parent who puts her first and makes it known how loved she is, will go so much further than you think. I can't imagine what it's like being a parent all the time, let alone a single parent, but from someone who's spent time with Sam one on one and with the both of you, there is no doubt in my mind that Sam is secure and knows how much her dad loves her," she said, shocking herself at how easily that had all come out.

Wyatt didn't say anything for a moment, and she almost thought maybe she'd gotten it all wrong. What did she know about kids anyway? Who was she to make these sweeping generalizations? But he blinked a few times and then grabbed her hand and started walking again. This feeling, her hand in his warmer, larger one, made her . . . want this. Him. More.

She wanted more Wyatt.

She didn't have the words to articulate what she wanted, and a part of her just wanted to enjoy this moment. Because she never would have expected this. She was supposed to come to Silver Springs to help her grandmother for the Christmas season. She was now knee-deep in family and friends and small-town life. This had been her worst nightmare a month ago. Never mind the fact that Wyatt was a cop. But now she was living a dream that she hadn't even known she wanted.

Wyatt held open the door to the Silver Springs Performing Arts Centre and they were barely able to inch their way in. They stayed huddled together as people lined up and waited for their tickets to be taken. As they stood together, Charlotte became aware of Wyatt's larger frame against hers, and she slowly allowed her shoulders to relax, to soften her back from its usual ramrod-straight position, and it was almost as though she was leaning against him.

Charlotte did not lean against or on anyone. Maybe it was just an inch or so, a gentle sway. But he was right there, his hard body against hers, and her breath caught as emotion and desire swirled together like the red and white candy cane decorations hanging from the ceiling. This feeling, this kind of contact, this kind of instinctive support . . . had this been what she'd been missing out on in life? Is this what she wanted?

"Hey! I thought I'd run into you," a man around their age said, working his way through the crowd to them. A woman with dark hair who looked somewhat familiar was by his side.

"Charlotte, this is Scott and Meghan."

Scott reached out to shake her hand and Charlotte shook it warmly, liking him immediately. "Nice to finally meet you. I was beginning to think Wyatt had made you up," Scott said with a warm laugh.

Charlotte joined him in a laugh while Wyatt gave him a deadpan stare. "I've heard a lot about you." She turned to Meghan, who was watching them with amusement. "And you seem so familiar."

She smiled. "I run the new Cheese Boutique in town."

They stood all together, making small talk for a little while before it was time to go inside. All of this felt so right. Every time she was with Wyatt it felt right. They were out in the world, in a crowd, and yet she still felt like they were in their own little bubble.

"Was Sam excited tonight?" Charlotte said as they finally made their way to their row.

He nodded with a grin and pointed to their seats. "Definitely."

"These are great," she whispered. They were in the fifth row with aisle seats.

"I learned my lesson the first year she was in ballet. I went online to buy the tickets literally five minutes after they went on sale, and I was in the back row. Now, I'm logged in with my mouse pointed to the 'purchase tickets' button five minutes before they go on sale," he said, leaning close to her as they spoke.

She laughed, feeling warm and excited. "I guess everyone wants to see their kids."

"I was thinking after the show, I could drop you off at Ruby's . . . or you can come over for a drink. Sam's sleeping at Scott's house," Wyatt said.

A blaze of heat tore through Charlotte as she stared at him. *This is what people do, Charlotte. You want to. You want him desperately. You've waited a lifetime for Wyatt.* She wanted to spend every moment with him. She wanted exactly what he wanted. "I'd like that," she said, forcing her voice to sound calm and not at all like her stomach was doing successive cartwheels.

He took her hand as the curtain opened and they were immersed in sugar plums and music and the magic of Christmas. At some point during the performance, Wyatt placed his arm around her shoulders, and she leaned close to him, taking every ounce of whatever he was offering. She breathed in the outdoorsy, fresh scent of his cologne and didn't think she'd ever get enough of him. Excitement swirled through her veins in time to the music, and she smiled as she spotted Samantha leaping across stage with the other soldiers. "She's fantastic," she whispered to him.

He smiled, pride shining in his eyes. One of the things she loved most about him was the kind of father he was. Watching him as a parent revealed so much of his character, his heart, and made her want to trust him with everything.

When the performance was over, they walked backstage amid the flurry of parents and excited ballerinas. Samantha spotted them and waved frantically, making her way through the people. "You were fantastic, sweetheart," Wyatt said, kissing her on the cheek.

"You were amazing," Charlotte said, laughing as Samantha threw her arms around her neck.

"We have flowers for you in the truck. I can drive you over to Scott's and can bring them home for you if you'd like."

Sam rolled her eyes. "Change of plans. Cat and I got in a fight, and I'm not going. I'll come home tonight."

Charlotte held her smile and glanced over at Wyatt. His jaw was clenched, but to give him credit he quickly smiled. "Sure. Uh, is this something Scott and I can help sort out?"

She shook her head. "Nope. Betrayal of the worst kind. But I'm going to go change," she said.

"Okay. I'll go pick up the SUV and pull up in the parking lot. Wait inside until you see me, okay?"

Sam rolled her eyes and turned back into the crowd.

Wyatt glanced down at Charlotte. "Welcome to my life. Ten bucks says she and Cat are BFFs by morning," he grumbled, and she couldn't help but laugh even though she was just as disappointed as he was.

They walked in the direction Wyatt had parked, moving with the throng of other theatergoers. "I don't think anyone does Christmas like this town," she said, wanting to break the awkward silence.

"Are you going to be here for New Year's?"

Her heart pounded and she nodded. "I am now."

He squeezed her hand. "I'm back at work that night, but my shift ends at 11:30. The whole downtown is blocked off and everything is open. The toboggan hill, the skating rink, restaurants. I probably won't be able to make it back to Ruby's to pick you up and get out here on time. But we can meet. Town square, in front of the clock tower?"

She'd meet him anywhere. "Perfect."

They reached the passenger side of his SUV, and he unlocked it. Instead of opening it, he hung back for a moment. "I'm sorry. I'm sorry that none of our time together has ever been . . . just the two of us."

Her heart squeezed in her chest and she took a step closer to him, drawn to him like that night on the deck when he'd looked so vulnerable. Wyatt made her want closeness when she'd been able to deny it for so long. He made her want to lean on someone, to love someone. He made her want someone to love her. Him.

Heavy, plump snowflakes—her favorite kind—tumbled out of the sky and around them, reminding her of her snow globe fantasy. She'd always wanted to be one of those people in those idyllic settings. Wyatt standing there, white snowflakes dusting his coat, brown eyes locked on hers, handsome face filled with tenderness . . .

it didn't get more ideal than this. Maybe this was once in a lifetime ideal. For her, it was.

His gaze went from her eyes to her lips, and her mouth dropped open, her breath becoming shallow. He swallowed up the distance between them and raised his hands to her face.

"I just can't let the night end without kissing you. God, I wanted to kiss you the moment we stopped kissing. I can't stop thinking about you." He leaned down to kiss her, and she was pretty sure each kiss was even better than the last.

His lips were hard and soft at the same time, his hands threaded in her hair, and she held onto him like she'd never held onto anyone. He kissed away every ounce of doubt and filled her with a promise of a love and passion so intense that she forgot who she had been before this moment.

Wyatt's phone vibrated in his jacket pocket and he pulled back with a groan. He took out his phone and stared at the screen for a moment. "It's Sam. Apparently we're taking five thousand years and she might as well go in some random person's car."

Charlotte laughed out loud at her sarcasm. "You know she's all you."

His lips twitched. "That's what scares me."

CHAPTER EIGHTEEN

DECEMBER 2004
SILVER SPRINGS

"I can't do this. Mac left us. You have to take the girls."

Ruby's mouth dropped open, her gaze going from her daughter's red-rimmed eyes to her two adorable granddaughters standing on the porch like orphans. She wanted to yell at Wendy for doing this to them, for not sheltering them from the harsh reality of what had happened.

"Come in," Ruby finally whispered, grabbing hold of the two girls and wrapping them in her arms. "It will be okay, girls. Everything will be okay. Grandma is here," she whispered over and over again, like a prayer, wishing it to be true. Oh, how she wished her old friends were with her, ready with advice. She hadn't come this far to have her family fall apart now.

She pulled back and looked down at their big, sad eyes. "You go into the kitchen. Grandma has fresh cookies for you both. See, it's like I knew you were coming!" she said, forcing a bright smile.

"Yes, Grandma," Charlotte said, putting her arm around little Olivia and giving Ruby a look well beyond her young years. She worried about Charlotte the most. She had a seriousness about her that told Ruby she had been absorbing the dysfunction in their family home for too long. She needed to be a child. She needed to play and dream.

When they were out of earshot she turned to Wendy. "What happened?"

Wendy pursed her lips. "Oh, that's rich. They get the royal treatment and you're standing here telling me this is all my fault?"

Ruby crossed her arms. Her daughter had a way of making herself the victim all the time and she was not going to have it. Not this time. "It takes two to tango, Wendy. Your marriage was on the rocks for years, and I never saw you make any real efforts at saving it."

Wendy shook her head. "I knew you'd blame me."

"Mac shouldn't have left. He shouldn't have. But you could have done more. Besides, how do we know he won't come back?"

Wendy walked to the door and panic filled Ruby. "We both know he's gone. I need to get away and figure out what I'm going to do. Tell the girls I love them. I'll be back."

*   *   *

Charlotte stood in the doorway of the kitchen, hands on her hips, and took in the bustle. It was Christmas Eve, the night that her grandmother's heart shone bright for everyone who entered the house. Baby Dawn was in her high chair, banging it every now and then, sending Cheerios flying to the floor in a high arc while everyone hurried around.

The kitchen was filled with the scent of turkey and fresh cranberry sauce and baking. It was the epitome of holiday spirit. It was everything she had feared for so long; it was almost perfect. She was happier than she'd ever been in her entire life. She was in love. Completely. If someone had told her last Christmas, while she sat on her couch, eating turkey and stuffing and cranberry sauce from the Whole Foods buffet, that this Christmas she'd be spending it with family and in love with the hottest, most amazing man, she would have laughed. And laughed.

She took a deep breath and walked in to help with another round. Because of Wyatt, she was so happy that her feelings toward her mother were dialed down and she was ready to enjoy the evening.

"Guests will be arriving momentarily," Grandma Ruby said, tightening the knot on her holly and berry apron and signaling to Charlotte to bring the cranberry sauce bowls to the table.

"Well, everything looks perfect, Grandma," Charlotte said, gathering the bowls that were to be spread in different spots on the table.

The doorbell rang and she ran to it, knowing Wyatt and Sam would be on the other side. She opened the door and thought her heart was going to burst at the sight of them. Wyatt held the door open for Samantha, who walked in, all dressed up in a red sweater and dark jeans. "Merry Christmas, Charlotte," she said and threw her arms around her.

Charlotte hugged her back, warmth for the young girl seeping through her. She loved Sam and all her quirkiness, and she felt so much kinship for everything she'd gone through. "Merry Christmas, Sam. I think my grandmother has saved you a special stash of cookies," she said as she took her coat.

Sam laughed. "Best. Grandma. Ever. Is my aunt here yet?"

Charlotte shook he head. "She texted to say she was on her way," she said.

Sam nodded and walked toward the kitchen.

Charlotte turned to Wyatt, who'd already taken his jacket off and was standing there looking at her like he did when they were alone. She forgot how to breathe because the combination of her emotions and desire was making it impossible.

"Come here," he said, tugging her hand.

Her heart raced as he pulled her onto the porch. Before she could even be chilled by the blast of air, he'd wrapped her up in his arms and kissed her. Her arms wrapped around his neck and delved into the hair at the nape of his neck as she kissed him back. He kissed her with a hunger that made her want so much more. His body was hard and warm against hers, and she never wanted this feeling to end. She had never felt so alive, so wanted, so safe. She held on tighter when her knees wobbled, and he made a noise deep in his throat that made her contemplate quickly escaping to his house for privacy.

"Now, that's what I call a Merry Christmas!" Aunt Mary's voice boomed theatrically from the other end of the porch.

They both froze.

"Damn," Wyatt said softly against her lips, slowly lowering her to the ground. "My family has the worst timing ever," he said.

"I'm sure my family will present their own problems at some point," she laughed.

"I'll give you kids a moment. No need to hurry," Mary said, as she walked into the house.

Charlotte lowered her head to Wyatt's chest as the sound of the screen door bouncing against the frame announced that they were alone again.

"Sorry. I couldn't help myself. I missed you and then you were just standing there in this amazing red dress and looking at me . . . with everything I feel for you," he said, leaning back slightly, looking down at her.

"I think it was the best Merry Christmas greeting I've ever had," she said with a smile, tugging him closer.

"You think? Maybe I should try again and make sure," he said, the corner of his mouth twitching.

She laughed. "Maybe you should."

He leaned down and kissed her again, this time softly, slowly before he lifted his head. "There is so much I want to say to you, but I want to wait until we're alone and I can be sure that no one is staring at us from the window," she said.

She darted her gaze to the window, jumping as she spotted his aunt there. "How did you know?" she whispered.

He shut his eyes briefly. "Years of training. Years of knowing my aunt."

She laughed. "Maybe after dinner . . ."

"You can come to my place and we can have a glass of wine together?"

She nodded. "Okay. Is it bad that I'll be looking at my watch all night?"

"I already set a timer on my phone. Five hours max."

She grabbed his hand, and they walked into the house as cars started pulling into the driveway. "Okay, let's get this Christmas Eve started."

Half an hour later, almost everyone had been seated in the dining room and they were about to start dinner. The dining room was filled with people they knew from town who were on their own this year, as well as people they had never met before. It was the amazing thing about what her grandmother had started—the idea that people could come together to share in the magic of Christmas no matter their situation in life.

The house was filled with the aroma of roasting turkey and fresh baking, and Charlotte was almost heady with happiness. There was nothing more she could have wanted. Her grandmother was the picture of health, she'd rebooted her relationship with her sister, she had gotten to know and fall in love with her little niece . . . and then there were Sam and Wyatt. People she'd never imagined knowing.

The doorbell rang again, and Charlotte called out that she'd answer it. As much as she loved the evening so far, she was anxious to get started with the second half of her night.

She opened the door and every part of her body went soft. The air, the light, the joy, had been plucked out in one swoop, leaving her barren and weak, with nothing but the girl she used to be front and center.

Her father stood on the other side of the door, holding a red poinsettia. His green eyes, the ones that had always brought her comfort, were the same, except now they had deep creases beside them, from years of laughing . . . with other people. He didn't seem as tall as she remembered, not as robust, but then maybe it was because he'd lost his hero status the moment she realized he was never coming back.

She didn't know if it was her gasp or if it was intuition, but when she recoiled she stepped back into the warmth of Wyatt's strong body. His hands were on her shoulders and she didn't feel so alone then, just like that, with that one simple touch.

"What are you doing here?" she finally managed to whisper against the heaviness in her chest, the tightness in her throat. Despite wanting to, she took in the sight of him, ingesting every detail that she had missed, a part of her wishing that he could some-how say something that would make this okay. His hair was more gray now, only a sprinkling of dark hair there to remind her of the father she remembered.

"I know I should have called."

"No," she managed, her voice sounding hoarse to her ears. "No, it wouldn't have made a difference. Nothing would have made a difference. You know what might have made a difference? You call-ing the day after you left us. Or you showing up for career day when I stood in front of my school, staring at the clock with my heart breaking. I thought you were coming. Then I told everyone that you must have been heroically saving a family or something. But the truth was you just checked out of your role as a dad. This? A *poinsettia*, almost twenty years later? This is pathetic," she said, ready to shut the door.

"Charlotte, I know you hate me. I know what I've done is unfor-givable, but I just want a chance to talk. Ten minutes. Just give me ten minutes," he said, his eyes filling with tears that she knew should not affect her. Nothing about him should have affected her.

But it did. Enough to make her stomach churn relentlessly, enough to make her palms sweat, to make her body shake. Everything about him affected her because she had lived a lifetime trying to forget him, to get over him, and now that her life was finally going well . . . he was here to rip her heart open again and expose all her weaknesses and vulnerability.

She heard the startled gasps around her and knew she'd been joined by the rest of her family, Mary, and Samantha. She couldn't look up at Wyatt or she would lose it. His hands didn't move from her shoulders.

"What are you thinking? Why would you come back here and ruin our Christmas? How did you even know we'd all be here?"

The second her dad's eyes connected with Olivia's, she knew. Olivia's face went red then white. "I didn't mean to, Char . . ."

"You've been in contact with him?" Charlotte said, the words painful, echoing through the heaviness in her chest.

Olivia's eyes filled with tears and she bounced Dawn in her arms. "Barely. Dad texted me a few weeks ago and . . ."

Charlotte rubbed her temples, trying to digest what her sister was telling her, what her sister had failed to tell her. She wanted to yell at her. Olivia had lied to her again, shut her out again. Even after their long chats together, she hadn't brought it up. This was why family was too much too handle. This was why she lived alone in the city. They were killing her every chance they got. "How would he even have your number?"

Her mother opened her mouth and then shut it.

Charlotte's heart lurched. "So everyone was in on this."

"It's not like that at all, Char," Olivia said, her eyes filled with tears.

"Samantha and I will continue the Christmas dinner, Ruby, you stay with your family," Mary said, taking Dawn from Olivia.

Samantha looked over at Charlotte, her eyes wide and filled with confusion and pain. Charlotte forced a smile for the girl, angry that she was witnessing this, knowing this must be dredging up so many emotions for her. Wyatt squeezed her shoulders, and she turned to him. "You don't have to stay. Maybe you should go to Sam," she whispered.

"You stay with Charlotte, Dad. I'm fine. I'll help Aunt Mary," Sam said, giving Charlotte a quick hug. That gesture and selflessness brought tears to Charlotte's eyes, and she stood silent as Sam and Mary left the room with the baby.

"I know that no one wants me here," their dad began once the others had left.

"I think that's pretty obvious," their mother said with a snort, the red punch in her glass sloshing over the rim.

Grandma Ruby walked forward, suddenly showing her age, her rosy cheeks slowly whitening. "Mac, this is very poor timing. It's very selfish," she said, in that tone that could make the toughest of men squirm.

Their dad winced. "I know, but it was the only time I knew you'd all be under the same roof."

"Oh, I see, so get it all done in one shot instead of speaking to each of us individually. It's always whatever is easier for you, isn't it? Just like it was easier for you to walk out on us instead of sticking it out," their mother said.

It was the first time in a long time Charlotte agreed with her.

"That wasn't my motivation. I know that I will never be able to earn back your trust or pick up as though I haven't hurt all of you, but I wanted to explain why I left. I know it won't take away the years of pain, but I can at least tell you where I've been, why I left. I know that sending money every month is nothing, but at the time it was all I could do."

The room turned silent, and Charlotte and Olivia turned to their mother, whose face had turned red. She had always told them that their father left them without a penny, that he'd abandoned them physically and financially. Not that the money would have made up for him walking away . . . but it was something. Something that should have been said. A small beam of light in the vast darkness they'd been left with. Maybe it would have given her some comfort knowing that at least he'd cared enough to make sure they wouldn't be left on the street.

"You never told us that," Olivia whispered, her voice shaking.

Their mother lifted her chin. "It didn't matter. Abandoning a family with or without money is the same thing."

Grandma Ruby let out a long, wobbly sigh. "It was something that should have been shared, Wendy."

Their mother threw her hands in the air, the punch spilling over the rim this time. "Oh, great, so now we're going to just let him off the hook because he sent a check every month, and I'm the bad guy!"

"Of course not," Charlotte snapped, trying to rein in her anger toward all of them. She was mad at her mother for always manipulating the truth and making herself out to be a victim. She was mad at her sister for *still* not confiding in her after all they'd been through. And she was mad at Grandma Ruby for allowing her dad in. This Christmas should have been hers. And Wyatt's and Sam's. They'd all had their chances at love, this was supposed to be *her* turn. "But it would have been nice for us to process the truth instead of your version of it," she said.

"None of this should matter, he walked out on all of us! The real person to blame is Mom, for this ridiculous open door Christmas Eve policy!" her mother said, pointing her glass at Grandma Ruby.

"Don't do that, Wendy. Don't blame Ruby. I'm the one who came here uninvited," her dad said.

Her mom rolled her eyes. "No need to play the hero, Mac. Years too late for that."

Grandma Ruby stepped forward. "The only reason I let him in is because—"

"Yes, yes, your altruistic policy about letting everyone in at Christmas. You always have to be so self-righteous, don't you," her mother said, bitterness seeping through her voice.

"Mom!" Charlotte yelled, unwilling to let her grandma take the blame for this, even though her policy had made her night even worse. "Back off."

"It's all right, Charlotte. Your mother never understood why I do this, even though I've explained it to her before. But I've never shared it with you girls. Maybe it's time I do. Follow me into the kitchen—all of you. We can't scare away the guests," she said, walking toward the kitchen, her face drawn, her shoulders hunched slightly.

Wyatt grabbed Charlotte's hand and she clasped it, like a lifeline, one she'd never had before. She couldn't bring herself to look him in the eye, but for once she didn't feel so alone.

"You don't have to do anything or explain anything you don't want, Grandma," Olivia said, sitting down beside Grandma Ruby in the kitchen.

"Maybe it will put a lot of things into perspective for you. At the very least, it will give you something to think about and give you the real reason of how The Christmas House came to be," she said, extending her hand to Charlotte as well. Charlotte sat across from Olivia but avoided eye contact with her; there was too much to process. Wyatt stood behind Charlotte, his hand on her shoulder. Their parents stayed still, at opposite ends of the table.

"When I was eighteen, I was supposed to get engaged to a young man—your grandfather," she said.

Olivia made a little noise and Charlotte looked at her—this was what they'd overheard during the argument.

"The night that we were supposed to announce our engagement to my parents . . . he hung himself."

"Oh, Grandma," she said as Olivia reached across and took their grandmother's hand.

Grandma Ruby shook her head and sat up a little straighter. "I was pregnant, and we knew that we had to tell our parents. We hoped that by announcing our engagement and having a quick wedding it would have spared the rumors and been an easy fix. It was a different time, a different era, remember, in a very religious community."

"He couldn't face his family?" Charlotte whispered.

Grandma Ruby shrugged her shoulders. "I guess not. He couldn't face the repercussions."

"I'm so sorry, Grandma," Olivia said, squeezing her hand.

Grandma Ruby's face softened slight. "Thank you. I . . . I should have known better. I can look back now and see that he wasn't a man to build a life with. He had no honor. No courage."

Her father cleared his throat. "I want to explain to you girls, not for my sake, for both of yours. My leaving had nothing to do with you. Early on after becoming a cop, I witnessed something horrible. I wasn't mentally prepared, and I didn't take the counseling that was offered. I struggled. I wasn't there for your mother. I took a lot of my anger out on her. I couldn't sleep. And that day . . . Charlotte, that day I told you I'd be at your school, I had a complete breakdown. I left town, and a week later checked myself into a hospital," he said, his voice cracking and his eyes watering.

Charlotte tried to breathe against the weight in her chest, but she couldn't get a breath deep enough to relieve the ache. "And after that?" she whispered.

"I was there for almost a year. I started a new life—"

"With a new family?" Olivia asked.

He shook his head. "No. Never. I was afraid to come back. By that point your mother and I decided divorce was the only option. I couldn't face you girls, but I also couldn't face myself. I didn't trust myself anymore. I knew that I couldn't come back and be in your lives and then disappear again if I started having problems. I thought it was better if I just stayed away," he said, clutching the side of the table.

"Mom, you had contact with Dad? You never told us any of this," Charlotte said, trying to remain calm. She was trying to process everything her dad was saying, but it was too much.

Her mother glanced away. "He didn't deserve you girls knowing the truth."

"Oh, Wendy," Grandma Ruby said in a low voice, shaking her head.

"I don't need judgment. I was trying to do my best too," her mother said.

"Can we leave now? I can't deal with this right now," Olivia said, standing, her arms crossed.

Her father stood up. "I'll leave. I just wanted you to know that I'm here. I'm in town if you ever want to see me or talk. No pressure. Whatever you're comfortable with. I'm sorry for everything. And I'm sorry for ruining your Christmas Eve," he said, walking toward the door.

"Wait. How long are you in town?" Olivia asked.

He turned around. "For good. I've got a job in town. I'm staying in Silver Springs."

CHAPTER NINETEEN

**PRESENT DAY, DECEMBER 24
SILVER SPRINGS**

Ruby walked to the front door, no one noticing that the doorbell had rung again. It was late to welcome a guest, but she couldn't refuse. There were leftovers in the kitchen. Her bones felt weary tonight, and the composure she'd been struggling to hold onto threatened to run away with the falling night. She was supposed to have brought peace to her family this Christmas, but had in fact done the opposite. No one was speaking. That was fine because she didn't exactly feel like speaking to any of them right now either.

All their secrets had come out, including hers. Harsh words had been spoken, and she knew this would all have to be sorted out. But not tonight.

Everyone had gone their separate directions and she herself was ready to change into her nightgown and call it a night.

She suspected that Charlotte would be gone by morning—her eldest granddaughter had more in common with her than she had ever believed. That girl did not want to have her heart broken, and she wanted to rely on no one. Ruby couldn't blame her. But it wasn't right.

Thank goodness for Mary, who had managed to run the rest of the dinner and help her clean up. Good friends like that were treasures, and she'd learned long ago, so many years ago, the power of good friends that turned into family.

She paused at the door and schooled her features. She needed to welcome a needy person with an air of comfort and warmth and reassurance. She opened the door and the man standing there . . . robbed her of all her breath, every ounce of her composure. The breath she let out, from the very depths of her soul as she clutched the frame of the door.

Harry.

"Merry Christmas, Ruby," he said. His voice was as deep as she remembered, his features still so impossibly handsome after all these years. He still stood tall, his hair all white now, but combed back, without a strand out of place. His dark coat clung to his broad shoulders, and he was every bit the distinguished man he'd promised to be way back when.

"Harry, come in," she finally said, holding open the screen. Her heart couldn't seem to catch a normal rhythm, and she was pretty sure her cheeks were flushed.

It was a good thing her granddaughters weren't here or they'd probably call an ambulance, thinking she was about to have a heart attack. She fought the urge to smooth out her hair or fix her dress. They stood there silently. Maybe he was taking in this new version of her just as she was taking him in.

Years seemed to float and dance between them, as though they were nothing, and it felt as though no time had passed. She felt like that young woman again, barely twenty, pregnant, and vulnerable. She could still hear his deep voice, just like she'd heard it so many nights as she lay awake staring at the dark ceiling, as she imagined what it would have been like to be his wife. Would they have fallen in love? Would they have had more children? Would life have been so much better with him? But she had gone it alone.

She had thought that the path where she relied on no one would be safer. But standing here now, with this man in front of her, she wondered if the risky path would have been so much greater, if loving him would have been worth the risk. She wondered until it was almost suffocating, that realization that she might have been wrong. Like Charlotte was running toward safety, she had done the same.

"You look as beautiful as you did that last day I saw you," he said, his voice thick before he broke into a small smile that tilted one corner of his mouth upward.

And darn it if her stomach didn't flutter like it had that day. "You always were a gentleman," she said with a smile.

He ducked his head momentarily. "I hope you don't mind me showing up like this. But . . . I had this overwhelming urge to see you. I never forgot you, Ruby."

A shiver stole through her, catching her by surprise, almost overwhelming her. She clasped her hands together in an attempt to control her emotions. "Harry . . . I never forgot you either. I never forgot the kindness you showed me that day or in the following couple of years. I can pay you back now. I never used the money. I saved it."

He held up a hand and she noticed there wasn't a wedding band on it, but she pushed those thoughts away because the life he had led wasn't her business. "I would never take a dime from you, and I would have kept on helping you if you'd let me."

She smiled at him, the sincerity in his voice, the softness in his eyes making her warm. "I know you would have. But I needed to make my own way in the world. I needed to prove to myself, I needed to show my daughter, that I was capable."

He returned her smile, his eyes crinkling at the corners. "I'd say you made it, Ruby."

She paused for a moment, her mind racing, her body tingling with excitement. "Would you like to come in for a drink? I have leftovers and desserts."

His smile widened. "I was hoping you'd ask."

*   *   *

Ruby sat across from Harry at the dining room table half an hour later. She had put together a tray of cheeses and fruits, and he had poured them each a glass of brandy. The fire was roaring and the lights from the garland twinkled in the windows. Her heart fluttered, reminding her of the girl she used to be, of a life that she'd lived so long ago it almost didn't feel real. Excitement coursed through her, and she couldn't wait to hear all about him.

"So how did life treat you, Harry? Did you get married, have children?"

He held up his glass, and she lightly tapped hers to his. "Merry Christmas, Ruby," he said, before they book took sips. "Yes, I did get married. We had three children together and I now have eight grand-children," he said, smiling, his eyes twinkling.

She ignored the stab of . . . she didn't know what. Maybe regret that she hadn't lived a conventional life like that . . . or maybe that he'd had that life with someone else. That was silly of her, she realized. Selfish, too. Because she was happy for him. He had always been a good man, and even though he didn't know it, he'd been a source of strength for her.

"It sounds like a very happy, very full life," she said, placing a small piece of cheese on a cracker.

He nodded. "It was. I'm very blessed. My wife, Ellen, died five years ago. Too soon, but my family was there, and we got through her loss together."

Ruby wanted to reach across the table and place her hand over his. If he'd been anyone else, she probably would have. But with Harry, it didn't seem . . . appropriate. "I'm sorry. After a lifetime together it must be hard to move on."

He cleared his throat and gave her a nod. "She was a good woman. A dedicated wife and mother and a true life partner."

Ruby swallowed past the lump in her throat and took a sip of brandy. "I'm happy for you."

"Ruby, I'm too old to lie and waste time. I came here because you were always somewhere in my mind, in my thoughts over the years. If I'm going to be completely honest, you were in my heart. Sometimes it felt as though I were keeping a secret from Ellen, because you were always there, hovering. If I could go back, I would have tried again. I would have come back to this place and tried to talk to you again. But the young man I used to be didn't have the confidence to keep trying to woo a woman like you."

Ruby was glad she didn't have an underlying heart condition, because she would probably have been on the floor. Her cheeks were burning and her stomach was in so many knots it hurt to take a breath. She had been on his mind? In his heart? He would have tried with her again? A woman like her? There was so much to say, so many things she was afraid to say, that she could only keep her mouth shut.

He winced, finishing the rest of his brandy and standing. "I'm sorry. That was out of line. It was inappropriate. I should get going and let you enjoy your Christmas," he said.

Panic jolted through her and, this time, she did reach for him. She reached for the only man's hand she'd ever reached for since Richard. Surprise flickered across his eyes and, for one excruciating moment, she wondered if he'd pull away. But instead, he wrapped his larger, warmer hand around hers and sat back down. "It wasn't out of line, Harry. I . . . this is the best Christmas surprise I've ever had."

*   *   *

"She's coming, right?"

Wyatt forced his gaze up from the black coffee in his Christmas mug, to answer his daughter, who hadn't moved from the window for the last half hour. Sam was wearing her reindeer flannel pajamas, and her eyes were wide and filled with a vulnerability he had a hard time looking at. He fought an internal battle to protect his daughter with a truth or a lie.

No, he didn't think Charlotte was coming. Their last words the night before, the shitstorm her father had caused by showing up, the pressure of that family, all of it, told him that no, there was no way in hell Charlotte was coming over here on Christmas Day. He couldn't blame her—if it were just him sitting here. But Sam changed everything. The other part of him, the one that believed that, despite her own pain, Charlotte wouldn't do that to Sam. She would know what that would do to Sam.

"I'm sure she's just running late," he said, deciding he was going to believe in Charlotte for his daughter's sake.

"Is the coffee good? I still think she'd want coffee over hot chocolate, right? Like, Charlotte *loves* coffee," she said, looking back and forth from him to the window. Her growing panic and nervousness were making it hard for him to remain calm himself. He didn't know what he'd do if Charlotte didn't show up.

"Coffee is perfect," he managed.

"What about the cinnamon buns? Did you take them off the cooling rack? Are they on the Christmas plates? You didn't eat all the icing, did you?"

He clenched his teeth and forced a smile as he nodded, not even finding it the least bit funny that she was worried he'd eaten the icing. Sam had woken up early and had baked a batch of frozen cinnamon buns for Charlotte and set out all the Christmas plates and mugs. When he'd walked into the kitchen and seen it all out there, and the hope and joy on her face, he'd hated himself. He had allowed both of them to fall in love with Charlotte. It had taken him forever to almost forgive himself for choosing the wrong mother for Sam once. He would never forgive himself for Charlotte.

Sam's shoulders fell, and she continued to stare out the window. "Dad, what if she went back home? That was crazy last night. I felt so bad for her. Like . . ." She stopped speaking and turned to him, her eyes filled with tears, and his heart broke a little more. "If that were Mom, who just showed up when I was all grown up, I'd be so mad. Like Charlotte was. Sometimes I wonder what I'd do if Mom showed up here one day. A part of me would be really happy too. That's messed up," she said, tears falling from her eyes.

He stood up and walked over to her, hoping that the hugs that had comforted her for the last eleven years could still bring her the security she needed. Just when he thought he couldn't love his little girl any more, she wrapped her arms around his waist and placed her head on his chest.

"It's not messed up. It's a normal reaction. We can't control what the other people in our lives do, Sam. All we can control is how we react. We have to rise above it, even when we feel like we're drowning, when we want to wallow in the injustice of it. Otherwise we only hurt ourselves. We have to live our lives and be happy and count our blessings," he said, kissing the top of her head. He took this moment and held onto it, tucking it away in his memories, reminding him that even though Sam was growing up, she still needed him, he was still important to her.

"I felt so bad for Charlotte and I wanted to tell her, but it was so awkward. But a part of me felt . . . safe or something. I know it doesn't make sense. But I didn't feel so sorry for myself."

He nodded. "Because you got a real-life glimpse into someone else's pain. Some people get lucky the first time around and get the perfect family. And some of us don't. But we don't have to have a perfect family to have a great family. I wouldn't trade my years with you for anything."

She looked away for a moment. "I know I've been driving you crazy since we moved to Silver Springs," she said, looking up at him.

He gave a small shrug and smiled. "That's a teenager's job."

She frowned. "I . . . sometimes I just feel like I don't even know what's happening with me. Sometimes I get angry or sad. Sometimes I feel like a kid and sometimes I feel like an adult. But so many days I just want to be a kid again, and I'm mad I can't be," she said, her voice cracking.

He smoothed the hair from her face, treasuring her honesty and openness. "You know I'll always be honest with you . . . everything you're feeling is perfectly normal. It's a rocky transition into teenage-hood, I remember it. It was kind of like hell on some days. But you'll get through it. We all do. Remember, nothing in life stays the same, nothing is permanent. And you know, even as an adult, I wish I could go back to being a kid. There are so many days I don't want to be an adult. That's why it's okay to have fun sometimes and not worry about what the rest of the world tells you. Just be you. I think you're pretty great," he said.

She lifted her large eyes to him. "You're the best dad, even when I act like you're not. I always know you are."

Emotion clogged his throat. "You will always be my girl. I will always be here for you. No matter what," he said, stopping before he actually cried like a baby.

"I wouldn't blame Charlotte if she left today," she whispered.

He tensed, ready to come up with something that would make her feel better, when he spotted Charlotte, her white pom-pom hat bopping with her march as she made her way up the driveway. "She's here," he said, forcing a tight smile. He knew just because Charlotte had come didn't mean this was all going to turn out the way Sam wanted it to. The way he wanted it to.

"She's here!" Sam squealed, running to the door.

Gratitude and love for Charlotte flowed through him as he stood and walked to the door. Sam had already opened it and Charlotte was walking up the path, snow gently swirling around her, landing on her dark hair.

"Merry Christmas!" Sam yelled as Charlotte made her way onto the porch.

The minute she raised her gorgeous face, he knew. He knew she'd done this for Sam but that she was falling apart inside. Her eyes were rimmed with red and her face was pale, and that gorgeous mouth that he couldn't get enough of was strained. Hell. He knew what this meant.

"Merry Christmas, sweetie," she said, her voice raw as she hugged his daughter tightly, squeezing her eyes shut.

Sam was oblivious to all of it as she chattered away and took the brightly wrapped packages from Charlotte. "I'll put these under the tree! You can kiss my dad or whatever and just tell me when you're done!"

Normally they would have laughed, but there wasn't an ounce of laughter to be had. But he couldn't shut her out, no matter what he was going to be facing. Instead, he walked up to her and wrapped his arms around her, relieved when she clung to him, her hands digging into his back. "Merry Christmas," she said, and it was almost laughable.

"Thank you for coming," he whispered in her ear before she pulled away from him.

"We have presents for you too!" Sam said, pulling the presents they'd bought from under the tree. His throat hurt as he watched Charlotte sit beside Sam as his daughter piled the gifts they'd bought onto her lap.

Sam had stayed up late, meticulously wrapping each gift, telling him his skills were lacking and he was only allowed to position the tape wherever she pointed. They'd bought three different gift wraps—each coordinating and with matching ribbon—all picked by Sam.

He stood on the sidelines, his hands jammed into the front pockets of his jeans, blinking furiously as Charlotte opened the first one, the new planner she and Sam had discussed, then the gift card Sam had insisted on buying for Greens on Main Street, followed by sets of markers and highlighters and stickers that Sam had picked out. He held his breath as Charlotte opened the last one and carefully pulled it out of the box. She didn't move, and then lifted her tear-filled eyes up to his and he wanted to tell her that it was what he was offering. Not just the snow globe, but everything the snow globe represented. She was perfect. They could all be as perfect as the people in that globe standing outside the house as snow tumbled around them.

"These are all so thoughtful," Charlotte whispered, reaching over to give Sam a big hug, before looking up at him with eyes filled with so much regret that it was hard to maintain eye contact with her. "Thank you."

He cleared his throat. "You're welcome."

"Okay, you guys open yours!" Charlotte said in an overly chipper voice, as she shoved a gift wrapped with vintage Santas skiing down a hill at Sam.

Sam ripped it open and squealed as she opened the exact same planner and a bunch of coordinating markers and pens and stickers. They both laughed. He really had no idea what was so fabulous about planners, but they were both obsessed with them, and that was all that mattered. His chest constricted as a gift card for Greens on Queen tumbled out of the planner and Sam laughed again, saying how alike they were. Charlotte reached over and gave her a hug again and it struck him—painfully—how much Charlotte and Sam had changed in the month that they'd known each other. In some ways Sam and Charlotte were similar in the way they had become almost hesitant to reach out to people. Charlotte had been almost resistant or awkward at first and now she was like . . . a mother figure to Sam. And it killed him because he knew she was going to break his daughter's heart.

"I've got to go text Cat anyway, so that'll give you some time away from me," Sam said, jumping up with an armload of gifts.

"Oh, you girls are speaking again?" Charlotte asked with a smile.

Sam rolled her eyes. "Yeah. It was a total misunderstanding," she said, bouncing out of the room.

He and Charlotte both gave what he thought was a pretty convincing smile and laugh. The minute Sam left the room, Charlotte exhaled and kept her head down.

"You're leaving, aren't you?" he said gruffly.

After a few tense moments she looked up at him, her chin wobbly, and nodded.

He cursed under his breath and turned away from her.

"Can we talk on the porch?" she asked, her voice thick with tears.

He didn't want to care. He didn't want to acknowledge that she was hurting. He just wanted to think about himself and the fact that he was in love with her. That Sam had trusted her and now Charlotte was going to break both their hearts.

But he wasn't going to let her go without a fight; without telling her everything, how much he loved her, his dreams for their future, everything.

He gave a stiff nod and walked over to the door, not bothering with a coat. The cold air felt like a harsh slap on his overheated skin. Charlotte came out a moment later with her coat on.

"I know you're going to hate me, but I want you to know that I'm not just going to ditch Sam. I . . . I know we've become friends, and I'd never just walk out of her life like that. If she wants one, I will always have a relationship with her. I won't leave town without telling her that and promising that I will always be there for her," she said, hastily wiping the tears that fell from her eyes.

He scrubbed his hands through his hair. "I trusted you. I trusted you with my little girl. I've never done that before. I've never let either of us put our guards down. I've never invited a woman into our home, into our lives. I can't let you ruin everything because of fear."

She covered her face with her hands. "It's not you guys. Wyatt, you are my dream. My dream man that I was always too afraid to wish for, and Sam is like a daughter to me. But I don't know how I can do this. I don't know how I can live in this town with my parents here. The feelings they bring out . . . I'm not proud. When I don't see them, I can handle life. I can be happy. But they . . . I'm so angry when I think of them. And my sister. And all of it. It's all too much," she choked.

He reached out to grasp her hands. "I know. It sucks, and I guess I'm a selfish ass for asking you to stay in a place where they are. But I've come to learn that no one has the perfect life, Char. That perfect family doesn't really exist—well, maybe for some lucky people, but for the rest of us? We make do. We focus on the good, and maybe because of that it makes the good even better. Maybe it makes people like us fight to get to great, fight for happiness, and maybe we're the ones who know true happiness because we've had to fight for it. It wasn't handed to us with that perfect childhood. I'm not going to beg you to stay, because I've done that once in my life and I know that if you don't really want to be here, it won't work. If you want me and Sam then you'll fight for us. You'll find your way back to us. But I can't do it for you," he said, taking a step back, that step feeling like a mile. But there was something else she was keeping from him and he could feel it, his instincts telling him he was right as he stared at her.

"I know. And I want to believe everything you're saying. More than anything, I want you to be right. But maybe I'm too damaged . . . to be what you need. What Sam needs. I don't know that I'm strong enough to deal with my family. I don't want drama. I hate drama. I grew up with drama. This Christmas . . . this is what I've been trying to avoid my entire life."

"Don't sell yourself short. I'm not perfect, Char. Far from it. But it doesn't matter. You don't need to be perfect for me or Sam. Just be honest."

She looked down. "I don't know. I don't know if that's possible."

"If you want me enough, it's possible."

She crossed her arms over her chest. "You are making this all sound so simple. Like I can just flick this switch and change. I have a life I was living before here. No one could hurt me. Then I met you and . . . Sam . . . and you both made me think that I was so wrong. You made me imagine a life that was snow globe perfect. I bought you the same snow globe," she said with a sad laugh.

He shoved his hands in his pockets. "But you couldn't give it to me because that's not going to be us anymore, is it?"

She bit her lower lip and shook her head.

Damn her. Damn her for already addressing his worst fear. Damn her for genuinely caring about Samantha and confirming what he'd known all along about her—that she could be trusted. He was expendable. His feelings came after Sam's.

"So that's it? Your dad comes back for a night and you don't want anything to do with us?" He tried to keep the harshness out of his voice. He wanted to sit down on the porch step beside her, but he was too angry. At her. At her family. At life, for making it so damn hard for them.

"Don't make it sound so simple," she said, her voice breaking.

"I'm not your dad; I'm not a guy who falls apart and walks away from my family. I would never to do that to you. I think your family being here is an excuse. I mean, hell, it'll be hard to deal with, but that's not it. Your dad walking back in brought all that pain to the surface, and you've been living in self-preservation mode for years. And you think the pain isn't worth it. The pain that comes from loving someone with everything you have. You loved him more than anything, and he walked out on you and destroyed your faith in people. But I'm not him, Charlotte. I don't walk away from the people I love," he said gruffly.

She let out a ragged sigh and lifted her face to him, her eyes glittering with tears and pain, but he stood still.

He ran a hand over his jaw. "I'm sorry that this Christmas wasn't what you wanted it to be, what you deserved. And I'm sorry your dad is here. But it doesn't mean *we* have to end. I'm not him. But I can't convince you of that. If you don't believe me, believe in me, trust me, then there's nothing left for us."

She nodded slowly. "No, I'm sorry. I'm a coward. I'm the one with problems. I'm the one who's built walls so high and thick that I don't know how to live without them, how to let them crumble to let you in . . . I won't say goodbye. I won't say goodbye to Sam permanently. I, uh, I'll just run in the house and let her know that I'm leaving for a few days," she choked.

"Don't lie to her," he said harshly.

She squeezed her eyes shut. "I won't."

"Wait, Charlotte," he said, his voice stopping her at the door.

She paused and waited.

He had to give it one last shot. Before she left for good. He had to put his hurt aside and make it clear how he felt. "I've made a lot of mistakes, but I've never run from them. I built my life around Sam. I can build my life around you. We can build a life together. If I have the two of you, I know I have everything. You can stay and try. I'll be here for all of it, for whatever you need. Or you can live in that pleasant color-coded world you've created and pretend that's living. But, baby, that's not living. You and me, when we're together, that's living. Think about that when you're alone in the city. Think of me, of who you know I am. You know I would never walk away from you. I won't give up on you, Char. I'll still be waiting. New Year's Eve. I'll wait for you for as long as it takes for you to realize we were meant to be together."

He held his breath, wishing his words would be enough for her to turn to him and choose him and Sam. But she didn't even face him. She fumbled with the doorknob. "I'm going to say goodbye to Sam. I'm sorry. Merry Christmas, Wyatt."

CHAPTER TWENTY

On New Year's Eve, Charlotte stared at the pile of empty coffee mugs and dirty dishes, and didn't even move a muscle in the direction of the mess. Normally, that kind of disorder would have sent her into a slightly hyperactive mode until everything was neat and tidy again. Surveying the open-concept living space, she spotted several different areas of disarray. On any other day, she would have taken out a notepad and made a list of all the areas to tackle, and then would have proceeded to highlight them off in coordinating Christmas-colored highlighters. Now the idea of doing that wasn't even remotely exciting. Who cared about markers or lists or color coordination at a time like this?

She picked up the mug of coffee she was currently drinking, the cute image of a red truck being driven by a dog wearing a Santa hat, with a Christmas tree poking out the back, doing nothing for her. She put the mug down with a sigh on the pristine white page of her planner, accepting the fact that she'd probably just created a coffee ring on the page. And she didn't even care. All of the accessories Sam had picked out for her were still sitting in their packaging. As if she could ever open them.

"You suck, Charlotte," she said aloud in her silent condo, the words, spoken to no one, sounding extra pathetic. But there was nothing that could fill the cavernous hole inside her. Well, there was something. Or someone. But she'd ruined that.

Or you can live in that pleasant color-coded world you've created and pretend that's living. But, baby, that's not living. You and me, when we're together, that's living. Think about that when you're alone in the city. Think of me, of who you know I am. You know I would never walk away from you. I won't give up on you, Char. How did he know her like that? He saw right through her and knew she was scared, that she didn't believe in him. And she had never been more alive, more real, more herself, than when she was with him.

Wyatt was everything she'd ever wanted. The opposite of her father. They may have worn the same uniform, but they were different men through and through. Wyatt had found a way to deal with pain and keep going. Wyatt knew how to love and knew how to fight for it.

And she had proven to Wyatt that she couldn't be trusted. She had run when she should have stayed. But what could she have done? Her one shot at having a perfect life—a life she had never even imagined could be hers—had been ruined by her fear. Her inability to trust someone with her heart.

"Charlotte, it's me! Please open the door!"

Her sister's voice pierced through her thoughts and the silence of the condo. She stood slowly, a part of her really happy that Olivia was here. The other part of her didn't know exactly how to feel. When Olivia had shut her out, she'd been deeply hurt, and she'd vowed not to let any of her family members, except Grandma Ruby, get close to her again, but then when she'd heard everything Olivia had been through, forgiveness had come easily and she'd let her guard down. Only to let herself be hurt again. But she wanted to believe there was an explanation. She wanted to understand. She didn't want to go through life without Olivia again.

She opened the door and smiled at the sight of Olivia and Dawn. Her heart swelled as Dawn's adorable face lit up and she smiled and banged her fists around at the sight of Charlotte. Charlotte laughed and held open her arms. A second later she was holding her precious niece and kissing her, inhaling her sweet baby scent.

Olivia scrambled into the condo, carting that pack 'n play and oversized diaper bag like a pro, dropping them on the tiled entry. Her sister looked as bad as she did. Her hair had probably been in some kind of ponytail at some point in the last twenty-four hours, she had dark circles under her eyes, and she was wearing pajamas under her winter coat. "I'm so glad you opened the door. I was so worried you were going to ignore me, not that I could blame you," Olivia said, taking off her coat and boots.

Charlotte felt comforted by the fact that her sister was worried. Maybe it wasn't nice of her, but it felt good to know that Olivia cared, that she knew she'd hurt Charlotte again. "As if I wouldn't open the door, Liv."

Olivia's chin wobbled, and her eyes filled with tears. "I've been such a crappy sister to you these last three years. I can't even explain how much I hate myself for ruining what we had and for not being there for you, like you were for me growing up."

Charlotte shook her head, her own eyes filling with tears, her throat feeling tight. She held onto Dawn a little tighter. "Don't say that," she managed to whisper.

"I have to. You need to know how deeply I regret shutting you out. And the Dad thing . . . it was completely unplanned. He reached out to me, and I didn't want anything to do with him. But I couldn't bring myself to tell you because I knew you would be mad, and I had just gotten you back in my life. I thought he'd just skulk off into the night again, I didn't think he'd actually show up and want to be a part of our lives."

"Really?" Charlotte whispered, those words meaning so much right now.

Olivia nodded. "Really. There was no plot. There was no secret relationship with him. Nothing. We didn't even talk on the phone. It was a text. You can even read it. I should have known that Mom was involved in all of this."

Charlotte rolled her eyes. "Yes, I guess we both should have seen that one coming. Do you want something to eat or drink?" she asked, leading the way into the sitting area of the condo, not wanting to keep talking about the past. Her sister had already given her what she needed to hear, she didn't need more.

Olivia nodded and set up the pack 'n play in pro speed. "How about we order Thai and drink and plan how I can help you fix your life?"

She let out a startled laugh before placing Dawn in the playpen while Olivia gave her a few toys. "Yes to the Thai, but my life doesn't need fixing, and you don't have to worry about that."

"*Right.* Okay, I'm ordering the Thai right now. You open the wine, for me—you're drinking coffee—because you won't be staying here long. I'm starving. I haven't eaten since last night. I'm going on coffee only," she said, pulling her phone out of her pocket.

"Sounds good. I haven't eaten either," she said, opening her favorite bottle of merlot for Olivia and brewing more coffee for herself, not even wanting to question the remark about her not staying here long.

"Okay, food ordered. Now, of course you haven't eaten, you have a broken heart. But hopefully I can fix that in under thirty minutes, so by the time the food gets here you can enjoy it and we've moved onto the planning stage," she said, taking a sip from the glass Charlotte held out for her.

Charlotte laughed nervously. Her sister could be pretty persuasive. "Liv, I don't think it's going to be that simple. I really messed things up. I pulled a Dad. I pulled what his ex-wife pulled on him," she said, flopping onto the white couch, her coffee swooshing precariously close to the rim, and her heart rate didn't even accelerate at the prospect of a brown stain on white upholstery. Who cared about her couch at this point? It's not like anyone actually came here. It's not like Wyatt would ever be sitting here. They were worlds apart, really. Just picturing him there was laughable. But she had so easily fit into his home and his life, and even though it wasn't one she'd pictured for herself, it was the best dream. She'd been living that dream for weeks. This sterile condo was her real life, though.

Olivia curled her legs under her body and took a drink of wine, her eyes not leaving Charlotte's. "That's not the way it works, Char. You really think that man is just going to hate you forever and get over you in a couple of days? Also, you're not his ex. You didn't marry him, give birth to his child, and then just check out forever. You told him you needed time."

She put her mug down on the coffee table with a thud and caught the giraffe that Dawn flung in her direction. Smiling at her niece, she handed back her giraffe and tried to not run from the feelings churning inside her. She didn't know how to talk about this, what Olivia was trying to draw from her. Wyatt had been able to bring out this side of her—he was the one who could dig deep and feel and love. But it felt . . . she felt like her thoughts and words were stilted and she desperately wanted to cling to them and keep them inside.

"I can't go back there. I said I needed time because it's true, but I can't go back. I can't live with Mom and Dad popping in at a moment's notice. That's like a nightmare, Liv."

Olivia choked on her wine. "Fine, I get it. But what's your solution? You're going to throw away a future with a guy like that because of your . . . eccentric parents? Seriously?"

The doorbell rang and Charlotte hopped off the couch to open it. After getting the paper bag filled with delicious-smelling Thai food plated, while Olivia handed Dawn a snack cup filled with Cheerios, they sat back down on the couches and ate.

"I'm still waiting for a reply, and you'd better hurry because then I'm going to have to feed Dawn and that'll take all my attention with the way she's been flinging food around these days," she said, shooting the baby a smile.

Charlotte laughed. "Okay, well, I don't have a reply you're going to like. It's not just Mom and Dad. It's . . . everything. It's exactly what Mom and Dad represent. What if Wyatt's ex shows up one day out of the blue, and he has a chance to reunite his family again?"

Olivia blotted her mouth with a napkin. "That's not going to happen, and even if his ex *did* show up again, do you really think

Wyatt would just jump back into a life with her? She broke his daughter's heart and is MIA. You can't just forgive that."

"But what about Sam? He might do it for her sake."

It was her greatest fear. Being left behind. Again. It had taken her entire childhood and so much of her adult life to get over her father leaving. Or maybe she never had. Maybe her actions right now were all because she'd never truly gotten over that abandonment. But Wyatt leaving her would rob her of the rest of her heart. She didn't know how she would recover. Coming back to this empty condo alone had already made her painfully aware of how hollow her life had been before he came into it. And she had come back on her own terms. If she were coming back here because Wyatt had left her . . . she didn't know how she would cope with that.

"There are things I've learned. It's taken me a long time to learn them, and I've made huge mistakes, but there are warning signs. There must have been warning signs with Dad too. We were too young to see them. But with Will there were warning signs that I already told you about. You can't tell me that Wyatt is the same. And the fact that he came back into your life is no coincidence."

Charlotte stuffed her mouth with a heaping forkful of pad Thai, wishing the carbs would actually bring her some kind of comfort. There was one man who'd been able to give her comfort in this world, whom she trusted, and she'd run from him. Like a coward. Everything Olivia was saying was right, but that didn't exactly help Charlotte now.

"I know. He's not the same. That's not fair to Wyatt, and I realize that. But so many of the . . . weird decisions I've made in my life are because of how we grew up. I mean, I know I'm an adult and I'm not going to sit here crying about what Mom and Dad should have done, but it's like, stuff I never realized until now. I thought I was living the life I wanted, but when I met Wyatt I realized I wasn't. I was living a life that was safe. I built this imaginary world for myself in a way. Because I didn't let anyone in, I controlled everything. I run my own business. I live by myself. Even the two girls I hired work remotely, and I've never met them. I don't date, Liv. Like, no one."

Olivia frowned, putting down her empty plate. "No, that's not true. What about that guy? You know . . . um, what's his name?"

Charlotte's cheeks burned. "There was no guy. Ever. I made him up. Well, okay, not entirely. He did ask to sit across from me at the coffee shop. Then he did ask me out for dinner. But I said no."

Olivia's face crumpled. "Oh, Char . . ."

Charlotte ate the rest of the pad Thai in an effort to collect her thoughts and take a break from the embarrassment she was feeling. She had projected to the world that she had it all together. She was a fearless go-getter, a successful entrepreneur who didn't put up with any nonsense. The truth was that she had been hiding from life.

"It's fine. Really," she said, putting her empty plate on the coffee table and crumpling up the napkin.

"It's a good thing I'm here. Time to save your life. Here's what you're going to do. You're going to take a shower, fix yourself up, pack your bags, get in your car, and drive to Silver Springs. I mean, like, not to Grandma's—avoid that house until after you have successfully made up with Wyatt."

A surge of hope coursed through her. That sounded like the perfect plan. It was what she wanted to do. She could make it to Silver Springs for midnight. She sat still.

"Up. Go. Now," Olivia said, standing and picking up Dawn.

Charlotte swallowed hard, past the lump in her throat, past the fear. "What if he rejects me? It's been almost a week."

Olivia lifted her chin. "He won't. Trust me. Trust him. Now, while you get ready, I'm going to tell you all the things that have happened since you left," she said, standing.

Charlotte's eyes widened as her sister swung her wine glass a little too wildly over Charlotte's planner. Charlotte thought she might die. "*No,*" she whispered as her gaze went from the drips of coffee to the perfect planner sheet. Now that her life was going to get back on track, she cared about her plans again.

Olivia simply *tsked* and shook her head. "This *is* life, Char. Real life. It's filled with dogeared pages, coffee rings, and smudged pens. It's snotty Kleenexes and, in your case, a hot man. Being afraid to take a chance, walking around hiding behind the hurt of our childhood? That's over. We take chances. Informed, wise chances, but still. This is not the narrative I want for Dawn. We need to do better. Go after that hot cop and just . . . live your life. I swear, if you don't text be by midnight, telling me you're in Silver Springs, I will send Mom after you. Oh, which reminds me, I need to tell you what's happening back home so you're not shocked."

Charlotte paused in her bedroom door. "I've been gone less than a week."

Olivia smiled mysteriously and picked up Dawn. "Mom and Dad are going out on a New Year's Eve date."

Charlotte groaned. "You have got to be kidding me."

Olivia laughed and shook her head. Dawn did the same. "I know. Talk about a train wreck. I give them one week, tops. I saved the best for last, though."

Her muscles tightened. She wasn't sure she really wanted to know. "Don't make me wait."

Oliva gave her a wide smile. "Grandma has a boyfriend."

CHAPTER TWENTY-ONE

NEW YEAR'S EVE, PRESENT DAY
THE CHRISTMAS HOUSE

"Happy New Year!" Ruby called out before stepping outside and quickly shutting the front door behind her. She didn't wait for their replies and the inevitable questions. Tonight her daughter would have to deal with her problems on her own. She took comfort in knowing that Charlotte was on her way home, that her granddaughters had made up and would find their way in the world. And she was slightly pleased that Wendy and Mac might be finding their second chance.

Tomorrow was a new year, and she would celebrate with all of them. But tonight was for her. She had spent a lifetime waiting, and she didn't have another one to spare. Just as she knew he would be, Harry was waiting on the porch for her. A giddy feeling, like the kind reserved for youth, coursed through her as he held out his hand. She clasped onto it for dear life.

"Ruby, you look beautiful," he said.

She smiled up at him. "You look wonderful yourself," she said, taking in the dark wool coat and suit underneath. He had always been so handsome.

"Before we go to the restaurant, I want to ask you something I should have asked that first night I saw you."

Ruby's smile dipped, not knowing what the question was, barely remembering the first time she had met him. "All right," she said softly.

"Will you dance with me?"

Her mouth dropped open. "Here?"

He nodded, slowly lifting her hand and, before she could even feel silly, she lifted her other hand to his shoulder. Soon they were dancing in the dim moonlight, under the twinkling white Christmas lights, on her beloved front porch. "That night, at the church social . . . Richard and I were standing together and you walked in, your dark hair pulled back with a black velvet bow, wearing a red velvet dress. I told him that I was going to ask you to dance and that one day you were the girl I was going to marry."

She gasped as the reality of what he was telling her sank in. Tears blurred her vision. He'd never asked her to dance. Richard had walked over to her. And the rest . . . she lifted her eyes up to his, the regret in them making her ache with the knowledge of what he had known so many years ago. "You never asked me," she whispered.

He clenched his jaw. "He beat me to it. But I'm here now. I can't let another new year start without you knowing how I feel about you. You may think it's crazy, but I fell in love with you that night, and each night that we spent in each other's company. I knew you were my soul mate, Ruby. Sometimes the heart just knows. I've spent a lifetime wondering about you, and now you're here. We have nothing stopping us anymore."

"Richard," *she managed to choke, emotion clogging her throat. Her mind was swirling as memories flooded her. So many years. She had told herself she needed no one. But throughout her life, she* had *needed people, Not the people she thought she had needed, but people who knew how to love without judgment, who knew what love truly meant. Maybe all she had needed were the* right *people. The people that The Christmas House had brought into her life. The man standing in front of her . . . he was the right people.*

He smiled gently, and they stopped swaying to the imaginary music as he cupped one side of her face. She couldn't help the sigh that escaped her lips. "I have so many things to share with you, so many stories. We have a lifetime of catching up to do. But someone very wise once told me that grace would lead me home, and maybe that's what's happened. This was always meant to be my home. And you were meant to join me here. Is it too late to take back every single 'no' that I told you?" *she asked, her stomach in knots, her chest aching with the idea that he would walk away again.*

His thumb grazed over her bottom lip and he slowly lowered his head, his lips hovering over hers in a heartbreakingly beautiful moment that been worth waiting a lifetime for. "It's never too late for a happy ending, Ruby."

* * *

Wyatt walked into the kitchen and tried to look like he was okay going in to work, not sitting on the couch enjoying his misery. Sam was sitting at the island, all dressed up in a dress that he'd preapproved after only ten *nos*, and texting someone. She quickly put her phone down and turned to him.

"You look beautiful," he said, getting a glass from the perfectly organized cupboard. A constant reminder of the woman missing from their lives. It was quite cruel, really.

"Thanks. You look like a disaster. You should shave and wear something nicer," she said with a frown.

He filled up his glass with water. He knew he looked like hell. "I'm going to work. I don't need to look good."

She made a *tsking* noise.

He shrugged. "I'll go shower. Not shaving, though."

"Here's what you're going to do, Dad. You're going to drop me off at Scott and Cat's house and then you're going to work and then you're going to meet Charlotte at the clock tower like you told her you would."

He choked on the water and stared at his daughter. "What?"

She nodded wisely. "Yup. You can't give up. You can't control the way people behave, but you can control your reaction. So, just because you're sad, you can't give up on Charlotte. You have to try one more time. She made you so happy. She made *me* so happy. And I think we made her happy, and you need to remind her of that. We are *really* cool people."

He put his glass of water down and let his twelve-year-old's advice sink in. He had planned on maybe just sitting in his SUV after work, parked outside the town square. But then he'd thought it might just break him, because he knew she wasn't coming. The wisdom in Sam's eyes was beyond her years. Hope trickled through him. Maybe Sam was right. Maybe Charlotte needed to be reminded of how good they were together, how happy they could make her too.

He cleared his throat. "I don't know that she'll show. She's not back in Silver Springs."

She shrugged. "Then after midnight, drive to Toronto. Do it, Dad."

Adrenaline started pumping through his veins. "Okay. I think you're right. I'm going. If you're sure you don't mind staying at Cat's tonight?"

She squealed and flew off the chair and into his arms. "I'm so happy you're finally listening to my advice. I knew this day would come. Also, I totally want to go to Cat's. Why wouldn't I? Now, go and make yourself look handsome. Hurry, it might take a while," she said, giving him an overzealous shove.

He almost laughed as he headed into the bedroom.

"Oh, and Dad?"

He turned around and waited.

"Also, remind Charlotte that families don't have to be perfect to be great. We can be great for her," she said, giving him a wink and a glimpse into his daughter as an adult.

He smiled at her, a rare prayer of thanks going up for the girl who had been his reason for getting up every day the last twelve years. Just for luck, he sent up another prayer for the woman he wanted to wake up next to for the rest of his life.

* * *

Charlotte replayed her sister's words over and over again in her mind like a mantra as her two-hour drive to Silver Springs turned into a four-hour, treacherous, nerve-wracking ride because of the poor road conditions.

Charlotte leaned forward, clutching the steering wheel tightly as the SUV moved with the wind. Her windshield wipers were going full force as she neared the outskirts of Silver Springs. Glancing at the clock, she guessed she was about half an hour out of town, maybe a bit longer because of the slick roads.

She was glad Olivia and Dawn were spending the night in the city at her condo. She would have been so worried about them driving back in this weather.

She eased her foot off the gas as the back of her SUV fishtailed slightly on the winding roads. *Everything is fine.* She had driven through countless winter storms. Besides, since it was so late there were barely any other cars on the road. It was just her and nature. Towering trees swayed on either side of the rural highway, and she could drive as slow as she wanted.

It was New Year's Eve and there was no way she was going to start her next year as Charlotte the Coward. She could do this. She did trust Wyatt. And she needed to tell him. This time tomorrow night, she hoped to be sitting on the couch with Wyatt and Sam, with the hope of the best new year ever ahead for all of them. If he forgave her.

She knew that she'd hurt him deeply. Yes, he had understood her reasons for leaving, but she'd still hurt him. He wasn't a man who threw his love around like confetti. He wasn't a man who opened his home to any woman. And he wasn't a father who let people get close to his daughter. But for Charlotte, he had. He'd trusted her and she had broken that trust.

Tears blurred her eyes as she made the last turn that would lead her into Silver Springs, and the snow died down, hitting the windshield in the prettiest, most erratic pattern. The streets were still slippery, but as she drove toward downtown, she could see they had been plowed. Streetlights led the way, and the tension started easing from her shoulders as a nervous anticipation filled her body. She still had half an hour before their midnight meet-up under the clock tower.

Slowing her car, she noted the cars along the side of the road and sidewalks filled with people. Twinkling lights on the storefronts beckoned her, filling her with hope. She pulled into a vacant spot on a side street close to the town square and got out of the car.

Cold night air hit her flushed cheeks, and adrenaline started flowing through her in a way that she hadn't felt in years. She picked up her pace, weaving her way around families and couples ready to celebrate the start of a new year. It was so much more for her. It was the beginning of a new life, a life she'd never before imagined she needed. But she needed this. She needed Wyatt and Sam and everything they gave her.

She paused for a second, a wave of nausea rolling through her when the clock tower came into view and Wyatt wasn't there. He would come. It was early. He was working.

"Happy New Year, Charlotte!"

Charlotte glanced in the direction of the voice and waved to Meghan from the cheese shop who was walking with a friend. She kept her smile as she stood in front of the clock tower. The sound of children laughing and yelling as they made their way down the toboggan hill and slid on the skating rink were a wonderful distraction as she stood by herself, people milling around her.

This was okay. She could stand alone. She had stood alone before.

"Hi, Charlotte! What are you doing here by yourself?"

Charlotte smiled at Aunt Mary, who called out from hot choco-late stand. "Just, um, waiting for Wyatt," she said, trying to sound confident.

Aunt Mary gave her the thumbs up before she and her boister-ous friends walked to the skating rink. For the next five minutes, Charlotte told everyone who asked what she was doing by herself, that he was waiting for Wyatt.

She glanced at the clock tower and, despite the cold, sweat trickled down between her shoulder blades as it had done so many years ago. She squeezed her eyes shut and tried to quell her wobbly chin as she remembered standing on the school stage, confidently telling everyone that her father was on his way.

Wyatt wouldn't leave her like this. Wyatt wasn't her dad. Wyatt would show up.

She opened her eyes and let her gaze scan the area, taking in all the people, all their joy. She lifted her chin and clung to her belief in him. This was it. This was her finally believing in someone. Tears filled her eyes, blurring the numbers on the clock. She stood still, waiting, letting her smile tell the world that she believed he was coming. She hiccupped and kept her eyes on the clock.

*   *   *

Wyatt cursed loudly as he approached the parking blockade. All the damn roads in town were blocked off because of the stupid New Year's town party. He glanced at the clock in his car. Shit. He had five minutes to get to the clock tower, on the crazy off chance that Charlotte would meet him. He'd go through hell and back for a chance. He was just going to have to leave his SUV here and some-how get there on time.

He parked and hopped out of his SUV and jogged along the sidewalk, darting around slow-moving pedestrians. He gave the occasional wave to people who greeted him, careful not to slow down. He stopped when he reached the toboggan hill. Panic filled him, and he knew there was no way he'd make it down to the town square in five minutes.

He surveyed the area, his eyes narrowing on the people milling around the bottom of the hill. It was almost impossible to see that far, but his heart started hammering when he spotted Charlotte's red pom-pom hat. It had to be her standing there in front of the clock tower.

"Hi, Sheriff Wyatt!"

Wyatt looked down at the young voice calling up to him. A little boy and his parents stood in front of him. The boy was holding a small sled. Wyatt recognized him from the class he'd gone to speak to as part of their outreach program before the holidays. "Hey there. Happy New Year," he said, not wanting to be rude, but knowing his time was running out.

"You too, Sheriff," the boy's parents said.

Wyatt stilled, his eyes going to the small plastic saucer. It was his only choice. "Hey, do you think I could ask you a big favor? Can I borrow your saucer? I need to get down that hill really fast."

The boy's eyes lit up. "Police business?"

Wyatt winced. "Maybe. Kind of."

The boy held out his sled. Wyatt glanced up at the parents. "I'll bring it back in ten minutes," he said.

They nodded. "No problem," they said as he took the saucer.

"Thanks," Wyatt said, giving the kid a handshake. Wyatt broke out into a jog, vaguely aware of the people turning to glance at him. In a town this small and this nosy, the sheriff's deputy taking a midnight ride down a hill in a tiny plastic saucer was sure to give them something to talk about.

Wyatt took a deep breath, his eyes on the one woman who made him feel like he could truly be home.

Grace will lead you home. Ruby's words that first Christmas in Silver Springs filled him and an odd sensation ran through him.

None of this had ever been a coincidence. Maybe they were both right where they should be, and this was their time. His and Charlotte's.

He sat down on the small saucer, filtering out the soft laughter around him and not giving a crap about any of it. He had to concentrate on keeping his large frame balanced on the child-sized saucer or he'd be a giant snowball going down that hill.

Here goes nothing.

He felt small hands on the back of his shoulders.

"I got you, Sheriff," the little boy said.

Wyatt was too nervous to laugh. "Thanks, kid. Give me your biggest push."

And just like that, Wyatt found himself flying down the toboggan hill on New Year's Eve, ready to claim a new life, to start the life he'd always imagined, the one that had always managed to elude him before.

As he tore down that hill, through his finely honed peripheral vision, he was vaguely aware of his aunt in the distance, of Ruby holding hands with a man at the skating rink, and Charlotte's parents arguing in front of the hot chocolate stand, and a peace filled him. An eerie calm in the midst of the wildest ride he'd ever been on.

That peace was unfortunately short-lived as he attempted to guide the saucer to the side in an effort to avoided colliding with a little girl. It wasn't going to happen. She was straight ahead and he would trample her.

He swore and abandoned the saucer, avoiding the little girl, and tumbling to the bottom of the hill like a snowman.

But he'd made it.

He righted himself and hopped up, not taking the time to brush the snow off his body, and ran toward the clock tower.

Charlotte turned around, and his gut clenched as he read the expression in her eyes.

She had waited for him. Even though there were only thirty seconds to New Year's.

He remembered her that day on the stage. He remembered her eyes. They were the same right now. Except today she stood there, and she believed in him.

Her mouth dropped open. "Wyatt," she whispered.

He limped over to her, cringing as his bad knee reacted to that ridiculous fall. "You came," he said, almost in front of her now.

She nodded, breaking into a gorgeous smile that would forever bring him home. He reached out and pulled her into him, not able to resist a moment longer.

"I missed you so much and I can't lose you. I'm sorry. I do trust you. I can't lose you again," she whispered.

He pulled back and raised his hands to cup the sides of her face. Fireworks went off in the distance, and people cheered as the clock tower chimed midnight. He lowered his head and met Charlotte's lips halfway. "Never again," he said before kissing her.

She held onto him tighter. "I knew you'd come," she said in between kisses.

"Always. Always for you," he said, emotion clogging his throat.

"I had to come back here and tell you how much I regret leaving. I was so wrong. I have nothing without you guys. I felt like I was giving it all up, Wyatt. That terrified me."

He smoothed a hand against her face. "Giving what up?"

"My control over my happiness, my life. I'm handing it over to you, and I've never done that before, with anyone. I can't color code you and schedule you into the appropriate slots."

"You can color code me. Red. For hot."

She burst out laughing, and he smiled with her. "I'll be sure to remember that. Keeping it all together was how I learned to survive, to just keep going. My life is so orderly and controlled, because that's the only way I know to keep it all together. Falling . . . in love with you has been the greatest gift I have ever received, but it scares the crap out of me, because I feel like I'm giving you all the power. I'm trusting you with everything," she said, giving him more than he could have ever wanted.

Wyatt blinked, clearing the moisture from his eyes, knowing what a gift she was giving him. He raised his hands to gently cup each side of her face. "Then I am the luckiest man alive, that you have trusted me with your heart once again. I would go to hell and back to make sure you are happy and safe and loved. You changed my life when I was a kid, and you have changed it again now. You changed Sam's life too, and for that, I will always love you. I have never before felt the way I do when I'm with you. Charlotte, you make me believe that happy endings are worth fighting for. I know life is scary, and I know there is going to be shit that we're going to have to face, stuff we can't predict, but I also know that I'm strong enough to get through anything and, even though you may not see it in yourself, I know you are too. I also know that if we're in it together, we can do anything we want. I love you."

He leaned down to kiss her, and this time it was so much more than desire, this time it was like a contract was being sealed, a bond was being forged. She stood on her tiptoes, and he held her against him tightly, her soft body feeling like it was made for his. "I love you too," she whispered.

"I didn't think you'd be here, and I almost didn't come. Sam convinced me. She also wanted me to tell you that we're really cool people."

She burst out laughing again. "I love her."

He kissed her again. "I know you do. Also, as much as we both love Sam, you should know that she's out for the night."

Her eyes sparkled. "What exactly were you planning?"

He forced himself to play it cool. "First, I need to return a sled. Then, talking. Obviously, lots of talking. Then I was planning on ordering us dinner."

She raised her eyebrows, smiling. "And then what? I'm sensing there was more to this plan."

He leaned forward, wrapping one hand at the nape of her neck, his lips brushing against her ear as he spoke. "I thought there were other areas of our relationship that we hadn't explored yet, and I was pretty certain I could make a case for myself from a completely different angle."

Her laugh came out breathless, and she leaned into him and everything he was offering. "Your plan might have worked, I'm not going to lie, Wyatt."

He smiled against her mouth, and she clutched his forearms. "Well, we can still try."

She leaned up and kissed him. "I can't think of a better way to start a new year. I thought I had blown it. That I would never get you back. That it was too late for my happy ending."

His lips hovered against hers, and he knew in his heart he'd never get tired of this, of her, or the promise of what they could be. "It's never too late for a happy ending, Charlotte."

ACKNOWLEDGMENTS

To Louise Fury . . . Thank you for always being so enthusiastic about my ideas and being a true champion of my books.

To Faith Black Ross . . . Thank you for believing in this book and for being such a joy to work with! Your edits and feedback were inspiring and motivating.

To Melissa Rechter . . . Thank you for keeping everything running smoothly and for being such a bright spot in my inbox!

To Madeline Rathle . . . Thank you for your marketing attention and ideas.

To all the other talented and dedicated people at Crooked Lane and Alcove Press: Thank you for believing in this book and me! I'm so excited to be working with you.

To my Readers and Bloggers: Thank you for joining me in Hope Springs! I hope this book brings you the joy of the season and leaves you with hope and happiness. All of your emails and reviews mean so much to me. I look forward to visiting The Christmas House again with you!